PRAISE FOR *DREAM EATER*

"*Dream Eater* brings much-needed freshness to the urban fantasy genre with its inspired use of Japanese culture and mythology and its fully-realized setting of Portland, Oregon. I'm eager to follow Koi on more adventures!"
—Beth Cato, author of
The Clockwork Dagger and *Breath of Earth*

"A timely book that happens to be a rollicking read. *Dream Eater* has it all: mythological and social diversity, strong characters, and a tender romance. I can't wait for the next one."
—Keith Yatsuhashi, author of
Kojiki and *Kokoro*

"I came for the Japanese mythology, and I was not disappointed. Readers who want variety in their urban fantasy beyond the werewolf and vampire staples are advised to pick up *Dream Eater*."
— Laura VanArendonk Baugh, author of
The Songweaver's Vow

"Lincoln infuses Japanese folklore into the Pacific Northwest, creating a fascinating world where a young dream-eating heroine, Koi, must learn to use her frightening talents to save her family in a tale of ever-increasing peril. By the end you'll be anxious for the next book!"
—J. Kathleen Cheney author of
The Golden City and *Dreaming Death*

"The characters really drew me in—Koi and Ken are intriguing on their own, but even better together. Overall, the book is as quirky and edgy as Portland itself."
—M.K. Hobson, author of
The Native Star

DREAM EATER

A PORTLAND HAFU NOVEL

K. BIRD LINCOLN

WORLD WEAVER PRESS

Published by World Weaver Press, LLC.
Albuquerque, New Mexico
www.WorldWeaverPress.com

Edited by Rhonda Parrish
Cover designed by Sarena Ulibarri.
Cover images used under license from Shutterstock.com.

ISBN-10:0-997788860
ISBN-13:978-0997788860

Also available as an ebook.

DEDICATION

This one is for all the Portland writerly folks who helped me while I was writing there: the Welorians: Misha, Tina, & Josh and the Wordos. And also for Stumptown Coffee and Dagoba Chocolates—'cause the book wouldn't exist without them, too.

DREAM EATER

CHAPTER ONE

The cashier held out my debit card, smiling with too-bright teeth.

"So terrible," she said, still turned to her floppy-haired manager. "He hardly had a career, and then on his one, big, movie break..." she let her sentence trail off, sighing.

I took the card, flinching as her fingers brushed mine. *Crap.*

Salty butter taste of popcorn on my tongue. Cheeks flushing with fear and excitement as an actor's garishly painted face loomed onscreen in a close-up.

I'd picked up a fragment from her.

Her Pepsodent smile had fooled me into thinking there was no real depth behind her chatter, but she was genuinely sad. Trying to make it look like something had gotten caught in my eye, I squeezed them shut and breathed in deeply. On the gray static behind my eyelids I pictured a brush dipped in ink. A broad, perpendicular stroke, followed by shorter ones coming together to form the kanji for "five." The popcorn taste faded—my usual trick had worked its magic.

I opened my eyes to the fluorescent store-brightness. The tabloids on the rack above the candy shelves headlined the untimely demise of a movie star with acne-scarred cheeks—the source of the blonde cashier's sorrow. The cashier, along with her manager, was now openly staring at me.

Marlin owed me for this.

I should have added one of the register display-bars of Ghirardelli 72% Cacao to Marlin's bill. Dark chocolate always made fragments go away quicker. All those endorphins and serotonin.

Too late now.

I was careful not to brush the clerk's hand again when I took the plastic bag. The gray-haired lady behind me cleared her throat, loudly. The receipt was waiting for me on the counter. I mumbled an apology, stashed my purchase inside my messenger bag, and swiveled to make a run for the exit.

Someone's midsection stepped into my path, I barreled straight into it and felt a warm shock pass through me.

The midsection was covered in a gray OHSU sweatshirt, but it was definitely hard, and male.

"Sorry," I mumbled again, flicking my gaze down from the man's startled face to the box in his hands.

Heat rose again on my cheeks.

Great. My first time outside my personal triangle of apartment, Stumptown, or Portland Community College in two weeks and what do I do? Immediately pick up a fragment from a star-struck cashier and bump into a guy buying condoms.

I pushed past the man. I had to get out, now. I tore through the candy bar aisle and out the sliding door.

Pacific Northwest damp gave the air a soggy, thick feeling. Douglas fir loomed over the rain-shiny blacktop of the parking lot, immense and aggressively green.

A weak fragment like the cashier's was easily corralled in the nether regions of my brain during daylight. As soon as I fell asleep, though, the emotional charge would rise to the surface, infiltrating my dreams like a dollop of real cream in a perfectly pulled espresso. Feelings would haunt me the next day. I wouldn't be sure if my reactions were my own or colored by the cashier's sad fragment.

Fabulous.

As if I needed more disturbing dreams. Despite being extra-special careful to keep my elbows in and hands folded since PCC's spring semester started, for the past few weeks I'd been haunted by a pretty bad one. A fragment I'd picked up somewhere at school. Or maybe Stumptown.

I'd honed avoidance to a fine art—Amazon Prime was my best friend—but at 9 this morning, Marlin had been on the phone, needling me in that little sisterly way that tripped all my guilt buttons. She needed Sudafed. Or. She. Would. Die.

Thus my live appearance at Rite-Aid.

I kicked at a pinecone on the sidewalk, and watched it roll into the soggy bark dust.

Marlin owed me really, really big.

Soon, afternoon school buses would disgorge tweens in spaghetti strap shirts and low-slung pants, despite the misty chill, but I managed to make it past the middle school to her condo without encountering more than a few curious glances from the LL Bean chic ladies lurking under the towering Douglas firs bordering the condo parking lot.

I'd dressed up for Rite-Aid in Nike workout pants Marlin had bought at the employee store when she interned last year, and a pink sweatshirt without any stains. I was presentable. I adjusted my messenger bag strap, heavy with textbooks, to the little hollow between neck and shoulder.

Marlin's door had a fish-shaped number plate. I traced the metal points of the sharp fins with my fingers. Mom had given Marlin the nameplate and me the pink sweatshirt, right before she went into the hospital the last time. We'd gone to Uwajimaya to get those sugared *senbei* she loved so much, but Marlin forced us into the gift shop first.

With Mom's chemo buzz cut and the dark circles under her eyes, she looked like a wizened waif. "You are too much like your father," she said, holding up a sweatshirt with my namesake painted in gold, sparkly scales.

"Wear this and remember your Pierce side," she said, apparently ignoring the irony.

"Mom. You guys gave me *your* last name, not Dad's. Besides, this is too flashy for me."

Mom whispered my middle name and cupped my cheek with her cold, dry palm. "Flashy? I suppose the metallic scales are more Marlin's style. But the fish's spirit, that's different. You have grown into that name."

I shook myself out of the memory, rubbing knuckles at the corner of my eyes. Mom and her marine-biology pop psychology.

A sharp rap on Marlin's door made it swing open. Unlocked.

"Koi?"

"Brought the Sudafed," I called out and made my way through the Ikea-furnished living room to the bedroom in the back. Marlin lay ensconced on top of her maroon sateen bedspread, propped up by a dozen cushions in floral and quilted geometric patterns that should have clashed, but didn't.

"My savior," said Marlin. She won the genetic lottery by getting Pierce eyes, amazing limestone-patterned flecks of blue, gray, and green—when she was in commando mode Marlin could bore holes through flesh with those eyes. My flat brown ones, like Dad's, didn't have the Pierce bite. Marlin complained they were too secretive.

We shared our mother's nondescript brown, wavy hair. Mine was a long and usually tangled mass hanging past my shoulders; easier to cut the split ends off every few months than bear the intimate and fragment-filled touch of a stylist.

Marlin's was highlighted with bronze and usually pulled back in a French chignon or ponytail, but today it was as unstyled as mine, loose around her shoulders in a way that softened my righteous indignation at the earliness of the hour.

"Here," I said, pulling out the Rite-Aid bag. Dark bags under her eyes gave her a bruised look. Not just a cold prompting her call for help, then.

"What's wrong?" I said, sitting on the edge of her bed. I'd picked up enough fragments from Marlin over the years that I could immediately tell when she was flavoring my dreams, but it still gave me TMI creeps seeing what haunted her sleep. Talk about awkward. Some things were never meant to be shared by older sisters, and Marlin's dream of her prom night date with Southridge High lacrosse player Taizo Kovach was one of those things.

"We need to put Dad in a home."

Oh. This again.

"We can't afford it," I said, picking at a stray blue thread fraying from her embroidered pillow.

If I would quit school and get a real-person job instead of the online coding gigs I scavenged we *could* afford it. We'd have enough left from Mom's life insurance to set Dad up in a memory care unit.

The whole argument where she very carefully didn't call me selfish, and I tried to explain that school was the only path out of the hole I'd dug myself into these past years, shambled into the room with us—a looming, unspoken monster. The thread I was wiggling tore away from the pillow, unraveling an intricately embroidered bird shape.

I just couldn't face that monster today. Not when I was gearing myself up for a class at PCC.

But Marlin didn't pull out her alphabetized file folder of nursing homes, or even the Willamette Weekly's classified section. She just waited, looking at me with Mom's eyes.

When Marlin played quiet and reasonable, I knew I was in big trouble.

"He disappeared for a whole day. I tried to call you," she said. I'd promised to pick up if she called me twice in a row.

"I'm sorry," I said, showing her my phone. It was set on vibrate.

"It figures. Look, he's either snuck out or slipped away from every home helper we've hired. This latest one only lasted two weeks! We can't take him to adult daycare every day and we can't leave him alone."

"He's fine. Ever since you got that plastic handcuff with his name and address on it, someone's always called the police—"

"That's not fine!"

I shut my mouth. But instead of the lecture on dire consequences I expected, Marlin collapsed into a fit of coughing. She grabbed a handful of tissues and pressed the whole clump to her face, drying tears and snot at the same time.

I teased open the Sudafed box with my ragged nail and put a capsule in my open palm. A peace offering.

"You are who you are," said Marlin. The bare tone more cutting than her eyes. "You're my sister and I love you. But. We all deserve a life. Even Dad." She plucked the capsule and slipped it into her mouth.

"What do you want me to do?" I said.

"Take Dad for two weeks."

"What? No, I mean, I can't. What about school?" I sucked in air, floundering. First the memory care monster, and now this? I'd been sucker punched.

She waved a hand at the mess of tissues and the box of Sudafed. "I have been managing Dad all winter. My clients are booked solid through April and May."

"You managed before."

"Ha," she said, "Managed." The word turned into a dripping sarcasm ball. "Just two weeks, Koi, that's all I'm asking."

"I can't do it."

Marlin looked down at her manicured thumbnail, picking at an appliquéd flower. Loose hair fell forward, covering her face in a glossy curtain. "He doesn't need me," she said quietly.

A bigger monster entered the room. Mom's reasons for leaving Dad, tangled up with the very careful way our family never, ever talked about the biggest thing I had inherited from him.

This was the closest we'd come to naming it since Mom died—a thin wisp of connection hovering in the air between us. I could reach out right now and take Marlin's bare hand, let all those unspoken things spill out of me. A yearning to share this burden, to explain somehow, flickered for an instant. But talking about it with Marlin would ignite her caretaker instincts, and I couldn't let her fix things for me anymore. I had to figure out my life on my own.

The moment dissipated. Marlin snuck a sideways peek at me through her hair. I reached out and stroked soft strands, careful not to brush the edge of her ear.

"And we'll try to work out some more permanent solution in the meantime," said Marlin, back to bossy little sister voice.

Permanent solution? "I was supposed to have spring off for my classes," I said. She just stared back at me, waiting, sick, concerned, and stubborn as Mom.

I flexed my fingers, trying to calm the little bursts of unease running up and down my arms. I couldn't fight this Marlin. She was deadly serious. "Okay. You can bring him by tonight."

"Can you just pick him up at Salvation Army at the end of his day program?"

"I've got classes." Even Marlin could push me only so far.

"Fine. I'll bring him. Now, I've got some serious binging to do with Leverage on my DVR. If you want to stay and play 'spot the downtown landmarks', that's fine. If not, you're dismissed." She fiddled with the remote. "And thanks for the Sudafed."

She kept her eyes on the TV, but I blew an air kiss to her as I left anyway. She drove me crazy, but she was one of the only people in the world since Mom died that I could call *mine*.

My smothering, meddling bridge to humanity.

I let myself out the door, ran down her rickety staircase and whipped around the overgrown pink-budded rhododendrons back toward the sidewalk.

And barreled headlong into somebody.

Somebody with a hard midsection covered by an OHSU sweatshirt.

I looked up, flushing for a third time that morning. "Sorry," I mumbled.

It was the guy from Rite-Aid. I hadn't had a good look at him before, but now there was no convenient escape-path. He had very dark brown eyes, almost black. Under the lack of a pronounced eyelid, his eyes tilted up at the corners. Asian, or possibly part-Asian. Medium-length dark hair, moussed up into tousled spikes at the top of his head.

He wore the sweatshirt like someone who didn't care what they put on because they had the body to pull off any look.

I glanced at his hands. The box of condoms was no longer in sight.

"This is becoming a habit," he said.

I bristled, but his mouth was curved into a relaxed grin, and he held one eyebrow arched up high in a way I'd wished I could emulate ever since I'd watched Spock on old *Star Trek* reruns.

"Sorry," I repeated with great emphasis. I stepped off the path to go around him, but he held out a hand to stop me.

"I was hoping to talk to you," he said.

"What?" I backed away, checking quickly to see if anyone else was nearby. The parking lot mothers had all gone inside. Not a soul was around. Unease prickled.

I'd touched him. Usually I only got fragments that lasted long enough to turn into dreams from people feeling strong emotion—like the clerk's sadness. This guy didn't have a drama aura, and I'd felt nothing at Rite-Aid, but all of a sudden I wasn't so sure he hadn't given me a fragment. Were crazy stalker dreams going to haunt me tonight?

"I'm new to town," he said, with a curious emphasis.

"I'm sorry," I repeated. *Is that all I can say today? Just placate him, and then slip away.* I was good at slipping away. "Do you need directions somewhere?"

"Directions?" he looked puzzled. "*Nihongo wakarimasu ka?*"

I shook my head, screwing up my face into a puzzled look. Crazy stalker who spoke Japanese? *Why the hell did he ask me if I spoke Japanese, anyway?*

It wasn't like Dad's heritage was stamped all over my face. There was only a slight lift around the corner of my eyes. Even my nose was the sharp monstrosity inherited from the Pierce side.

"Ah, *dame ka*," he muttered. Those perfectly formed eyebrows fell, and his face changed. Not just the expression, but I swear his eyelashes got thicker and his mouth got wider, the lips more generous and the cheeks rounder. I blinked and looked again.

It was the same guy, but his expression now fairly screamed "attractive and amiable." As if he were the ultimate life insurance salesman.

"Ah, I have to go...ah meet someone for coffee." I gestured vaguely at the apartment complex. "I'm pretty sure all the apartments are labeled with names. You shouldn't have any trouble finding anything."

"Actually, I was going to ask you for directions to the nearest café," he said, his smile was genuine, but a hint of a smirk crinkled beneath his eyes.

Seriously? I rubbed my hands on the sides of my sweats. This guy was weird, but he hadn't given off scary vibes when I bumped into him those two times. If only Marlin were here to give me a clue about how to handle this. Was it more normal to blow my rape whistle or walk with him to Stumptown?

He was patiently waiting, smiling in that way that made me feel included in a secret joke.

Okay, Stumptown it was. Once we got there I'd order first and then slip out while he was waiting for his.

"Follow me," I said, moving forward so he had to fall into step beside me. My head barely reached the bottom of his chin. Walking side by side meant I didn't have to meet his gaze.

"Do you live in one of these condos?" he said.

I stumbled a bit over a non-existent sidewalk crack.

He coughed. "Ah, that's not a comfortable question, is it? Let me try again. Okay, how about, do you know a cheap but nice apartment complex around here?"

I considered my scant knowledge of the neighborhood where I'd been living for most of my post-high school life. Nope. Not a clue.

Best cold buckwheat noodles in Portland? Grocery stores that delivered? Back stairwells on PCC's campus? Navigating databases and academic search engines? I was your girl. Knowledge of the real world? Not so much.

"Can't help you. But there's some great apartment-finder websites for Portland. There might even be some of those real estate booklets at Stumptown."

We stopped at the intersection and I waited, looking at him expectantly. He grinned back, but made no move to push the crosswalk button even though he was closer. Sighing, I reached past him to hit the button with an open palm. Instead of backing away when I invaded his personal space, the guy leaned in, flaring his nostrils like he was…smelling.

I pulled back abruptly.

His brows knit together in puzzlement. "You…you aren't only human. Why don't you—"

The light turned red, and I strode away from him across the intersection.

Okay. Line officially crossed into whacko-ness. Only human? What?

Even Marlin wouldn't tell me I needed to be polite to Mr. Sniffer-Stalker now.

Stumptown and relative safety was at the end of the street, the bright yellow rooster-bedecked sign visible from here. He could find his own damn way.

My back prickled again, but I refused to turn around and look. No acknowledgement, no encouragement was the best policy. I reached Stumptown and stepped around a bicycle trailer, banging my knee against the protruding handle of a kiddie scooter. *Stupid inanimate objects, always getting in my way in a social crisis.*

Inside the calm, blonde wood interior, I stood sideways in line to make other customers less likely to crowd up behind me. And to keep one eye out for Mr. Sniffer-Stalker.

"You're next," said the lady in line behind me. I looked up to see the puzzled faces of Greg-ever-chipper and Sai-can't-be-bothered peering at me from behind the glass case of pastries.

"What can I get started for you?" said Greg, in a forced version of his chipper voice that indicated he was repeating something for an embarrassing-teenth time.

"Large latte," I said. I whipped out my debit card to hand to Sai.

Ever since I passed her in a PCC hallway three weeks ago, I'd been working my way up to chit chat with Sai. I needed to say something normal. Something interesting and witty.

"How are classes?"

"You know, pretty easy so far," said Sai. Her smile seemed genuine. I glanced around the displays, looking for something to ask about.

My eyes came to rest on a man at one of the little tables. He was familiar in a way I couldn't place. A professor, for sure, decked out in a plaid jacket with suede elbows and an armful of coffee-stained papers in loose folders. Probably I knew him from walking the halls at PCC. A little shiver ran down my spine.

Why did the sight of him make me uneasy? Nothing in the way

his gray-speckled hair curled over his collar told me anything.

I walked to the corner to wait for Greg to finish my latte.

"Ah yeah, I guess your classes must be okay, too then," Sai called after me. A thin undercurrent of sarcasm laced her voice. Oops, preoccupied with studying the back of the professor's head, I must have missed Sai's continuance of our chit chat.

Not even a quick flash of the patented chipper grin as Greg put my latte on the bar. Maybe they'd chalk up my spaciness to caffeine deficiency. I could always hope.

When my hand touched the warm cardboard of the latte, the aroma of cinnamon suddenly intensified. The strange, horrible fragment that had been giving me nightmares bubbled up from the depths of my mind. I froze.

The bright red of the espresso machine bled into the brown walls and counters, streaks of watery smudge blurring everything.

Oat bran and molasses on my tongue. A hint of exotic spice...cardamom? Brown and red seeped into the brown-on-black shadows of a darkened hallway. My hand gripped the cold metal handle of a giant jagged-edged knife, like the kind in old Rambo movies. Blood dripped from the blade onto the pale, motionless body of a woman with long, black hair and a prominent, hooked nose.

Scalding milk spilled down my arm and I yelped. The lid of my latte had popped off. Someone pressed a towel to my arm. I murmured apologies and closed my eyes hard until the dead woman's glassy eyes faded into black ink.

Ki, yama, tsuki; the firm strokes of my old Saturday school teacher's ink-tipped calligraphy brush painted kanji on the fuzzy light leaking behind my eyelids. That horrible fragment was haunting my waking moments now? How had I gotten such a strong one without realizing? This had never happened before. A whole week's dreaming hadn't lessened any of the visceral details.

Breathe. Paint a black line. Defining spaces of white contained within black helped banish the hallway, the scent, the terrible pale skin.

After a moment, I opened my eyes. Greg stared at me, dripping towel in one hand.

"Should we call Ben?" he whispered sideways to Sai.

Any progress I'd made in the past month at Stumptown was just completely obliterated. Time to beat a strategic retreat. Give people time to forget the weirdness.

I spun around clutching my half-full, soggy latte.

The professor guy was also staring at me, and I suddenly knew where I'd seen him before.

He *did* teach at PCC. I'd bumped into him outside my Japanese lit professor's office last week. He'd just barreled through the door, flustered and flushed. Before I could dodge, he'd patted my bare arm in apology. For once, the mishap hadn't been my fault.

I'd first tasted that disturbing fragment in my dream that week, the molasses-oat, and the jarring figure of the dead woman.

It was *his* fragment, this professor with the suede elbows. But it had to be a nightmare, right? Not a memory-flavored dream like Marlin and Taizo Kovach on prom night. I mean, PCC professors didn't actually murder people.

The professor stood up, gathering his things. He was handsome in an older-guy, tousled curls kind of way. I imagined rows of blonde undergrads staring up at him, drinking in his every word. The image was replaced by those same undergrads sprawled across a blood-streaked floor.

Morbidness issues much lately?

To cover my confusion, I brought the latte to my lips.

Yuck. It was tepid, and the cup's rim was so saturated with milk it threatened to break off in pieces on my tongue.

If there was any kind of fairness in the world, I could retreat back to the safe haven of my apartment, but I had a class. Time to find some of that strength Mom talked about when she gave me this sweatshirt, now streaked with latte.

I navigated the towers of burlap-sacked beans without brushing against any waiting customers. *Almost home free*, I thought, just as I noticed the front glass windows reflecting a shadow right behind me. A strange tingly sensation, like I'd had with Mr. Sniffer-Stalker, swept me from shoulder blades to scalp. The professor, following me?

I stepped out the door. There had been ample time for the professor to leave already. Why would he be waiting around?

Not only was I morbid, but paranoid too. There should be a new entry on Wikipedia for me. "Morbanoid."

I turned a corner. The strange tinglies got stronger. Was someone actually behind me? I slowed down, slipping my sopping drink sleeve off so I could fumble it into the garbage can and allow whoever it was behind me to pass.

The person halted in front of the garbage can.

"Don't I know you from campus?" the professor said. I recoiled and stepped back, my messenger bag thumping me in the thigh. He turned up the wattage on his smile, extending his hand. "You were in Kaneko-sensei's office, right?"

He meant to be friendly, but the idea that this man remembered me, noticed me in a chance encounter gave me the willies. I left his hand hanging in midair. No way was I touching him.

"Ah, yes, um…" I said, searching for an escape. "I…uh…"

"Ah, there you are!" said a voice behind me. I turned around to see Mr. Sniffer-Stalker giving me a dazzling grin. "Time to go."

He gave a little wave to the professor. "Sorry to interrupt, but I've come to whisk her away." He cupped my clothed elbow with his palm and warmth spread from his touch up my arm to my rapidly beating heart.

The professor frowned slightly. A whiff of cardamom. That pale, too-still body. Mr. Sniffer-Stalker was whacko, but he felt infinitely safer than the professor.

"Yes, I have to go," I mumbled. The professor tensed, as if to protest. Instead, he flashed me a polite smile, and gave Mr. Sniffer-

Stalker a curiously formal nod before turning back to the parking lot.

Panic receded. An escape...but from what? From an awkward conversation with Kaneko-sensei's colleague? When fragments impacted the waking world this much, that's when I knew I had to force myself into some kind of interaction other than Marlin or emailing Todd, my Java freelance job headhunter.

Stick with reality. Ignore the fuzzy-edged stuff.

I shook my head, wishing I could cast all this off of me like Mom's black lab, Sukey, shaking water after a dip in the Willamette. This wasn't my normal morbanoid self. Other people's fragments didn't do this to me—it was something particular to the professor.

A hand squeezed my shoulder and pulled me back onto the sidewalk. I went with Mr. Sniffer-Stalker, trying not to slosh more latte foam.

His hand was on me. Bare skin touching bare collarbone where my sweatshirt gaped open.

Where was the panic? The instinctual recoil? Only Dad could touch me like this and not force feed me fragments. But Mr. Sniffer's hand didn't feel awkward. It felt heavy. Warm. No tingles. No scents. No fuzzy static swimming across my vision.

"Why did you do that?" I blurted.

He blinked at me. "You didn't want to talk to that man."

"How could you possibly know that?"

"Does it matter?"

"Yes!" I jerked my arm away.

This guy was just so...coolly rumpled looking. Like Marlin's lacrosse-playing boyfriends. Those dark-on-dark eyes pulling me in, making me feel guilty for being so abrupt.

Why should I feel guilty? He's the weird stalker, not me. But the truth was, I wasn't afraid.

No desire to harm me lurked behind the openness in his dark eyes. I was sure of it. As sure as if he had given me a fragment and I'd dreamed of green, open spaces filled with cuddly, white bunnies hopping amongst the daisies.

Be wary, be wise. I shouldn't feel this warmth, this urge to relax into his presence, like I was at home in my lumbar-supported, cushioned computer chair. Maybe the professor's fragment had shorted out my brain.

"I apologize for interfering then, ah…er…"

"You can't go around stalking people without even knowing their names!"

"Stalk?" he said. Another eyebrow raise. He mumbled something in male-slang Japanese so quick I couldn't catch it. "Tell me your name, then."

I glared at him. Here's where Marlin would order me to strut away in a huff. Blow him off.

But a trickle of that horrible oat bran and molasses smell still coated my tongue, and I didn't want to be alone in the vicinity of the professor.

"I'm Ken," the guy said, and bowed in a formal way that reminded me of Dad at his sushi restaurant.

Ken? The name did not fit him in the least. "Ken" should be a shaggy-haired, blonde hulk of a football coed. Mr. Sniffer-Stalker's hair was that deep, deep brown that could be black or could lighten in the sun into a chestnut. His tall, slim build was more like an Olympic swimmer's than a football player's. Thick-fringed, glinting dark eyes and the barest hint of an eyelid. I still couldn't decide if he was mixed or full Asian. Either way, "Ken" was not him. There was nothing boy-toy Barbie about him at all.

At least my name wouldn't sound ridiculous now. "Koi," I said.

His wide lips curled into a smile. "As in 'flirtatiously modest'?"

"No, my mother had a fish fetish. 'Koi' as in 'carp'."

He bowed again, and I had to stop myself from bowing back. Exactly like Dad when he got together with the other Japanese business owner geezers for endless pints of *nama* Sapporo Ichiban at Yuzu. Or, at least Dad before.

"Well, *Ken*," I said, "I guess I owe you one. Thanks for rescuing me from that professor guy."

"A professor, huh?" The amused glint sharpened. "My pleasure," he said in a low, rumbly voice. Warmth crept down my neck, spreading flushed wings across my back. Where did he get off having a voice like that? Like actors in one of Dad's samurai dramas without the gruff undertones.

"Thanks again," I mumbled and downed the last of my latte. *Definitely* time to get out of here before I actually started scoping out my own stalker. Ken probably wasn't really a stalker or crazy, but there'd been enough time for the truly creepy professor to clear the area. I had places to go. Non-creepy Professors to dazzle with lit critiques.

Ken's steady gaze didn't waver. Was my signal too subtle? "I'm off to class now." I thought that was more obvious, but he just stood there. An oncoming lady with a double stroller forced me to step off the sidewalk onto the bark chip-lined flowerbed.

Ken was still there after the lady passed. "I don't have anywhere to go," he said. His sharp amusement softened into an aggressively open expression, inviting me in to confirm nothing fishy lurked deep inside. My guilt wires tripped. Mom's islander hospitality had been drilled into us at a young age. Never let a neighbor escape without a cup of coffee. Always 'make plate' of the leftovers at potlucks for the homeless. A thousand ways not to say 'no.' Something she had in common with Dad.

"Oh," I said, my cheeks flushing a bit. "Wish I could stay and hang out, but I really do have a class to get to."

"No, not like that," he said. "I've just arrived in this territory."

Territory? What was it with this guy? He was homeless or something? What did he want me to do? Inside my jacket pocket, my phone buzzed. I reached in and checked the screen. Text message from Marlin.

"Hold on a minute," I said, and flipped my phone open.

Drop off Dad. Tonite. 8.

Tonight? Crap. I forgot I had lab tomorrow. I couldn't spend all day babysitting Dad. Marlin was acting as if I had no life, nothing important to do. Okay, so maybe for the past few years that had been true. My freelance work had given me a very flexible schedule, but things were different now.

I was finally doing something with my life.

"Bad news?"

Oh, yes. The other gift today had given me still stood there.

"No. Yes. I mean, my sister's dumping my Dad on me, and I have classes and he can't be left alone." And there I went confusing boundaries. I shouldn't be pouring out my troubles to a probably-not-a-stalker, no matter how safe I felt.

Ken looked confused. "Why can't you leave your sister alone?"

"Not my sister, my *Dad*. He's got Alzheimer's. He gets confused and wanders off."

"Ah, yes. *Bokette iru. Yoku wakarimashita.* I looked after an uncle like that," he said. "For a year I lived with him."

"Seriously?" Sketchy coincidence, but my imagination had taken his words and run with them. All of a sudden lab tomorrow didn't seem an impossibility. And it would only be for one day, until I could find another home helper for Dad.

Breath whooshed out of me, deflating my fantasy bubble. *Crazy.* No way was I going to ask this stranger to look after Dad. Dark eyes or not. Marlin would kill me.

"Your father is the Japanese one, right?" said Ken.

Okay, he could have guessed that from my name.

"I speak Japanese," he pointed out.

New to town, no job or place to stay, and experienced with senile, old Japanese men.

The part of me that was doggedly determined to do well in lab tomorrow pointed out there was no way Ken could have engineered the situation. It wasn't like he had control over Marlin's clients.

"Well, he speaks this really rare dialect of Japanese from Aomori Prefecture and we really couldn't hire a caregiver who he couldn't talk to in his less…lucid periods."

"I've lived in Northern Japan, the dialect won't be a problem." He paused, lowering his gaze, giving me room to decide without the pressure of those eyes. His left foot kicked at bark chips that had strayed onto the sidewalk, a movement full of repressed energy. "I'll watch him just for a place to sleep. I really do have no place to go."

This was too temptingly easy, such a tidy solution to my problems. Dad could sleep in my bedroom on a foldaway like usual, and Ken could bed down on the couch, or—he was at least a *hafu* like me, if not full-blooded Japanese, wasn't he?—we could roll out a futon on the floor next to the bed, and I could sleep on the couch. Then Dad would trip over Ken and wake him up if he started night-wandering.

The sane part of me forced my lips open to say *no,* my tongue ready at the top of my palate.

Ken's eyebrow arched.

I just couldn't take care of Dad right now. He was the only person I could touch without getting fragments, but every moment I spent with him lucid rubbed me raw. For the past year he'd have these weird, raving fits; crying in a hoarse voice about hiding from sea monsters and burning dark-eaters and other crazy stuff. As if he'd pushed through Alzheimer's right into schizophrenia.

I am not considering this. Am. Not.

Marlin would freak if she found out. *Maybe I could pass Ken off as a school chum?* I snorted.

"I'll give you a two day trial," I said. *Think about uninterrupted sleep. Think about not failing classes.*

"I am at your service, then," said Ken, holding his bow low at the waist for far too long.

"Well, yes, then. Here," I flipped open my messenger bag and ripped a piece of paper out of a notebook to jot down phone and apartment numbers. "I gotta go to class now, for real, but if you could come to my apartment tonight…um, I could give you dinner. Say around 6:30? It's just ten minutes away from here walking."

"I'll be there," said Ken.

"Bye."

"Bye, then."

Neither of us moved. Like I was a high school freshman waiting for my senior boy crush to move first. I grabbed my bag strap determinedly and thrust past him. Two steps and I had to turn back to see what he did.

I watched him walk toward Stumptown Coffee. Maybe he really was going to get coffee. Most likely a caramel macchiato type; a layer of sweetness on top, but dark, rich bitterness on the inside.

Focus.

I booked it down the sidewalk. It sucked having everyone's eyes on me when I came in late. Kaneko-sensei considered himself a comedian. I'd laughed along with him when he made snide comments about other late arrivals before, but I didn't know if I could take his brand of sarcasm today on top of everything else.

Luckily, Kaneko-sensei must have been having a bad day, too. He was oddly subdued when I rushed in the door, barely giving me a glance as he strode to the podium.

He slapped a transparency on the projector and a chorus of groans erupted from the students scattered around the classroom. Pop quiz. Mishima and Kawabata. Both suicidal lunatic authors, but at least I'd read the short stories Kaneko-sensei assigned two weeks ago.

Scratching pencils and frustrated huffs of air filled the room. My mind kept bouncing between shots of the professor's eerie fragment and my own personal lunatics; Dad and Ken.

The dribble of latte I'd rescued wasn't enough to cut through my jumbled thoughts. Maybe there was still Dagoba chocolate hiding in my bag. I'd stashed a lavender-blueberry tasting square package last week when Marlin had taken me shopping at New Seasons.

Theobromides to the rescue!

But a moment of rooting around in my bag squashed all hopes.

Concentrate. You need to pass this class for elective credits, with or without chemical help. I didn't have the energy or money to waste on a different class; everything had to go for core classes in my accounting degree.

An accounting degree equaled a real life. A job I could do mostly surrounded by papers and computers at a desk, well paid, but with minimal risk of actually touching customers.

I pressed the backs of my hands into my eyes until the darkness flowed into a little burst of gray static. Right. Mishima quiz. I could picture the row of slim, paperback Japanese books on Dad's shelf. Mishima's last works were…Sea of Tranquility…

"Excuse me," said a man's voice from the corridor outside the open door. The professor from Stumptown Coffee. He stepped into the classroom and turned to face the class, staring straight at me.

CHAPTER TWO

Kaneko-sensei's furrowed frown relaxed into a smile. "Professor Hayk. What can I do for you?"

"I was hoping you'd let me make that little announcement about my research project."

"Yes, yes, of course," said Kaneko-sensei. He gestured at the podium at the front of the class. His fawning attitude was irritating. Snarky pants Kaneko acted like the professor was the university president or something. Kaneko-sensei didn't even warn us to close our quizzes. His eyes were focused entirely on the professor, on Hayk.

The girl who usually sat next to me, Elise something-or-other, sneaked a peek at her copy of Kawabata's *Snow Country* under the desk. She glared when she caught me looking.

"Professor Kaneko was kind enough to let me borrow time from his class. I'm doing linguistic research, and I'm looking for Japanese speakers familiar with lesser known dialects."

Elise had stopped her glare and was now as focused on Hayk as Kaneko-sensei. *Okay, so he is attractive, but can't she feel how creepy his vibes are?*

"Of course anyone who participates will be eligible for extra credit," said Kaneko-sensei. He all but wagged his tail at Hayk. *What is wrong with everyone?*

Hayk stepped away from the podium and walked down the aisle toward me. My scalp tingled. I shifted back in my seat.

"Koi, isn't it?" he said. I blinked at his black-and-red striped tie, unwilling to meet his eyes. *He knows my name?* Did he overhear Ken's and my conversation? Had he—worse—asked Kaneko about me?

My stomach tightened. "Yes," I said. My hands on my desk, my legs poised to get me up and walking away.

Simmer down now. Walking out on Kaneko-sensei's crush during a quiz was a straight path toward failure.

Hayk put a hand on my desk and I flinched.

He sniffed.

I risked a glance at his face. Amused disdain. He let his little finger stray closer to my hand grasping the quiz paper. I scooted back.

His eyes stayed hard, but the corners of his mouth twitched.

"Oh yes," said Kaneko. "Koi, your father is Issei, isn't he? From somewhere in Aomori?"

Shut up. Shut up! I wished my Japanese professor's overpriced Nikes would fly up and strike him in the mouth. Unfortunately, they just walked him closer.

"Is that so?" said Hayk.

"Yes?"

"Yes," said Elise, pushing her silky blonde hair behind a multiple-pierced earlobe. "Didn't you so kindly tell the class what was meant by that Northern dialect passage the translator flubbed in the *Dancing Girl of Izu?*" The full wattage of her smile was solely directed at Hayk. He barely even turned.

"Great. Then you'll help me?" said Hayk.

"Of course. I'll bring her down right after class," said Kaneko-sensei.

Hayk took his hand from my desk to wave it in a negative motion in front of Kaneko-sensei's face.

"No, no, that's not necessary."

Kaneko-sensei's expression turned from sloppy puppy to hangdog in a matter of seconds.

"It would really be no trouble," he said.

The bitter scent of cardamom layered on top of the rotted-cantaloupe smell of old blood. *Gag.* The dead girl's glassy eyes rose up inside my mind and swam over my vision. I gripped the edge of my desk so tightly my pinkie nail bent to the point of breaking.

"I'm so sorry," I ground out between clenched teeth. *Just breathe. Breathe and it will pass.* "I've got pressing matters to attend to after class."

Someone snorted. Probably Elise, but fragment static still lingered in the corners of my eyes.

"Oh, it will only take a moment, I'm sure Koi has the time," Hayk said, and this time his voice was warm and low-pitched.

Hayk inhaled audibly, and suddenly the cardamom and molasses-sweet oats was overwhelmed by the salty tang of the ocean.

Energy coiled in the air, tightening around my desk. Hayk slowly lifted his hand to where a jade Buddha tie clip held his tie in place, and pressed his finger to the back of the clip.

He winced, and I caught a slight smear of red on his thumb. My hackles raised, my heartbeat speeding up. *Damn the quiz.* I'd make it up somehow. *Danger is here. Get away, get away...*

"I'm sure you have *a-short-time-before-an-important-errand* to lend me," said Hayk, his voice sonorous, brushing over the skin of my face and neck before sinking in deep. Biting tingles skittered up and down my arms.

I blinked. For a moment everything in my visual field flickered, like the room spun a faster-than-light 360 degrees and ended up the way it was before, only somehow more focused and sharply clear.

My fingers unclenched. Puzzled faces of the class surrounded me. Fear melted away like butter on Marlin's waffle griddle.

All of a sudden the fact that I had fifteen minutes to spare at the end of class became a glaring beacon in my mind. Of course I had a short time, before my important errand of...of...I swallowed down a strange, salty thickness in my throat.

"Y-yes, I'll stop by your office before I leave," I found myself saying. Unease curled around the edges of my words, making them hesitant and soft. My hands were tingling. I flexed my fingers, and then pulled the band off my braid, running my hands through the tangled strands just to give them something to do other than break nails on my desk.

"Now that we've got that all worked out," said Kaneko-sensei. "Everyone back to the test." His words came out a bit pouty.

Hayk gave me a long, slow smile that didn't quite reach his eyes. His front teeth were pocked, like he'd spent hours sucking lemons or had bad dental care in childhood.

"I will see you later," he ordered, and then strode to the door, dropping a crumpled tissue in the garbage by the door.

The rest of the class passed in a blur. When the clock ticked over to 4pm, I stood and gathered my things.

"Sure you don't need someone to walk you down to Professor Hayk's office?" said Elise. She reached for my books, and I jerked them away.

"I guess not, then."

Not making friends again, here. I already had the Rite-Aid clerk and Ken fragments to deal with tonight, I didn't think my mind could deal with whatever Elise dreamed about at night. What did such a white-bread, ex-cheerleader type dream about anyway?

Most people dreamed the same things; flying, missing class, being chased, falling. There was something just a tad off-kilter about Elise, despite her flawless skin and perky smile. Elise probably dreamed of haunted, gothic mansions or axe-murdering.

I tried to shake off the dark thoughts. Kaneko-sensei told me Hayk's office number as I left, and before I knew what I was doing, I found myself standing in a deserted corridor in the basement of the Social Sciences building, running a finger over a frayed place on my bag's strap.

My calves were strung tight with tension, ready to take me down that silent hall and back up the concrete stairs to the bustling student courtyard. At the same time, a sea-deep voice inside me kept insisting, *you do have a short time.* The voice was heavy, outweighing all my silly fears.

The door opened.

"Ms. Pierce, come in," said Professor Hayk. His presence was solid and unhurried, standing there as if he'd known I was wavering outside his door. I carefully looked everywhere but his face.

He stepped back into his office, leaving the door open.

"Of course," I said, caught in the spell of polite convention. Too hard to get out of this with him halfway across the room already.

Hayk's office was not professorial. Geometric-patterned rugs hung in rich golds and crimsons from every wall. A pair of desk lamps with swirling star shapes painted in dark blue on the shades cast strange shadows under the bare-bulb fluorescent lights. Against the wall behind the desk was a huge chunk of gray, scarred stone, thick as two men and taller than Hayk by a few feet. At the top was a stylized image of some animal with huge, curling horns.

It was like stepping into the luxurious lair of a sheik from one of Marlin's paperback bodice-rippers.

Hayk's monotone-gray desk and chairs jarred with the sensuous feel of the room.

The image of that pale, dead girl flashed through my mind, her broad, high-arched nose, and the blood streaking her torso. *Just five minutes. What could happen in five minutes?*

"Sit down," he commanded. I found myself obeying his order, taken off guard by his impatient tone, so less smooth than he'd been in Kaneko-sensei's class. The folding chairs in front of his desk seemed to be there to discourage sitting. I squirmed, the metal seat-edge biting into the backs of my knees through the soft cotton-spandex of my workout pants.

Hayk lowered himself onto the edge of his desk, his presence filling my field of vision; on purpose, I was sure.

"I'm looking for a list of words in an obscure Aomori dialect, the one spoken in Herai-machi."

I blinked. Coincidence that the dialect he was looking for happened to be Dad's native tongue? Or had he checked me out somehow before, did he *know*?

Frown creases appeared around Hayk's mouth. He looked unpleasantly surprised I hadn't just gushed out my impatience to help him.

Yeah, there's a crack in that hot professor façade. Deal with it.

The last thing I wanted to do, no matter the urge to come here, was to tell him anything about Dad or my background.

I shivered. Despite the boiler-overheated spicy air in the room, a damp feeling pressed in on all sides, like I was swimming in Hayk's smarmy regard.

I couldn't just sit here, silent. My left leg jittered on the floor. Tension coiled in the air. I would rather sit through a Leverage marathon with Marlin than tell the professor anything about myself.

"My father's from Herai-machi," ground out through clenched lips.

Hayk's frown eased into that disdainful smirk.

"Of course he is," he said. "Then you will help me." It wasn't a question. He swiveled, and took a sheaf of papers from a neat pile. A quick glance showed the papers on his desk were lists; words in multiple languages, some that didn't look Indo-European or Romantic or Germanic.

Prickles moved down my arms. Hayk totally creeped me out for no reason at all I could justify. *Just say yes to anything he wanted and get out of here.* I had dinner to worry about, and Dad and Ken the not-a-stalker…

"What can I do for you?"

Hayk held out the papers, clearly intending for me to take them. I did, carefully. Even so, that molasses-oat bran scent, tinted with cardamom hit me full in the nostrils. I coughed behind a clenched fist.

"I need some translations, the Herai Dialect equivalent of these Japanese vocabulary. It's all explained on the paper."

Why did he need Aomori dialect translations? What kind of research was he doing? If I asked it would only prolong this encounter.

"Okay, then. I'll take a look," I said. I couldn't stand up with him sitting on the edge of the desk like that without running the danger of brushing against him. He made no move.

Narrowed eyes pricked my skin. A thousand questing needles. I met his eyes this time, willing myself to look innocent. Like oh-so-helpful Elise. An ex-cheerleader, completely free from any images of dead girls in hallways.

"There's something about you," he said. He reached forward and grabbed my wrist.

He is touching me. Touching *me!* My brain gibbered, helpless. A fragment washed into me like an arctic wave. I was sinking…sinking…down into the depths of an endless aquamarine.

Breathe. Get a hold of yourself. Patterned rugs and the gray-metal desk swam back into view.

"Something different," he said, his voice taking on a tinge of that sonorous *otherness* I'd felt in Kaneko-sensei's class. I'd thought his eyes brown, but thin rings now glowed bluish-green around his pupils.

"No, sir," I said, gulping for air. His fragment filtered all the way down to the pit of my stomach. A feeling like I'd eaten too much wasabi all at once burned just under my navel. I stood up abruptly, kicking the chair back. I felt the heavy presence of the dead girl, her cold, glassy eyes.

Hayk looked at his hand on my wrist, frowned and then released my arm, rubbing his hands together as if he'd bruised his palms instead of my wrist. I hooked my hands in my messenger bag strap, wanting the sharp points of my elbows between us. I took another step back, my head roiling with scents and sights I couldn't process.

I should never have left my house this morning.

"I'll...just be going, then," I mumbled. All of sudden I felt a strange, irritated energy. Like I'd downed Greg-ever-chipper's favorite concoction of espresso and Red Bull. Hayk's blue-ringed eyes drilled into me, but he stayed intensely still as I made for the door. Like the coiled power of some predator content to let its prey escape...for now.

My back prickled, my skin expecting the sharp slash of the knife from his fragment any moment. I turned the knob, relief flushing through me in a hot wave. *Escape.*

"Bring those translations back in a week, Ms. Pierce," Hayk called out.

I nodded, shutting the door behind me very, very carefully, not exhaling until I heard the latch click.

Immediately the tension simmering in my belly traveled up to my temples where it started a pre-headache throbbing.

What was that? Oh god, I am losing it. A professor asked me to translate some words and I freaked out. So he touched me. So maybe I got another fragment. Did I have to rush out of there like he was a serial killer or something? I gulped. *Okay, bad analogy.* But it wasn't like he was researching medieval torture instruments or germ warfare.

I glanced at the sheaf of papers in my hand. He just wanted the Herai Dialect equivalent of these words. Poetic phrases that had no direct English equivalent. "The feeling of a memory you know you once had but have forgotten," and "an instance of total surprise," and "the poignancy of an ephemeral beauty just before it passes."

I squinted at the bottom sheet. A whole list of scientific looking names, possibly plants? Nothing I couldn't handle with my own grasp of Herai dialect and black-belt google-fu.

Hardly research to make me queasy. I shook my head. It was easy to run away from awkward situations. Much harder to stay and deal with my stupid paranoia. And I'd determined not to take the easy way out anymore.

Marlin's exasperated voice piped up in my brain. *Don't be the 'noid' in 'paranoid,' Koi Ne-chan.* A weird, high-pitched giggle escaped my lips. Time to follow Marlin's advice. Head home and find comfort in the safety of my apartment.

The shuttle bus was crowded, and I had to concentrate on my breathing and keep very, very still not to accidentally brush anyone. Down the street from my apartment, a thought finally percolated through my exhausted fugue.

Ken. Crap. And Marlin dropping off Dad. *Holy crap.* Even the sanctuary of my apartment was breached.

I took a deep breath. *Okay, first things first.* Sort dinner, and then tackle the other problems. I could detour to Trader Joe's and pick up some of that pre-packaged bulgogi Dad loved, and hope Ken wasn't a vegetarian.

Somehow the image of Ken with veggie sticks and tempeh didn't quite mix. I imagined him tearing the flesh away from a bulgogi rib, wiping sauce from the corner of his wide mouth.

Inside Trader Joe's sliding doors I stopped, my heart pounding for no good reason at all, causing a guy with two squirming toddlers in his basket to crash into me.

"Sorry," I mumbled. He gave me an exasperated look. I quickly took a hand basket and made for the relatively less crowded snack aisle. I sifted through my encounters, thinking about Ken, and how I'd not been afraid of him even when I thought he was a stalker. Outside of Stumptown Coffee when he'd touched me while rescuing me from Hayk, I hadn't once flinched. Like the deepest part of me held no fear of his fragments. His hand on my elbow had been a cocoon of warmth.

I squatted to reach some of Dad's favorite sesame-flavored *senbei* crackers on the bottom shelf. Ken was coming to dinner. Inside my apartment.

The plastic-wrapped *senbei* crackers crinkled loudly under my grip. *Big deal.* People went into other people's apartments all the time. It was normal. I liked normal.

Make the dinner, lock the door on your bedroom tonight, and try not to make things all morbanoid and dramatic. Drama was Marlin. I was supposed to be the rational one. I gave a firm smile to the Hawaii-shirted clerk at the only open check-out counter. Of course it would be the one with Trader Joe's current chocolate display.

Their dark chocolate left a gritty aftertaste that wasn't my favorite, but I snagged a tub of chocolate-covered dried blueberries.

Antioxidants were important.

Outside the store I popped open the tub and ate a few before stuffing the rest in my bag.

Velvety bitter-sweet washed the last tint of salty cardamom from my mouth. I walked down the almost empty streets not caring about the sprinkle of light rain coating me.

Ken was sitting on a bench under the double-blossom cherry tree outside my apartment building's garage when I walked up the sidewalk with my grocery bag.

My weariness drained away and something suspiciously bubbly welled up in its place.

Ken stood up, a smile lighting his face. He gave a little wave, his smile turning to a sheepish grin. That grin, the flash of white teeth peeking through his lips, did something to my insides. I frowned.

Why did the sight of him feel so normal?

"Don't tell me," I said, "You've been waiting here the whole time?"

He pointed to his shirt, no longer an OHSU sweatshirt, but a short-sleeved button down shirt in a black and white geometric pattern. "Not the whole time," he said. Maybe it was just the drizzle in the air, but he seemed less round-cheeked, as if the rain stripped him down to cleaner lines, sharper-boned features.

He reached for my grocery bag.

"It's okay," I said, pushing past him to cover my awkward flinch. "I've got it."

"I was being careful," he said. "I wouldn't have touched your hand." I heard him take a deep breath. "Why don't you…why won't you acknowledge what you are?"

I swiveled around. I remembered very clearly Marlin in our backyard, recoiling from me, her own sister, as I told her of what she'd dreamed the night before.

A lesson burned into the marrow of my bones. Don't tell, don't speak of it to anyone. Even Mom had skirted carefully around any hint of my strangeness, as if this was the one thing even she couldn't wrestle to the ground.

Let it go. Smooth it over. Act like nothing's out of the ordinary. First Hayk, now Ken. Everything that I'd kept secret all these years was threatening to explode all over my new-and-improved life. *Hell to the no.* I was going to get my degree. I was going to have a normal life. No more scared hermit.

I flung myself around, hefting my bag toward Ken. He grabbed it just before it hit the ground. Wide irises of French roast brown searched my face as if answers were written in the pores of my skin. My cheeks tingled. *Please play normal for now. Please.*

"Well, come on," I said, in Mom's no-nonsense, let's get on with it, voice. I ran up the stairs to the second floor and paused outside my door. Had I left underwear anywhere embarrassing? How messy was my apartment?

No help for it now. I fumbled the key in the lock.

Behind me, Ken hovered, a warmth on my back in the chill of the covered corridor. I'd already touched him twice today. Would I dream his fragments tonight? My back bowed into an awkward curve to get the door open without backing into him.

Not fear of a fragment, this skittish energy. Certainly not afraid to touch him. It must be natural hermit reluctance at the intrusion into my lair.

Really, that's all it is.

I directed Ken toward my galley kitchen and he started unpacking groceries. He opened my fridge and laughed.

"Do you survive on coffee alone?"

"It's been a busy week." And Subway was cheap.

Ken perched on one of my second-hand barstools, sitting with a straight posture I usually saw in people who did yoga or were ballet dancers.

I took things out of the grocery bag, setting the *senbei* snacks on the counter. After a moment of silent reconnaissance, Ken got up. "Here, let me help with dinner," he said.

"It's okay, I'm just heating up bulgogi in the microwave, and then some marinara and spinach noodles."

There wasn't room in my galley kitchen for two adults. Too little space between us, and every particle of it charged with the tall length of him, towering over me this close. His long limbs rested on a barstool, waiting, patient. For now. How much time and space would he give me before whatever had sharpened him, sitting under the Portland rain, won out over this amiable façade?

Whatever this was, this unspoken tension filling the room, it certainly made me feel awake—like a double shot Depth Charge espresso awake.

I coughed, turning back to my distorted reflection in the metal sink. Evidently he was content to let this simmer. *Small talk. That's what we need.* I pushed the jar of marinara toward him and indicated a saucepan hanging from a hook by the stove.

"I guess you can heat that up," I said. The bag of baby arugula ripped down the middle, so I dumped it all in the salad spinner. Then, in a passable approximation of Marlin's cheery chatter voice, I said, "So…where did you arrive in Portland from?"

He stopped in mid-unscrew of the jar.

"You really don't know, do you?" he said.

My hands crept up to rub over my upper arms, trying to soothe goose bumps prickling all over me. "Illuminate me."

Ken bowed his head for a moment, taking a deep breath. He muttered something in harsh, male, Japanese. He didn't strike me as high-strung, but there was definitely a battle going on behind those dark eyes.

After a tense moment, he looked up, evidently having decided to go along with the inane small talk instead of letting out whatever was brewing. He poured sauce into the pan and took down my wooden spoon to stir. "I was born in Tochigi, at the base of Nantai-san, but I grew up all over Japan. I'm usually based out of Tokyo now, but I've just spent some years in Kyoto." He said Kyoto gingerly, like he was expecting me to nod knowingly or arch an eyebrow or flinch or something. A test of some kind?

Instead I bent over the sink, filling my spinner bowl with water. I was going to fail this test. "That sounds nice."

Ken's presence behind me felt close, too close. My back went all shivery as if it were cold, but the kitchen was warm, too warm. "I didn't spend much time touring the shrines and palace. It was more of a…duty than a pleasure."

What to say next that isn't inane? I rubbed my eye with the back of a damp hand. I was reacting to his presence like a hormonal high school girl. He was just a nice, weird guy reheating spaghetti sauce. I was just a nice girl a tad more introverted than most. We should be able to make conversation and dinner.

Ken closed in behind me. I tensed, clutching the plastic spinner bowl to my stomach for protection.

"Koi," he said, his voice a soft breath on the back of my neck. I felt the pressure of a hand on my shoulder, and then the spiciness of male aftershave swallowed the bitter arugula smell.

"Koi?" he said again and this time his voice delved all the way inside and made me want to lean back into him, enfold myself in that warmth and scent. His palm lightly trailed down my back, and then fell away. My breath caught. A rush of awareness swept down my body, curling my bare toes against the chill floor tiles.

"I'm not here in my official capacity," he said. "There's no need to be so wary."

"I don't understand." *Space, I need space.* I couldn't keep up this façade of normality with him invading my personal bubble.

"This wall between you and the world, it doesn't hide your nature," he said. "But you have nothing to fear from me."

I whirled on him, sharp words about strangers and their unasked for advice ready on my tongue. The open bewilderment in his eyes stopped the words, but we were too close, pressed together in each other's space. It was like he gave off an ambient glow, and my skin soaked in that warmth like a sponge. Our breath mingled for a jittery moment; coffee and wintergreen.

"Who are you?" he whispered, an urgency twisting between us, forcing me open and vulnerable. The laugh crinkles were gone. His eyes bored into me, really *seeing* me.

Koi Pierce didn't do vulnerable.

"I'm Koi." The hard syllables of my name lanced the tension in the air. "And existential questions of existence can wait until after dinner."

Ken laughed, his features softening "And just as self-sufficient and full of gravitas as your namesake, I suppose."

I squinted at him. "How the hell did you come up with a word like gravitas?"

He leaned forward, sniffing. "I think the sauce is burning."

I elbowed him out of the way and grabbed the wooden spoon. A burnt crust had formed on the bottom of the saucepan. I switched off the burner.

"Hope you aren't too hungry," I said.

"Actually, I'm ravenous," he said, and circled to the other side of the counter.

I gave him most of the rescued sauce and covered my own noodles with a boatload of parmesan and cracked pepper. We sat on barstools at the counter. Ken hardly touched the salad at all. He slurped up his noodles Japanese-style, proving once and for all he wasn't American-bred. Mom had complained a million times when Dad did the same thing.

Between bites we talked about school and my sister. Every time I probed into Ken's life, he steered the conversation back to me. There was no way to fend off his skillful chatter without being direct and rude. The twinkle in his eyes told me he enjoyed watching me try to wrangle words.

A knock sounded at the door.

I flinched. I'd forgotten entirely about Marlin. And Dad.

Ken pointed to the door with a fork burdened with noodles. "Aren't you going to answer that?"

"Of course," I snapped, savagely spearing a piece of lettuce.

I dropped my fork, lettuce uneaten, and pushed away from the counter, almost knocking over my water glass.

I clicked open the two locks and slid the sticky deadbolt. Marlin stood in the hall, one hand clasped around Dad's middle.

I gave her my most baleful big-sister stare.

Marlin sighed. Dad sported a scraggly, half-grown beard and gray-translucent skin stretched tight over sharp cheekbones. My always fastidiously clean father, even at the worst of his spells, never left the house unshaven. One of Mom's Hawaiian flag quilts draped across his shoulders like a lifejacket.

"I can't handle Dad like this," said Marlin. "The Daycare program nurse won't take him anymore."

"Damn it, Marlin," I said, stepping forward and putting my arms around Dad. I could feel him trembling slightly, like an alcoholic in withdrawal. "How long's he been like this?"

"A week."

"Is he taking his meds? Why didn't you take him to the doctor?

36

You can't just let this go for so long!"

"Don't," said Marlin. "Of *course* I took him to the doctor. Of course his meds are fine."

I blinked back tears. This wasn't easy for Marlin, either. Miss Fixer not able to fix one of the people who mattered most. I shook my head and pulled Dad into the apartment. Ken stood up, but I waved him back out of sight. Marlin didn't need to meet him right this instant.

Dad fell onto my couch like a limp jellyfish. Marlin turned away like she was leaving. *What?* I lunged out into the hall. "Look, I know Dad's difficult. But I'm trying to make something of myself here. I can't take him like this and still get to classes."

"*Really?*" said Marlin, spinning around to reveal red-rimmed eyes and her own tears making wet trails down her cheeks. "This time is going to be different, how? You're not going to start skipping classes when things get too *difficult?* You're not going to stop returning calls? Ignoring all the boring details of life that just weigh you down, like, maybe, oh just off the top of my head, something like Mom dying of cancer?"

"You don't understand what it was like."

Behind me, I heard Ken shift, murmuring something in Japanese to Dad.

"Save it," she said, palm out as if she could physically stop my protests. "You've given up on every course you've ever taken. You copped out on Mom when she needed you most. You can just suck it up for once in your life, for Dad."

"Marlin," I said, anger turning to a leaden pain. It wasn't true. I didn't just give up. She didn't understand how difficult it was every single damn day for me.

I shuddered. How could I explain what it felt like when Mom was dying? At first she kept wanting me to touch her, and I'd hold her hand and feel a chill, crawling emptiness pass into me.

But even worse was when Mom figured out something was wrong.

She looked at me, and slowly, her fingers had loosened in my hand.

"Do you know why I named you Koi?" she had said. "Because you were always so sturdy, so strong, even when you were just a keiki. And I wanted you to remember, when it got hard," here Mom's voice had cracked. She coughed, and I took her water tumbler from the side table and carefully held the plastic straw to her cracked lips.

She swallowed with such an obviously painful effort my own throat ached.

"Koi can live on any continent, in almost all temperatures. Survive even in the muddiest water. And that's what you've got, eh?" I looked through the glass window where the OHSU nurses in their cheery scrubs hustled back and forth down the corridor. "Muddy water," Mom repeated.

"It's okay," I said, moving to hold her hand again.

She batted weakly at my fingers. "You've got to take care of yourself when you spend all day stirring up what lies on the bottoms of ponds."

The morphine was messing with her brain. Mom was being all emotional and fuzzy and skirting dangerously near topics best kept packed away. I hugged the stuffed red devil I'd sewn with a cape and giant A when she'd started her Adriamycin chemo. Captain Red Devil. It was supposed to kill all those pesky, metastasizing cells.

"Sometimes being strong, my little fish, means settling down to the bottom of the pond and sitting tight through winter," she said. "Surviving has to be done alone, in the end."

My heart broke into a thousand painful shards there in that room. Mom was giving me permission. Not to come to the hospital. Not to touch her. Not to get those bone-sharp chill fragments from a dying woman.

She would never say it out loud, but she knew.

Dreaming her death night after night had hollowed me into a shell of bone and grief.

Tears burned at the corners of my eyes.

I curled my hands into fists. *Stuffed toys or blubbering isn't going to help Marlin or Dad. Keep it together.*

"Please," said Marlin, pleading. "See if you can help him."

"I'm..." I bit back the word "sorry" forming on my tongue. If I apologized, it would be like admitting everything she accused me of was true.

Marlin took a quick, shallow breath. The polished mask she usually only used with clients slid into place. "Two weeks," she said firmly and strode off down the hall.

Behind me, Dad was mumbling. The tempo of the stumbling words increased until they streamed from his mouth in his incomprehensible, gravelly, Aomori village dialect. Just as I turned around, he stopped.

Eyes wide, face pale with tension, Dad spoke in clear, accentless, English. "You've got to get away, Koi. Before it's too late. Run away!"

CHAPTER THREE

Ken sat next to Dad on the couch. Dad had his arms wrapped around bent knees, rocking back and forth, mumbling gibberish in Herai dialect again.

My cheeks flushed hot. We were a family of lunatics.

"Can you get a glass of water, please?" I asked Ken.

There had to be tranquilizers left in my bathroom cabinet from my last stint as caregiver. Marlin had reminded me to update the prescription but I…yes, here they were. I grabbed the plastic bottle and raced back to the living room.

Ken stood in the kitchen with an unreadable expression, water glass in hand. I grabbed the glass and headed back to the couch.

"Dad?"

More mumbling. All in that Aomori prefecture Herai dialect. Whatever burst of energy had prompted that crazy warning in English, it was gone now.

I pulled him onto the floor next to me and gathered him close, pinning his elbows to his sides with one arm, while with the other I pushed a small, pink pill into his mouth. So thin. Like his bones might poke through the frail parchment of his skin.

Dad fought me, spitting the pill back out.

"Let me," said Ken, coming round the couch.

"No, it's fine," I said, tone biting. "Just leave us alone for a minute."

Ken backed away, heading to the bathroom.

Without the audience, the panic inside me eased.

"Dad, you have to take this pill, okay? Please just take it." I repeated both in English and Herai dialect. On the third repetition, Dad let the pill in through the barrier of his lips.

He swallowed, his Adam's apple convulsing, but when I tried to get him to sip water, he dribbled it all down the front of his shirt.

I let go, keeping the burning behind my eyes from spilling out in tears by biting my bottom lip.

Dad could sleep in my room tonight. But I had to unfold the couch for Ken.

A flush sounded in the bathroom.

The faster, the better.

In record time, I had the couch unfolded, threw blankets and a pillow on top, and pulled Dad into my room.

"Make yourself at home," I called to Ken as I shut the door.

For a moment, I just sat on the edge of my bed next to Dad, breathing in and out, feeling like my tiny room was the safest place in the universe.

Safer than out there, where I would have to find something to say to Ken and his carefully neutral expression.

Dad yawned, his eyelids heavy with tranquilizer-doziness. I helped him lay out on my bed, tugging off his flip flops. *Crap.* The Japanese style futon was folded up in the closet out there. No way was I going back out there. I grumbled like an old lady while I made a nest of blankets on the floor to sleep in, but the tranquilizer must have worked on Dad. He made only the hitching rhythm of sleep-breathing, and there was no sound from the living room at all.

Despite the leftover adrenaline in my system, I only had a few moments to wonder about what Ken wore as he lay on my couch bed outside the bedroom door, before I, too, fell asleep.

And dreamed.

A flash of the dead movie star's face in his movie-villain's makeup, streaked with inky tears. I ran from some nameless, shadowy terror, before a part of me recognized this wasn't my dream, but the Rite-Aid clerk's fragment.

The dream blurred, coalescing into a dark forest.

Yellow eyes peeked from behind a canopy of dark branches. Overwhelmingly heady scents of musk and bitter green, the old dry must of moss leaving a patina on my tongue.

Urgency filled me. I crouched low against the pine-carpet, my arms and legs awkwardly angled, but strong, shaking with the need to run...and then I did. A blur of motion, breath burning through my lungs, and a speed like falling through misted air.

There was another, terrible dream after that. Then I awoke, sweating and gasping for air, feeling bloated and swollen like I'd just had a Thanksgiving feast.

None of the bad dreams from last night were gone this morning. They crowded together at the corner of my eyes, pressed on the inside of my skull, spreading creaky dark-wings over me. Daylight shifted in through the shuttered window. From my sprawl on the floor, I craned my neck to see the lump of Dad's shape buried in the blankets under the brush-and-ink Baku drawing, the only decoration in my sparse bedroom.

I gave a ragged laugh. This was the first night in ten years I hadn't slept under the Baku drawing.

As a young girl, Dad used to put me to bed with tales from Herai village's version of evil dream-images. Two snakes twined together, a fox with the voice of a man, blood-stained garments, a talking rice-pot; just your common, Hicksville Japan, every day version of terror. Those images didn't frighten me, and I never had nightmares when

Dad tucked me in.

But on the nights he had the evening shift at Marinopolis, I had terrible, awful nightmares; not the full-on tangled and sweaty fragments I had after puberty, but dreams where nameless things chased me through dark places.

When, at eight years old, even the sight of Mom in my doorway at night made me burst into tears, Dad took out his calligraphy brush in the middle of the night. In *seiza* posture on my shag rug he ground ink on a stone and with careful, powerful strokes, brushed an ink outline of Baku, the Eater of Evil Dreams from Japanese folklore, onto thick rice paper bought at Kinokuniya. Baku looked like an elephant crossed with a tiger. Awkward, ungainly, and vaguely menacing, but if you said "Baku, come eat my dream" three times in Japanese upon awaking they were supposed to protect against the ill effects of bad dreams.

Dad hung that picture over my bed and the nightmares receded. They never went completely away, but they didn't cause me to startle awake in my bed in the morning, sweating and gasping for air.

At the beginning of 6th grade I got my first period, and other people's dream fragments started invading my night times. The mornings I woke with fear like a sour miasma surrounding my head and a bevy of electric eels swimming in my stomach, I opened my eyes and looked first at my Dad's ink drawing of the Baku.

It was oddly soothing to see the squashed-together, uncomfortable looking parts of its body echoing the disjointed feeling in my own limbs. Stark, black ink on creamy white a crisp contrast, helping me tease out other people's fragments from my own reality.

Sadly the sight of the Baku was doing nothing for me this morning.

I took a deep breath, feeling it catch in my lungs on pockets of phlegm like cotton ball stuffing. Sticky trails of dried tears streaked my face. Just turning my head to check Dad had made my shoulder muscles scream like I'd paddled the entire distance of the Willamette.

That forest dream, as incomprehensible as it was in the bright morning light of day, was not the cause of my nausea and unease.

The last dreams I'd experienced, in the early morning hours before I'd clawed my way through clinging dream cobwebs to consciousness had been Hayk's fragment.

No longer just the dead girl in the hall.

A young boy, too. My perspective had been from above. I'd seen him lying far below me down some kind of well or mud hole. Thick, black hair turning to shiny curls against his head where viscous blood welled.

The boy was dead. And all I felt was a satisfied glee, a sick triumph.

Remembering it now made my stomach clench.

Hayk is a bad, bad man.

Hayk dreamed of death, dreamed of killing people and was pleased by it. These were not nightmares, they were too…excited. Strong emotions characterized fragments that weren't purely fantasy, but echoes of reality. Memory-dreams. Wicked memories. That wickedness sat heavily, making my stomach roil.

I was not over-reacting about this project. It seemed so innocuous, just translating some words, but I didn't want to help Hayk. I didn't want to get anywhere near him again.

Swallowing nausea, I managed to sit up without the room spinning more than two or three times. I pressed thumbs into the inner eyebrow ridge near my nose, trying to keep my head from splitting apart by sheer force. It helped a little.

My need for the bathroom outweighed any embarrassment over risking Ken seeing my morning bed-head. I staggered to the bathroom and dry-swallowed three ibuprofen. The detangler Marlin had forced me to try felt cool in my palm, but it didn't seem to do much for the rat's nest of my hair. At least it smelled nicer than sleep-musk.

After a few minutes of pulling a wet brush through the worst snarls, I pulled everything back in a neat ponytail.

I had to get Dad to the bathroom, too. He sometimes wet the bed if I let him sleep too long in the morning.

When my head settled into a dull, throbbing ache, I risked moving over to kneel by the futon.

"Dad," I said. There was no movement. I poked at him through the covers, but the form under the blankets was strangely mushy. I ripped the top cover off completely. Underneath was a rolled up set of sweatpants and a pillow.

Oh god.

I rushed out the bedroom door and ran smack dab into a very familiar gray OHSU sweatshirt covering a hard and warm stomach.

"Oof," said Ken, his arms coming up to rest on my shoulders, "ever try actually looking where you're going?"

"Dad!" I said to him, my heart pounding. His morning scent was faintly bitter, and I couldn't stop myself from breathing it in deeply, savoring that bitterness.

"He left about ten minutes ago." Ken's eyes darkened, holding mine, the line between pupil and iris bleeding together, becoming obscured. Black eyes, like an animal's. I had a flash of pine needles on a forest floor, a gathered sense of power in my legs. Moss tasting like stale matcha and dirt on my tongue.

"He was very lucid. He knew his own name, the date, and that this was your apartment. He told me not to wake you and was out the door. I didn't see how I could protest."

"His nervous breakdown the night before wasn't a reason?" My hands curled into fists. I took another deep breath and closed my eyes. Punching Ken wouldn't get Dad back. "I have to find him. His lucid periods don't last long."

I made a move to go around Ken, only to be held in place with his hands heavy on my shoulders. I looked up and saw him sniff the air, then he looked down at me with a penetrating, direct gaze that made me squirm.

"Not like that," he said, his voice husky.

Oops. That's right. Underwear and a t-shirt were all that I had slept in last night. I hoped to god that the t-shirt at least covered me past my panty-line, but I couldn't pull my gaze away from Ken's to check. A furious flush crept down my neck on its way to my toes.

Ken laughed, low in his throat. A warm awareness washed over me, my flesh goose pimpling all over in places I knew were exposed. Those thick lashes lowered, narrowing his eyes into dark crescents that just barely betrayed movement as his gaze flickered over me from head to toe.

The hands on my shoulders slowly twisted me around and pushed me back through my open bedroom door. He shut the door between us silently. Controlled.

Dad could be lying in a ditch somewhere. Or singing Enka half-naked in the fountain at Pioneer Square. This was not the time for an awkward awareness dance with Ken.

I tore through my pile of semi-clean clothes on the floor in front of my dresser. I pulled on the first things that came to hand; a pair of jeans and short-sleeved, black hoodie with stylized wrasse swimming across the back. Another gift from Mom.

I was out the door again and down the steps of my apartment building before I realized Ken was close on my heels. He'd taken the time to mousse his hair up into spikes at the top and put on a pair of black jeans, though where he'd stashed them I had no idea since he'd shown up without any bags.

"You don't need to come," I said.

"Two people can cover more ground." Apparently he was taking his role as caretaker seriously.

"I can find him, wait there," I threw back over my shoulder. But Ken wasn't behind me anymore.

He was bent almost double near the mailbox at the end of the sidewalk. He was sniffing again. I halted my headlong rush. He pivoted, testing the air all around him. It should have looked ridiculous, but there was a sense of energy coiled in every muscle, as if he was holding back. Storm clouds pulsing just before they broke.

How had I not noticed before that his hair was long enough to curl at his neck? Or his shoulders so angular at the joints?

"He's gone down the street this way," Ken said. I shook my head. *For real?* What, he could sniff Dad out?

I pointed the opposite direction. "He almost always tries to get back to our old house in Tigard. He'd have gone south to Scholls Ferry."

Ken took a step toward me, his features sharp with that coiled intensity. "Are you some kind of test? Did the Council set this up? What do I have to do to prove—"

"I don't know what the hell you're talking about," I snapped. I took a step onto the sidewalk and somehow Ken was again in front of me. I blinked up at him.

"I didn't come here to stir up trouble. I am showing my willingness to cooperate," he said in a low growl.

"You are seriously freaking me out. I need to find my Dad. Let me past."

Ken's face relaxed into a careful blank, his eyes widening from those dark crescent moons of anger. Still disturbingly black, no white at all showing.

"I know your father, Koi. I'm not sure about you, but he is unmistakable. Even if you are as ignorant as you pretend, you must know that I am not exactly what I appear to be. I can *smell* him."

Ken twisted me around the opposite direction. *What was with him and the man-handling?* I pulled out of his grasp. Fine. I didn't know for sure which way Dad had gone. I just had to get moving before I burst.

Ken had that same air of capability as Marlin, as if he knew exactly what to do at all times. I was the queen of denial, but there was no denying something wasn't quite normal about him. Something not normal in the same way it wasn't normal to dream other people's dreams and to *know* you were doing it. To *know* that some dreams were just bad nightmares, and some truly memories of evil deeds.

I stalked down the sidewalk deeper into the residential neighborhood, past the middle school grounds. Freshly mowed, I could see no trace of my father's purple *jinbei* pajamas in the open expanse. And he'd never hide in the thorny border of riotous blackberry vines around the fence. Still I kept walking in the direction Ken indicated with a jerk of his chin.

Ken was impossible to ignore and write off as totally bonkers. And not just because something about his eyes made me shiver. So he wasn't normal. He could join my club. Hell, I'd elect him president if his sniffing actually found Dad.

Past the school we entered the small shopping district. No sign of him here. I stopped abruptly, but that dancer's grace served Ken well; he halted without missing a beat. He wasn't even breathing hard from our fast-paced walk.

"Now where?" I said, indicating the major crossroads past the row of shops.

Ken bent his head close to my ear and breathed in deeply. I arched away from him.

"What the hell?"

"Your scent is very strong, mixed in with your father's. I was just trying to distinguish the two." He arched an eyebrow at me.

"And?" I tapped my foot.

"This way," he said, pointing across Scholls Ferry to the shuttle bus stop for PCC.

Please, no. Please don't let Dad have gotten on a bus.

Touching Dad never gave me his fragments, but he sometimes dreamed mine.

One Friday evening in my teens, after I'd started dreaming fragments, I'd been at his house for the weekend and fell down his steep basement stairs with a six pack of coke bottles. Picking out the glass bits and cleaning up my knee had required him, reserved as a monk, to touch my bare skin.

And that night when I'd dreamed the inevitable fragments picked up from classmates at school, there had been a dark dream, a nightmare.

I had woken up exhausted. At breakfast, Dad casually asked me who I'd eaten lunch with the prior day. I knew something was up—Dad never asked about friends or school work or activities, that was Mom's territory. I blathered some answer about my current best, actually only, friend Lisa.

The next Monday at school, Lisa didn't sit next to me in English. In P.E. she avoided my eyes.

She wasn't at school the next day.

Whispers finally reached me a week later. Lisa's family had moved away suddenly. An anonymous caller had left messages at the school, and welfare services charged Lisa's father with sexual abuse.

I wasn't surprised about Lisa's Dad. It wasn't until after high school that I learned to separate truth memory-dreams from fantasy, but Lisa's nightmares had never been usual. Her dreams had been a shifting fog of pale, slender limbs posed naked against flannel sheets, and looming, cruelly twisted faces leering with stagnant eyes the same exact shade of green as Lisa's.

My surprise came from realizing Dad had dreamed Lisa's fragments—just from touching my wounded knee. Then he'd gone out and acted on the fragment; this man who'd never even showed up for a Parent's Night or Teacher conference once in my whole life.

If Dad had picked up the fragments I'd gotten from Hayk, there was only one place requiring a bus ride he'd be headed now.

Hayk's office.

I hoped to god he was lucid. "He's on his way to PCC," I blurted.

Ken gave me that searching look, like he was trying to see past my skin, directly into my brain. To keep from squirming, I bit my lip, curling my fingernails into my palms.

An urge to explain welled up so thickly inside me it was a pressure in my throat. For so long it had been only me and Dad, with Mom's suspicions unvoiced, a gentle wall between us and the world. Then Mom died. And Dad's lucid periods grew further and further apart.

Standing there, his eyes back to a macchiato brown, Ken's gaze searched *inside* me like he wasn't afraid of what he might find, like he wanted to know. A soggy lump settled under my breastbone—the urge to tell Ken the truth. The whole truth.

I felt…the opposite of scared.

Words welled out in a rush.

"That professor you saved me from yesterday, Dr. Hayk, Dad's gone to his office."

"Because…?"

What could I tell him? Because Hayk had evil murder dreams and they terrified me? This thin limb I had climbed out on was shaking, threatening to snap off entirely.

How quickly could the warm interest in his face turn to condescending shock?

"Because he must have seen some papers from Dr. Hayk I had yesterday. I agreed to translate stuff for Hayk into my father's Herai dialect, and maybe my father latched onto that." That was close enough to the truth.

Ken wasn't fooled. He arched a devastating eyebrow at me. "Is this some game you're playing with the new guy in town?" His lips curled into a smirk. "Not what I expected of Herai-san at all." He lowered his chin to his chest and took a deep breath. "All my instincts are telling me I should walk away."

Heat rose to my scalp line. I was such a fool. Marlin always teased me about my unclear boundaries. One close moment in the kitchen over spaghetti sauce, and all of a sudden I had to fight the urge to tell Ken secrets I'd been keeping my whole life.

No more crazy sniffing and eyes that saw too much. I would find Dad on my own. Safer all around.

"So why don't you?" I snapped.

Ken reached for my hand, but I jerked away. He straightened the entire, long length of himself, and then crowded me so I was trapped between the bus stop bench and his chest.

"Because I've never met anyone like you," he said in a low, growly voice. "Because you and your father are hard people to leave alone."

What the hell does he mean by that?

"And," he continued, "because Herai-san is one of only three known Baku left on the Earth, and you are terrified that he's gone to this professor, Hayk's, office."

I blinked at him.

"Terrified beyond mere concern over him just getting lost," said Ken.

"Baku?" I said, only able to process that one word. I floundered, caught between incredulity-fueled irritation and fear for Dad.

The shuttle bus pulled up to the stop, and Ken lunged through the open door.

Words flung themselves against my skull like bluefish in a feeding frenzy. I stood there, staring at the open door. The driver let out an exasperated cough.

Okay, one step at a time. Get on the bus and *then* force Ken to explain what he meant by calling Dad a Baku.

Climbing the bus steps felt like crossing an irrevocable boundary. The annoyed driver gingerly accepted two paper tickets from the little booklet I'd stuffed in my hoodie pocket. He regarded me with all the jaded amusement of Portland bus drivers, as if it wouldn't surprise him if I suddenly sprouted wings or turned purple. Ken sniffing out Dad's scent like a bloodhound and calling him 'Baku' wouldn't have made him blink. Like he was a character from that TV show *Grimm* or something.

The seats were packed. A group of obvious exchange students, Korean probably, took up the entire back. Ken stood next to a pole attached to the seat of two girls with orange-dyed streaks in their glossy, smooth hair, and matching Coach bags.

"Tell me about Hayk. Why does the thought of your father with him scare you?"

I stood facing him, back to the front of the bus, trying not to bump into the Korean girl's knee. "You said *Baku*."

Ken sighed, and ran a hand through his hair, tousling the brown waves. The girl by the window smiled up at him, and he gave her an answering flash of teeth.

I cleared my throat as meaningfully as I could. The girl smirked, and then said something in rapid Korean to her companion. They giggled, the sound like a cheese grater on my already frayed nerves.

"Do you really need me to spell it out?" said Ken. "Focus on telling me what to expect when we reach PCC. Just exactly what kind of danger is Hayk? Is he Kind?"

Kind? Why the hell does that matter? The bus lurched, and I stumbled forward a little. Ken caught me with a light grip on my shoulders. His eyes went through that transformation, darkening so that iris and pupil were indistinguishable, a pool of intensity that spilled black into the white.

He wasn't just crazy. *I* wasn't just crazy. Something definitely *not normal* was happening here.

"You really don't know," he said, his voice husky. "Herai-san truly kept you ignorant?" His hands tightened on my shoulders. "Stupid fool."

I gasped. "Let me go." A squeak more than a command.

There was no air in the bus. He pulled me closer, only the cold metal of the pole between us. Somewhere far away, the Korean girls giggled again. My whole being was focused on Ken. He didn't feel safe at all, now; he felt volatile. Energy twisted in the air, like a thunderstorm's humid electricity before a sudden downpour.

"Tell. Me. Everything," he said.

The bus pulled to a stop in front of the student union, and I was torn from his grasp as the entire group of Korean students rose as one and shoved themselves out of the bus. Caught in the wave, I stumbled down the bus steps, little pricks of energy dancing over my skin.

Go. Go. Go. Get away. Away from Ken, away from those questions. Answers lay at the bottom of a deep whirlpool of madness, and I had deep scars from crawling my way out of that whirlpool before. *Holy crap, all I want to do is go to school and get my degree and live like a normal person.*

Scratch that self-pity whimpering. All I want right now is to find Dad.

I half-jogged through the bark chipped border of bayberry bushes, uncaring of the thorns snagging my jeans. Down the grassy slope toward the gray, concrete-and-brick buildings blurring into the even grayer Portland spring rains-clouded sky. Past the cafeteria to jump down the steps leading toward the two-story social sciences building. One step toward the lobby and I saw Elise from Kaneko-sensei's class loitering in front of the glass door, looking my way as if she wanted to snag my attention. Uh-oh, no time for her. Swiveling mid-step, I made for the outside staircase.

When I reached it, the area was deserted except for Ken, leaning against the door with his arms crossed in front of his chest.

"What took you so long?" he said. He wasn't even breathing hard. *How did he get here first?* His features had taken on that feral sharpness from when he'd been sniffing out Dad. Not a happy Ken.

Too bad.

"Get out of my way."

He straightened up and made an elaborate bow. "After you." I brushed past him to open the door, and felt his hovering thunderstorm energy flickering at the skin along my arm. A musk, familiar, rose to fill my nose and an acrid tang coated my tongue. For an instant I was crouching on a bed of pine needles, my fingers flexing with the urge to run.

Ken's dream.

I risked a quick glance at his face as I entered the building. His eyes were completely dark, not a bit of white showing.

Allrighty, then. Whatever it meant that I dreamed others' fragments, I was sure I was human. What was Ken? And what did it mean, despite his weirdness, that having him at my back felt safer than looking for Dad alone?

"Your father's scent is strong here," said Ken from behind me. I kept up a rapid stride down the hall. It was deserted, most of the frosted glass panes on the office doors showing no light. It was too early for professors to be in their offices. A glimmer of hope. Maybe Hayk wasn't here. Maybe Dad was already on his way home.

Hayk's door was ajar, light spilling out into the dim hallway.

I'd gotten this far in a panicked rush, but suddenly the idea of entering Hayk's lair was a pressure in my chest, forcing me to halt abruptly.

The dead boy at the bottom of the hole, his curls shiny with blood. The hawk-nosed woman in the hallway. The nauseating mix of cardamom and rotted cantaloupe.

"It's okay," said Ken, still in that husky voice. He put his hand on my shoulder.

Warmth spread down, unlocking my chest and allowing me to gulp in a deep breath. Just like that, the fragments went out like a match stuck in a glass of water.

A muffled sob came from inside Hayk's office. Dad. I stepped through the door. The same, cheap metal desk taunted me amongst luxurious crimson hangings. The ginormous stone pillar loomed against the wall. No Hayk. The sob came again. My dad was crumpled in the corner with his head between his knees.

"Dad?" I knelt beside him. My palm hovered over his back. A few times in the past when Dad had been in one of his 'states' he'd reacted violently when I touched him.

"Blood...she's covered in blood," said Dad. He'd for sure latched on to one of Hayk's fragments. It would only get worse if I touched him. I settled back on my heels.

"Dad, you've got to get up. We can't stay here."

He lifted his head. His face was mottled in patchy blotches of red, and shiny with tears.

A painful lump settled in my throat. I hated him like this, hated that I had to see it. Bear it. Torn between wanting to shake him and fold him into my arms, all I could do was kneel there, my fists clenched so tight I was trembling.

"Who's covered in blood?" said Ken. His legs, warm and solid, pressed into my back, supporting me.

"The girl in the hall," Dad whispered.

I gasped.

"The boy in the well."

Ken would assume this was dementia talking, but if Hayk overheard…

"Hayk can't find us in here," I said.

"Hayk's just a human," rumbled Ken. He moved around to crouch at Dad's side, my back chill without his supporting warmth. "No danger to Baku."

"Danger, Koi," said Dad. Shaking hands twisted themselves into my hoodie at the neckline. He stood up, wiry muscles still strong enough to bring me up with him. "Blood, everywhere," he ran a hand tensed into a claw through my hair, snagging tangles at the back. "Soaked through her blouse, ripped and torn."

"Stop," I hissed. "I'm right here. I'm fine."

My father ran a thumb clammy with sweat down the center of my forehead to the bridge of my nose.

"Koi," he said, his pupils focusing into black pinpricks. "Still alive."

Damn it, he isn't lucid. Touching him was a necessary risk. I grabbed his wrists and pulled Dad away from the wall.

"There's something here," said Ken, one hand on my shoulder. His musky smell overpowered the dusted, old spice and mold smell of Hayk's office.

"Yes, us," I snapped. "And soon Hayk, too."

Ken glared, his lips parted to show those white teeth. His nostrils flared, and his tongue flickered out, tasting the air. He slowly swiveled around. "Something not human or Baku."

He took a step toward the stone pillar.

Ken could stay here and play mystic psycho-dude, but I was getting Dad out of here. I pulled at Dad, but he locked his knees, focused entirely on Ken and the stone.

"This isn't just dead rock," said Ken. His palms hovered just over the surface of the stone, as if it were radiating a heat he could feel. "There's something here…something that feels like Kind, and doesn't."

"Vishap," said Dad. "I can't…I can't reach the dreams…I can't protect…" His whole body tensed, and shuddered, and I put an arm around his shoulder to take his weight as his knees buckled.

"The stone-scent is wrong," said Ken. "Like strange spices and salt-metallic. Something strong sleeps in this stone. We should leave before it wakes."

I gave an exasperated sigh. "Ya think?"

Ken shook his head, but took Dad's other arm and tucked it under his own. We pulled Dad away from the stone pillar and turned to leave.

Hayk stood framed in the doorway, his face a blank mask. It must have been his version of surprise, because a beat later I watched, a sinking feeling in my stomach, as his features flowed into an expression I thought only existed on animated TV shows; evil glee. He even rubbed his hands together.

"What a pleasant surprise, Ms. Pierce."

"Uh, Professor Hayk, ah, hi."

Dad mumbled something under his breath in Herai dialect. I couldn't quite catch the meaning, but Ken gave a slight jerk of his chin in Hayk's direction.

"Um, this is my father. I thought he might be able to help with the…uh translations."

"Excellent," said Hayk. He took a step into his office, and reached out like he was going to take my elbow. "Let me just—" he said, and Ken snarled.

He snarled.

I scuffled back, Dad's entire weight on me. Behind us, I heard a shifting sound, like stone foundations settling.

Ken growled again. Then he flowed in front of me, a shield between us and Hayk. All semblance of normality was in tatters. Ken crouched, one leg back, his body angled sideways, both hands curved into claws at chest-level.

"And what might you be?" said Hayk. No fear spoiled the rumpled professor vibe. He looked pleased.

"Leaving," said Ken hoarsely, his words strangled through a clenched jaw.

"No, no, you just got here," Hayk stepped forward, but came to an abrupt halt against Ken's claw. *Claw?* God, Ken's hands weren't just curved like claws. Quarter inch long, thick nails the color of old ivory extended from his fingertips. Hayk looked down at one claw pressed against his chest and blinked.

"We are leaving," Ken repeated.

"But you haven't even told me your *name*," said Hayk. The way he said *name* made me shiver, bringing to mind the strange way the room had spun in Kaneko-sensei's classroom. My mind went on red alert, skin prickling. Heightened awareness chafed against the roughness of Dad's corduroy shirt and choked on the cardamom stifling the room. Behind us, the stone shifted again. Followed by a loud cracking noise.

Hayk's smile deepened, and for an instant he broke away from the staring contest with Ken to glance at the stone pillar. What he saw made him step closer, unmindful of Ken's claws tearing tiny holes in his shirt.

Get a grip. I shook my head and eased Dad's weight against my hip.

"Don't make the mistake of thinking me ignorant," Ken said.

Hayk's pleased expression faltered for a moment. "Never fear, I do not mistake you, nor Ms. Pierce at all. I am insanely curious who you might be."

"The Kitsune will help us, he won't let you die." Dad had spoken in Japanese, but not his Herai dialect. His eyes were clear from murky confusion. Ken gave an exasperated huff.

"Kitsune," Hayk repeated. His voice pressed in, underlaid with jarring harmonics and weirdly enough, a fiery smell like smoked paprika. "How fascinating." Shivers ran down my arms and back. "Let me show you something I think you might be interested in here."

I blinked furiously, trying to clear away the paprika sting.

Hayk's resonant voice continued. "I'm sure you have *a-short-time-before—*"

He can't finish that sentence. "Let's go," I broke in, panting with the effort of speaking through the spicy fog. "Come on."

Hayk's words stuttered to a stop, anger breaking through the pleasant mask.

Ken straightened up. With the flat of his palm he pushed Hayk hard out of the doorway. Hayk banged into the opposite wall with an oomph, breath knocked out of him.

I dragged Dad by the arm, skin at the back of my neck prickling and goose pimply. We scrambled past Hayk and through the door. I hurried down the still deserted hall, sure Hayk was going to charge out of his office any second and tear Dad from my grasp.

I glanced back once before we turned the corner. Hayk stood outside his office, his gaze hard and hungering.

CHAPTER FOUR

"You're a Kitsune?" I said in Japanese. No point in freaking out the taxi driver.

Dad sat quietly between us in the back seat of the taxi. His eyes were clear, like he was in a lucid patch, but his mouth was a bloodless, white line. Lips pressed tight against words threatening to break free. Or he was going to upchuck.

I had tried talking to him in Herai dialect. No answer. I needed him more than I ever had in my life, and he was gone. Gone into the dementia fog. Traveling down that thought path only took me into the forest of anger and sadness. Desperate for a distraction, I had turned to confront the craziness that was Ken.

"The simple answer is yes," said Ken, replying in the same language.

"Yes, you're a red fox?"

Ken laughed. "You saw the claws." He lifted one hand and turned it back and forth in front of me. I expected to see it morph into some monstrous, hairy appendage a la *American Werewolf in London*, but it stayed well-formed, the fingers slender and strong, the forearm lithely muscled. No sign of the ivory claws. Did they retract?

I tore my eyes away from his hand and looked out the window. I'd always had a thing for hands. Ken had nice hands, strong, long fingers. Claws. Kitsune. If only this was a reality prank show or something.

"Don't be willfully obtuse," said Ken. "You can't speak Japanese like a native without knowing something of the culture. Obviously not Kitsune, not in the sense of being a red-haired vulpine, but Kitsune in the sense of being an illusionist and shape-shifter."

"A were-fox, then?" I had no idea where this giggly voice came from. Maybe it was hysteria. Maybe I was totally flipping out.

"Yes," said Ken in English, "on the nights of the full moon I turn all hairy and rummage through people's garbage cans."

Irritation spiked, killing the giggles. "Don't be condescending."

"Don't be block-headed, then. You're the daughter of a full-blooded Baku, I'm a Kitsune. We're both of the Kind. I don't know the extent of your heritage's expression, but if you're Herai Ahikito's daughter, then you have at least tasted people's dreams. Probably tasted *my* dreams." From the grimace accompanying his last sentence, the thought of me dreaming his fragment unsettled us both.

But Ken wasn't done with me. His rant continued even as Dad's head slumped forward, eyes half-closed. "And Hayk may be human, but he's got something of the Kind about him. You're definitely not safe. Don't hide behind ignorance, it only makes you more vulnerable." The fervor in his voice reached inside my belly, stirring up sensations until I couldn't distinguish anger from fear in the murky depths.

"You can't just ignore this like Herai-san did with anything that threatened to infringe on his precious *human* life," he said, settling back against the seat.

How dare he? He met me yesterday. He has no right to—

The taxicab drove past my complex's driveway. I switched to English and got the driver to make a U-turn and paid the fare.

60

As the taxi drove off, Ken stood there, one arm around my Dad, and the carefully neutral expression I was learning to hate on his face.

Willfully obtuse? Block-headed? Who was Mr. Mysterious Kitsune to call me out for being less than open? Like he was so forthcoming. He knew much more about Dad then he was letting on.

But he wasn't avoiding it. He wasn't hiding in an apartment somewhere, trying to pretend everything was normal.

He was right. Dad and I had skated around this my whole life. If I let any dreams or not-normalness percolate up into my conscious brain, if I acknowledged that I had more than an inkling what Ken meant when he threw out words like *Kind* and *Baku*, then I would have to acknowledge the whole package.

I dreamed other people's fragments. A talent I got from Dad who was most likely a mythical dream-eating creature. And Hayk had used something other than just words to command my presence in his office. So he was not-normal, too. Not to mention evil.

I wasn't prepared to deal with real Evil. Or to imagine Dad's ramblings were anything other than tangled, plaque-clogged neuron misfires.

Or to consider what it meant I should do with other people's fragments. I choked back a sob midway up my throat. I wanted my real Dad back, one without crying spells and a brain filled with cotton, who could tell me what the hell I should do.

"So," said Ken, impatient with my silence.

Dad took my hand, pressing it to his chest. I felt the warmth, the easy familiarity of him; the one person in the world I'd been able to touch. The one person I didn't have to flinch away from in daylight because of what I dreamed in the dark. Because I never dreamed his fragments.

Not once.

Dream eater.

"Dad," I said, so tense I could only manage English. Ken blinked in surprise. "Do you dream my dreams, do you...eat them?"

Dad let out a long breath. "I used to dream the world wyrm's dreams," he rasped in Japanese. "I used to dream the lady of light."

My shoulders loosened. Not quite the answer I was looking for. This raspy voice only came out during a confused spell. This was the Alzheimer's speaking, not Dad-the-Baku. The awful fear ratcheted down a notch. A medical problem, not a mystical one.

"Of course," I said. Things were never simple. I guided Dad up the stairs.

"Don't bury your head in the sand again," said Ken.

"Give me some credit," I snapped back. Dad's arm was thin and vulnerable under my palm, but he was quiet, as if anticipating the next question. Calm and serious. Not like the irritated fidgets he got during a confused spell. *Oh god.* It wasn't dementia. He was serious.

The only thing more awful than Dad confused by Alzheimer's would be if all these years he had been trying to tell us the truth.

The hand gripping Dad's wrist felt wrong, awkward. A little girl tugging her wiser parent down to a child's level.

"Why did you run away? What were you doing in Professor Hayk's office?"

"Hayk?" said Dad. His face went slack, the deep shadows under his half-closed lids making him look like a waxen statue of himself. His tongue worked convulsively over his front teeth. I thought of smoked paprika and yellowed linen and the tang of blood.

"You dreamed the fragments I had last night, didn't you?"

"Yes," said Dad. "I tasted the dragon. But I couldn't...I couldn't reach the dreamer." He was getting more agitated. Ken came up behind us, putting a hand on his shoulder to steady him, but Dad flinched away.

"You're in danger. It knows—the dragon's pawn—knows about you."

"Knows about what?"

Dad's eyes closed all the way, scrunching up in his face like he was in pain. Tendons stood out on the side of his neck. Every muscle in my father's body strained to the limit doing...something. I'd seen this before. It was the beginning of one of his particularly bad spells, when the Alzheimer's fog made him into a different, crazy-talking person.

Or, was this the real Dad coming out, one he'd hidden from his family for so many years until it became too late?

"What's wrong? Dad?" I put an arm around his shoulders and pulled him, his body rigid as stone, with me through the front door. "He needs to sit down."

Dad vulnerable like this was too awful. The sight of his hands shaking at his sides made me bite my lip. Those elegant fingers that used to wield a fillet knife like an artist were now splayed out and useless.

Dad collapsed on the couch.

Long limbs tightly held together, curling into himself, Dad looked like a dried up husk. His eyes rolled wildly under closed lids.

"Where have you been?" said a voice. I whirled around to find Marlin stepping out of the bathroom, adjusting her gypsy skirt.

"Great," I said. 'Cause Marlin's deep-seated need to know everything was just what was missing from this family revelation. "What happened to I'm-dying-and-I-can't-get-up?"

"I recovered," she said. "And I forgot to bring Dad's prescriptions last night." She nodded to Ken. Her delighted expression made me curl my fingernails into my palms, but her smile abruptly morphed to a frown as her eyes fell on Dad. He had his head buried in his arms and was rocking back and forth, muttering.

"What did you do to Dad?"

"Nothing," I said, feeling the defensive gates come crashing down. "He had one of his spells and went a little walkabout, that's all."

"That's all?" repeated Marlin, scornful. I bit back the impulse to apologize and explain. The less Marlin knew about Hayk, the better. I didn't want that man anywhere near my family.

Marlin gave an exasperated sigh. She pushed past me to enfold

Dad in her loving embrace.

"You can't just leave him alone."

"He wasn't left alone," said Ken. "I saw him leave. I didn't know there was any problem. Herai-san acted in a normal manner."

Marlin raised an eyebrow at Ken. "So who is this, then?" She turned the full force of Mom's Pierce glare on me.

"His name is Ken," I said.

Just how was I going to explain this without Marlin jumping to wild conclusions? It wasn't like I picked up men all the time. Ken was probably the first non-blood relative Marlin had seen in my actual, physical company in years.

Ken and Marlin stared urgent messages to me, both demanding things I wasn't capable of giving.

"He's going to help me out with Dad's care."

Marlin returned Ken's formal nod, looking him up and down like he was a bolt of fabric she was choosing for a client's easy chair.

Ken did that nostril flaring thing. "You are Koi's sister?" His eyes went dark with intent. "What do you know of Baku or the Kind, then?"

Marlin's mouth froze open in surprise. "I'm sorry?" she said.

Right. Time for me to sweep in with damage control. No way could I let her in on the full blown nutsoid happenings of the morning.

Semblance of normal was what we needed. I was good at that. I'd been faking my entire life. "Ken's a student in Japanese studies at PCC," I said. "He's a little passionate about his work." I glared meaningfully at Ken, willing him to back me up.

"Put some of that passion into watching my father and we won't have a problem," Marlin said.

"That is my intention," said Ken, his tone formal.

Marlin harrumphed. She ran her hand down Dad's neck and back, murmuring something in Japanese. After a moment, Dad stopped rocking and settled again on his side, supported by the cushioned sofa arm.

"Koi," he said. I came to the couch to kneel next to him. But when I reached for his hand, he pulled it away. "No," he said through gritted teeth. "Don't touch me. The dragon fragments…"

Stung, I fell back on my knees. Dad's eyes clouded over, going blurry at the corners. Tension wrinkles appeared at the corners of his mouth.

"I know your true purpose come here," he said to Ken. He was speaking English in the slightly broken, uncomfortable way he did when he used to argue with Mom. "I taste the water dragon there, in Koi's dream fragment. You know what I say?"

I turned to Marlin, schooling my features to match her expression of indignant surprise. *Now we're in for it. So much for semblance of normal.*

Ken nodded, his expression carefully guarded.

Dad clenched his hands into fists on top of his thighs. "I'm not…I may not have able to help," he said. He let his chin fall to his chest, gulping air like something constricted his chest.

"Dad?" Marlin smoothed a hand over his fist, working it loose with small rubs. Anger made high spots of color in her cheeks, a Pierce on the warpath. "Don't feed into his delusions. It's not good for him—"

"Let me finish, Maru-chan," said Dad stiffly in Japanese.

Ken went down on his knees next to me, legs folded underneath in formal *seiza* posture. "I'm listening, sir," he said.

Marlin's glare could have melted glass.

"When I left Aomori," said Dad, focused on Ken, "the Kind rubbed their hands of me, and others who did not only believe full blood ways."

Close-lipped, stoic Dad, saying these intimate things in English. For Ken, a stranger. Resentment burned.

"I did nothing to, to mend that," continued Dad. "And then I married a human. And then she birthed children."

"Human?" Marlin repeated in a choked voice.

65

"They know nothing, then," said Ken, not hiding his disapproval.

Dad bristled. "Better they living with no knowledge with the humans than living the *welcome* they'd find with full blood Kind."

"Koi experiences other people's dreams. You left her vulnerable to that with no guidance? No explanation?"

Dad's shoulders slumped. "I thought it was…manageable."

Manageable?

I choked back another sob. Or was it a laugh? It tasted like sour persimmon. All those classes I skipped because I couldn't face the risk of accidentally touching someone. People's fragments blurring everyone around me. Never being sure if my reactions were my own or caused by another person's fragment. I thought of how I'd retched over and over again into the toilet when I'd felt Mom's fragments of dying, and how Lisa's dreams of her dad made me ache to tear at my skin, as if I could peel shame off in onion layers.

Manageable.

"Dad," I said. Everyone's eyes swung to me. Marlin furious and Dad's clouded not with confusion but grief. I swallowed past the obstruction.

"You're a Baku." I said baldly. After everything he'd confessed to Ken, I had no gentleness.

"Koi, don't be an idiot," snapped Marlin.

"Hear me out. Just hold off trying to smooth things over for just one second."

Marlin blanched. *My tone too harsh? Whatever. Marlin can suck it up for once.* I turned back to Dad.

"I'm a Baku, too?"

"Maybe yes," he said. "What you are, I don't know for sure. How much of you is from me. How much is Andrea."

"All these years…you never thought that might be important information?"

Dad shook his head. Anger pricked, turning everything in the room sharp and defined, outlined in light. It felt good, far better than the dragging confusion from before.

"I thought I was a freak! All you had to do was say, 'Koi, you're not a psychotic weirdo, you've just got a mythological dream-eating elephant for a father.' Would that have been so hard?"

"What would your life be if I showing you to the Kind? You have no idea," said Dad, his English even worse than before.

"You think so?" I gestured at Ken. "He doesn't seem so terrible." I pressed knuckles into the sides of my head. I wanted to growl or yell or punch something.

"Stop it," said Marlin.

"Why not her?"

Dad shook his head. "It is rare thing for Kind to mate with humans. We keep ourselves to ourselves." He blinked several times.

My Dad, tearless even at Mom's funeral, had moisture gathering in the crow's feet at the corner of his eyes.

Anger turned to astonishment. The whole world turned upside down and inside out. I let my hands fall to my sides. "Ha, right," I said, but my heart wasn't in it. Dad had never seemed so vulnerable, so human as right now. My knees gave out. I came down into a sprawling heap next to Ken. His arm snaked under my ponytail, around my shoulders.

I couldn't summon the strength to shrug him off.

Dad's hands tore at the frayed edge of his plaid shirt. "Andrea? Don't cry honey," he said.

Marlin tightened her grip on his arm. "Dad?"

He pounded his fists into his thighs again like he could chase the confusion away with pain. "Koi, yes, ah no." A deep, shuddering breath racked his frame. "I've left it too long. It's too late," he whispered in Japanese.

"What's too late?" cried Marlin.

Ken made a shushing motion at her. Dad went on in that thin, wavering tone.

"I call on you, Kitsune, as one Kind to another. I guess your purpose in Portland. But I am without recourse. You must help my daughter. The water dragon can't have her."

"I so swear," said Ken, slowly, using archaic Japanese that I'd only heard spoken by actors in historical TVJapan dramas.

Dad answered in the same style. "I will know, Kitsune, whether you honor that promise. I will taste it in the dreaming."

Those last words must have cost him, because his eyelids fell closed, rapid movements underneath a sure sign of his agitation despite the bloodless clench of his lips.

The sudden drumming of a rain shower pelted the roof. Dad folded his limbs more tightly against his body, closing up like a clam at the sound. Marlin tucked the sofa's hibiscus-patterned quilt, another one of Mom's, around him.

I felt Ken settle his weight back on his heels.

"What have you done?" Marlin tore open the silence. "He's so exhausted he's passed out."

"You mean what has *Dad* done," I said under my breath.

"You've had him for one night and already he's fallen apart. Why is it so hard for you to take care of this? Why do you act like everything has to stop just for you? Other people have *problems*."

I thought of her harsh words about me abandoning Mom. Was this how she saw me?

Marlin made an exasperated cluck. "Don't you shut me out like that, Koi. Say something."

I looked at her, so many words crowding along my tongue there was no room for any of them to escape. An awful layer of heat pressed down on me. I wished everyone in the room gone. I needed to be alone, needed to understand what Dad had been saying. What it meant.

"Fine, then. You can have your precious solitude. I'll take Dad. He can stay with me—"

"No!"

Marlin flinched. "I'm doing you a favor."

"I keep Dad," I said. I fiercely craved to be alone, but I wasn't going to give up. That's what the whole PCC thing meant. Even with all this Kind and Baku craziness. There was no going back now.

If Marlin took Dad away, it would prove she was right about how pitiful I was, about how I abandoned Mom. Being filleted by Dad's sushi knives was a preferable fate.

"He's not wounded or insane. Just one of his spells," I said. "You know how he gets."

"It wasn't just him with the crazy talk."

Ken shifted off his knees. "Your father has kept from your family an entire history."

No way was I going to let Ken mix it up with Marlin. "Okay," I said. "There's stuff going on here. Weird stuff." See how she'd like a dose of her own blunt medicine. "Stuff about how Dad and I dream other people's dreams."

"Koi," said Marlin, years of avoidance crammed into the word.

My self-righteous wave of indignation crashed right over the Pierce tradition of keeping unmentionables unmentioned. "And apparently we're Baku. You know, those creatures that eat bad dreams?"

"Why are you being like this? I'm trying to help." Marlin indicated Ken, still sitting quietly beside the couch. "You've obviously got a lot on your plate right now, and I just thought I'd…"

"What?" I said, "Make it all better? Take away poor, overwhelmed Koi's problems? Smooth everything over so on the surface it's okay?"

Marlin blinked, like she was clearing something from her eyes. Like she was trying to clear *me* from her eyes.

"Don't be a bitch," said Marlin. "As if I could leave Dad here with you when you're obviously wound up tighter than a hibiscus bud."

The rain intensified into a drumming sound. Hail? In a Pacific Northwest spring? The kitchen window's glass blurred, the whole world drowning outside.

How could I get Marlin to understand? I didn't want her to take things over, to be the fixer-upper sister. This was my problem. Dad was my responsibility, now.

I thought of Hayk's hungry gaze following me down the hallway as we escaped.

The drumming rain was stunningly loud in the tense silence. Marlin glared. Ken waited, perfectly still, half-crouched near Dad's knee.

What would come out if I dared open my mouth with this frustration roiling around, so strong it crackled in the air?

The tinkling notes of the Swan Lake theme filled the room. Marlin flipped open her phone one-handed, glanced down and grimaced.

"Damn. A new client wants to meet in fifteen minutes." She transferred the grimace to me. "This. Is. Not. Over." One perfectly manicured nail poked me in the chest. "I mean it."

"I know," I said, trying to make my face less fierce.

Opening the door let in the damp-mold smell of heavy rain. I handed Marlin an umbrella from the bottom of my closet—a peace offering. She raised an eyebrow at me. Only tourists and Asians ever used umbrellas in Portland. It was a standing joke in our family that we upheld that stereotype.

"Take care," said Marlin, hesitating outside my door.

I breathed in, the wet weighing down my lungs, squinting to see through the downpour. "He'll be okay," I said.

"I didn't mean just Dad," she said, and left.

CHAPTER FIVE

Dad was dead to the world, like our conversation had taken as much out of him as a Portland Hood to Coast marathon; the only sign he still lived was the uneven rise and fall of his chest.

Ken pulled the quilt up to Dad's chin, tucking him in with a surprising gentleness. He exuded such a fierce vitality. Every movement sure and strong. Like he had spent years learning a physical discipline like ballet or Tae Kwon Do.

Or was it a Kitsune thing? Whatever that meant.

"So?" he said, catching my over-long perusal.

"So?" I repeated. I would handle this. I could handle this. Whatever this was. Because if I didn't, I was truly as pathetic as Marlin said.

"So," I said again, taking a deep breath. "I'm starved. What do you say to eating?" As soon as the words left my mouth, I realized it was true. I could eat a cow.

Ken's gaze flickered over Dad on the couch. "Your fridge is empty."

I deflated. "Oh. Well, I guess one of us could walk over to the

Black Bear Diner or something."

Ken's eyes flickered over to the window.

Right. Heavy rain. Okay. I couldn't even handle getting us food. How the hell was I going to handle whatever Hayk was, whatever it was he wanted?

Ken sat down on a bar stool in the kitchen, leaning back against the counter, legs bent underneath, arms crossed. Very carefully tucking himself away from my space.

Were all Kitsune so expressive with their body language?

"How about a cup of coffee?" he asked.

I sighed and reached in the cabinet for the Nescafé I kept for emergencies.

Ken stared at the Nescafé. "I was warned American coffee was horrible, but when I saw you with the latte I had hope."

I pushed the Nescafé back into the cabinet and closed the door with more force than I intended. "Fine. Water it is." I banged open another cabinet door and grabbed a couple of plastic tumblers.

The hiss of breath drawn through closed teeth; the Japanese male sound of distress. "I don't agree with how Herai Akihito has kept you in the dark," Ken said slowly. "You are now upset, but it wasn't my place to tell you these things."

"And now?"

"It's still not my place," he said, brushing a hand through his hair, making it momentarily lift into a messy tangle. "But finding Herai Akihito with that Vishap stone changes everything."

Here it came. I would never really be ready for any of this, but pain and trouble would always come. Like Mom said, it's how you meet and greet it that counted. "Lay it on me," I said. "Really. I promise to listen with an open mind. No wisecracks."

Ken smirked, and then after a beat, his mouth loosened into a comfortable smile. Real this time, not Kitsune illusion.

"Your father and I, and you, to some unknown extent, are of the Kind."

"Yeah, I got that much," I said, handing him the tumbler of tap-water.

"No cracks." He patted the stool next to him, but I went around to the other side of the counter, gripping it so that the cool laminate against my palms would help ground me.

"What is, are, the Kind?"

"Have you read Joseph Campbell?"

I blinked. "The Power of Myth guy?"

"That makes it easier to explain. If you've read Campbell you know about universal myths like the hero quest, vampires, and dragons."

"You're saying the Kind are vampires and dragons?"

"Not exactly, but in a general way, yes."

"Baku aren't a universal myth."

"Morpheus? Ojibwe dream catchers? Incubus? Nocnitsa?"

"Morpheus is for real?"

"No," said Ken, arching an eyebrow in what I was learning to recognize as amusement. "But your father is from a powerful family lineage. He left Japan decades ago due to a disagreement and hid himself away from Kind society."

"He didn't get along with the other Baku?"

"Baku are rare. In Japan, the Kind are mostly Kitsune and Tengu, with a scattering of Kappa. The disagreement was with the Council."

"Which is a what? A Kind United Nations or something?"

"Something like that. All powerful beings. And your father was one of the last few known active Baku before he left." Ken was stepping carefully around any talk of Baku.

"Dad always said he immigrated to the States like 25 years ago."

Ken shook his head slowly. "Your father left Japan right before World War II, when Japan invaded China."

"But that would make him over 90 years old."

"Some Kind age a bit slower than humans."

"I see." But I didn't. I looked over Ken's shoulder to the quilt-covered lump on my sofa. How old was Dad? What else had he hidden from us? How much of the father I had known was a lie?

Anger flared. I glared at Ken. His words had taken my Dad and left some kind of weird changeling I wasn't sure how to feel about.

"Why did you come here?" I leaned over the counter, wanting him to feel hounded. Spicy aftershave, like ground, cinnamony *kinako* powder on the rice cakes at Uwajimaya, warmed the air between us.

He looked over at Dad's quiet form. "That's really not important right now, I promised your father—"

"It's important to me!" I said, and slammed a closed fist on the countertop. Water spilled from Ken's tumbler.

He covered my hand with a light palm. I wanted to jerk away, but at his touch, all my frustration and anger fled toward the pit of my belly, knotting itself into a heated ball. Electricity charged the air accompanied by the primal drum beat of the rain. Ken leaned in, his fingers smoothing their way up my wrist to the sensitive crease of my inner elbow.

"You are going to need my help," he said, deep voice and delicious *kinako* scent drawing me infinitesimally closer.

"I need answers. I need truth," I said, my voice catching a little.

"You've tasted my dreams." His fingers tugged me gently, pulling me closer to his side of the counter. "You know my truth."

The dark irises of his eyes widened, bleeding over into the white, pulling my gaze into his as inexorably as his hands pulled mine to his chest, trapping them there. They throbbed, beating like trapped doves in the cage he made of himself.

Whoa, hold up. Back away. Press him for answers. The sane voice was small, and far away, as most of my mind was busy trembling on the edge, poised to fall into the intense darkness of his eyes. Ken's strong, slender fingers caressed mine in slow circles, the rhythmic thud of his heart beating under my palms.

So warm.

I *had* dreamed his fragments—slipping through some primeval forest. Unblemished by ill intent. Safe.

"You, you only dream of running. Under the green trees. I've never—" I swallowed something hard-edged and bitter, "—touched a man and felt only that wild rush. Stripped bare. So simple."

Ken turned to the side, presenting a sharp profile; tense jaw, aquiline nose. The Kitsune, there, but more, a man using every muscle in his body to hold in something powerful, to surrender nothing of some dark vitality.

"There is no other dream for me," he said, finally, a fierce-edged whisper from a bowed head. Hot breath, the harsh scrape of his stubbled chin on the back of my hand.

With a quick intake of breath, Ken closed the distance between us. His lips grazed mine in a light brush. He pulled back to scan my expression, but then it was my hands tangled in his shirt tugging him back.

He kissed me more fiercely, the feel of his mouth firm, urging me to let him in. He opened his mouth over my bottom lip, sucking it, using gentle teeth and tongue to tease me open.

My hands gripped and released his shirt, taking on an urgent rhythm. After a few more minutes, or an eternity, he slipped inside my mouth.

Earthy *kinako* and his familiar musk made my heart thud violently against my ribcage. His mouth moved on mine in an insistent pattern, a rhythm of tension and release that gave me no room to slip in a breath.

I released his shirt so my hands could trail their way up his shoulders to the warm width of his neck. Skin on skin. I gloried in the fearlessness of the touch.

Ken pulled me halfway across the counter, his hands smoothing up and down my sides.

Oh god, this is crazy, this is out of control. Kissing him was making my body riot like I'd jumped naked into the Willamette.

The loner's danger; touch was so momentous. And his mouth on mine, the feel of his hands on me was too much. I was overloaded with sensation, feeling dizzy. Out of control. Part of me didn't like this helpless feeling. Like I was trapped on a rocky cliff with an ocean storm swirling around me, threatening to sweep me away.

The edge of the counter bit into my waist as Ken's teeth grazed my lip just a bit too sharply. The frenzy drained away, leaving me eyes open, horribly aware I was *kissing Ken*. He stiffened, paused with his lips at the corner of my mouth and pulled back.

He held my gaze, not moving, not changing his expression. So goddamn *patient*. So careful. Like I was a fragile butterfly. I didn't want *concern* from him, like he was taking over for Marlin. I slid down the countertop to stand on my own feet, disentangling my hands from his shirt.

Kinako tickled the back of my throat. I coughed. Ken sighed and ran his hand through his hair. The gesture ended in a curious awkwardness, like he didn't know where to set his hands afterwards.

Awkward. God, awkward sucked. Could I run to my bedroom and shut the door on all this?

No, that was what old Koi would have done. I was the new, stronger, Koi. There was the motionless figure of Dad under the quilt, and then Hayk was somewhere out there, and neither of those things would get resolved by hiding.

Okay, so deal with the aftermath of kissing a Kitsune. Right. And me with no chocolate stash.

"So. Pizza delivery?" I said. Maybe this restless, empty feeling would get better if I had food.

Ken smiled, his hands settling onto the counter, folded calmly. "I have four sisters," he said.

"And they all like pizza?" I said.

Ken shook his head. "And you would think that I would have learned how to deal with women by now."

A huff escaped me. "I am not someone you can just...just *deal* with," I said.

"No?" he drawled, the word somehow encompassing everything—Hayk, my sleeping father, the tension that still crackled in the air.

I glared at him. "Believe me, you will have your hands full trying to deal with a very cranky woman if we don't get food soon." I sighed. "And coffee. Preferably a triple latte."

"Okay. Don't think you'll get to avoid what just happened forever," said Ken. He leaned forward, the corner of his mouth quirking up when I flinched back. "But we do have other things to worry about, right now."

"Like what toppings for our pizza."

"Like why Herai-san thinks Hayk is a danger."

I rummaged through the drawer where I stuffed the fliers the battling pizza companies hung on my doorknob and held up a finger at Ken as I dialed the number. Ken sat in that perfect, eerie stillness for the few minutes it took me to order. When I put down my phone, he stood up, went to the couch to check on Dad, and then came around to lean on my side of the counter.

I breathed in deeply, trying to settle my roiling stomach.

"You dreamed Hayk's fragments, didn't you?" he said.

The breath came out in a rush. "Yes," I said, crossing my arms in front of me.

"Tell me."

"There were two." I closed my eyes, trying to hold myself together against the flavor of cardamom, the sickly-sweet smell of blood, the *absence* in the eyes of the dead girl in the hallway and the boy at the bottom of the hole.

"They felt different from the usual fragments I get from casual touches. I mean, I'm not sure," I swallowed down nervousness. Hearing myself talk about this stuff out loud felt like I was careening head first down the 20-foot pink slide at Oaks Park. "But somehow these were more real. Like they were memory-dreams, not just the dreams everyone has, you know, like flying or running, or being naked in class."

Ken arched that darn eyebrow, and I felt a flush creep down my neck.

"What did you see in Hayk's fragments?"

"Murder. He murdered two people." Nausea rose in the back of my throat. I hugged myself tightly. "There was a feeling of completion, of satisfaction in the fragments. Like he's accomplished some task, and he's *happy*."

"Did you eat those dreams?"

"Did I— What?"

"You're Baku."

"You've got to be kidding me."

Ken shook his head, his jaw tight with frustration. "Eater-of-dreams. There's a reason you're called that."

My hands came up, palms out, pushing away his words.

He continued. "Baku eat bad dreams and take the power of the dream into themselves."

"That's absolutely crazy. Freakish."

"Yes," said Ken, his voice gentle, but his eyes darkly serious, pinning me against the cupboards. "Not human at all."

Flashes of Dad in his black skull cap, filleting salmon into paper-thin slices, the quiet anger trembling in his long limbs during arguments with Mom before he left, the awkward bundle he made on my couch, sleeping.

Dad ate dreams? Evil nightmares like Hayk's?

"My father is not a monster. I am not a monster."

"You are not entirely human. The story of why Herai Akihito left Japan, left the *Council*, is his to tell. But it is no coincidence that he left so soon after Japan invaded Manchuria. Evil accompanies invading other countries."

"He left to escape evil?"

Ken nodded, slowly. "I don't know that much about dream eater ways, but I do know that many of the Kind believe there must be a balance in all things. And for the Baku, eating innumerable nightmares, taking untold evil into themselves, could upset some balance. It could be dangerous."

I shivered, feeling the relentless rain outside somehow creeping into me, like a chill even Ken's warm presence couldn't dispel. Dangerous, how? Dangerous like eating away Dad's memories in a way doctors misdiagnosed as Alzheimer's?

"When you say 'eat', just what are you talking about?"

Ken closed his eyes, holding up a finger in blatant imitation of how I'd silenced him earlier. "I am Kitsune. Illusions are my strength. Herai-san is going to have to answer your questions."

The doorbell rang. I used frustration to propel myself out of the kitchen to answer, scooping up my checkbook from the black-lacquered side table beside the door.

A drenched young man stood in the hall. He clumsily undid the thermal outer pocket, his fingers slipping on the wet material, and I exchanged a check for a piping hot pizza box. His fingers left wet smudges on the check paper.

"Wait," said Ken. He was suddenly beside me, his arms braced in the doorframe. "The rain."

"It's a downpour," said the pizza guy.

Ken leaned his head out the door, running his tongue over his lips, slowly, tasting. A flush crept down the back of my neck, my hands tightening on the box, wanting to *do* something.

"What the...?" said the pizza man, taking a step backwards.

"This is no ordinary rain," said Ken. "Smell it."

I took a step into the corridor and stuck my hand out from under the overhang. The rain coated my palm with a warm, syrupy feeling. I snatched back my hand and sniffed.

Cardamom.

"Uh, yeah," said the pizza guy in a careful voice. "Y'all just enjoy your pizza, now." He lit down the corridor, leaping down the stairs.

"Hayk," I said. "It smells like his fragments."

"It tastes of power," said Ken, the tip of his tongue appearing again to touch his bottom lip. "Something of the Kind."

"Kitsune? Baku?"

"Not Japanese. Not the first peoples I'd expect here in the Pacific Northwest. Middle Asian."

Ken drew me back inside, closing the door firmly behind us and leaning against it like he could shut out the rain with his body.

"Hayk sent the rain," I said.

"No. Hayk is human. Whatever was in that stone in his office sent it, the rain tastes of what I smelled there."

"The Vishap stone?"

Ken pushed himself away from the door and stood in front of me, too close for casual, his gaze crawling like angry ants over my skin. "What does he want from you?"

I tossed the pizza onto the counter as I stumbled back to the couch and sunk down next to Dad, still immobile under the quilt. "He wanted translations into Dad's Herai dialect. Not really sinister, but kind of weird and creepy."

Ken shook his head. "A ruse. He knows of the Kind, he knew of the Kitsune. He knows you're related to the Baku. The rain searches for *you*. The Vishap stone wants you for something more than translations."

"The stone?"

"Whatever's in the stone."

My stomach made an embarrassingly loud gurgling noise.

"I don't know enough," said Ken. "They sent me here blind."

"These questions aren't getting us anywhere. Let's eat and I'll get my laptop. Maybe the interwebs know what a Vishap stone is."

Ken dished out slices onto the green melamine plates Marlin had chosen to "match" my wallpaper.

I went to check Dad, still snoring gently under the quilt. Too pale, his cheekbones cut too sharply. But still Dad, still human on the outside. Not a monster, I told myself firmly. I brought my laptop to the kitchen counter. Hot oil burned my hand as I folded a piece of pizza so it wouldn't drip on the keyboard.

Ken delicately dissected his slice with a knife and fork. He blew on a piece, put it in his mouth neatly, and handed me two napkins.

When my browser powered up, my Gmail account icon was blinking. It was full of new emails—mostly from Ed. My coding broker. He'd be pissed I wasn't answering, especially because I had a project due in one week. Maybe he'd give the contracts to Violet or Hopper; neither of them had a life outside of the Portland Perl Mongers.

I had a life now. Ed would just have to wait.

"What does Wikipedia say?"

I gave Ken a startled glance. He arched a brow at me.

"The Kind are wrapped in myths, but we aren't clueless noobs," he said, flashing me a plastic-wrapped bundle he pulled from his pocket. Slowly he peeled back the plastic...er...actually was that a condom? A DoCoMo phone. Encased in a condom. I shook my head. Unique, waterproof way to travel with a phone.

I thought of how he'd asked me directions to the nearest café. He'd had access to GPS this whole time. Ken stabbed a black olive and chewed, holding my gaze with an eyebrow arched in challenge, daring me to comment.

I wrenched my eyes back to the screen. A few queries and I was scanning Wikipedia's entry for "Vishap."

"Not much, actually. This article's a stub. Give me a moment to use my Google-fu." My napkins were already filthy, so I snagged his napkin to wipe sauce dribbling down my chin. "Okay, here's something. Looks like some grad student's seminar project. Armenia has these stones, like the one in Hayk's office from like prehistoric times. Nobody knows exactly what they were used for. This grad student thinks the bull-shape carved on the top is a thunder god. And the wavy lines surrounding it are meant to represent water, no, actually a water dragon. Ulli, Ullike..."

"Ullikemi," said Ken.

"Yeah, what you said," I squinted at the screen, licking grease from my fingers. I didn't even know the Middle East had dragons.

"Ullikemi was birthed by Aramazd to defeat the thunder god," said Ken. He stared down at this empty plate.

"That's what it says here," I said. "You know all this already?"

"I didn't know about the Vishap Stone. Ullikemi, I have come across before." His lips cured into a brittle smile that didn't quite reach his eyes. "I know all the names of dragon Kind."

I blinked at him. Raw anger pulsed behind those words, but he resolutely cut another dainty piece from his slice and chewed.

Dad had mumbled something about a water dragon. Alzheimer's raving, I'd thought, but he'd been trying to warn me. I cleared my throat. "Ullikemi rained all over Portland just to find me?"

Ken put a hand on the pizza box, resting it there as if the debate whether to eat another slice or not was weightier than he could manage. "Yes, you or your father. Not the human myth Ullikemi, of course. Humanity has made up stories to explain the Kind all over the world. We're not actual gods," he said, his voice low and gravelly.

"Oh that's a relief, then. Not really a god. It's so much better that some Armenian dragon Kind thingy is looking for me, instead." I batted Ken's hand away so I could take another slice.

My sarcasm worked. The heaviness lightened. He shook his head at me the way Marlin did whenever she dropped by the apartment and discovered I'd been on a hermit streak lasting over a week.

I prattled on. "Good thing I'm a slave to melted cheese. I'll just hole up here with Dad and this pizza for a few days. Hayk will get bored and find someone else to pester."

Ken slid the barstool back. "It's not that simple, I'm afraid."

"I figured. But denial's always my first strategy."

Standing balanced on the balls of his feet in my kitchen, energy coiled tightly in his limbs, Ken lost the last vestige of amiable-salesman. Feral sharpness lit his face. The heavy scent of musk gathered in the air, along with an electricity that didn't come from the gathering rainstorm.

Kitsune, his *otherness*. That was the reason little hairs stood up along my arms. Yes, definitely it was the Kitsune in him manifesting, not any other reason at all. Not the graceful line of wrist and hand, or the way his sharp cheekbones carved out a strange masculine beauty in the planes of his face.

I remembered the press of his lips on mine, making me vulnerable and sensitized and aware of each square inch of my body, like I was swelling through my skin.

"The Vishap Stone is the key." Ken made a fist. "I've heard stories before. A perversion of Kind nature. Someone bound this dragon Kind to the stone."

"Wait, we can do that to Kind?" I was trying not to picture Dad going all smoky and being sucked Aladdin-style into a glass bottle.

"The knowledge to do such a thing has been lost for centuries. It is the worst madness. The dragon Kind would change, become a twisted thing locked into the human story."

"Are…are you locked into Kitsune form?" I said.

"No," Ken said. "Human Kitsune tales do not limit me. What I am is just easier to explain by using traditional folk tales. A kind of shorthand, if you will. No, Ullikemi is something else. No matter what it was before, Ullikemi now is only what the human myth tells it to be. The dragon is no longer fully Kind."

"Ullikemi's myth," I said, wanting to turn back to the screen and skim down the rest of the page. I needed to know how the dragon's story turned out.

Ken was on a different track. "Hayk is most definitely the stone's servant, a human doesn't have the power to enslave a dragon Kind. He knows your father is Baku, and so Ullikemi must be directing him. They aren't going to just leave you two alone."

A tight knot formed in my stomach, like I'd eaten the whole pizza myself. "Out with it," I said. "Just spit it out, whatever horrible thing you're not telling me." Ken leaned over the counter toward me, his eyes dark and cold and hard.

"The dragon is driven to fulfill its part in the human story of Ullikemi. It needs to defeat the thunder god, whatever it perceives that to be."

"I'm not a thunder god."

"No, but Ullikemi must be weak bound to that stone. It needs power."

"How can it get that?"

"Power enough to defeat something it perceived as a thunder god could only come from a sudden release of life energy. Birth or death."

"It's after me, right? I'm not pregnant."

"You're human and vulnerable, yet you are an eater of dreams. Your blood would offer a potent mix of mortal and Kind power at death. Ullikemi wields Hayk to take you for a sacrifice, and with the power of your life's blood, he would defeat the thunder god."

CHAPTER SIX

The red sauce-covered crust on my plate suddenly didn't look appetizing at all.

A sacrifice. Like the hawk-nosed girl and the boy in the well? Had Hayk murdered them for some magic compact with Ullikemi?

"Who is the thunder god?"

"I don't know," said Ken. "We need to find out what Hayk's been up to." His fingers curled into claws on the counter.

"Is there a Kind association you can get in touch with here? A secret society?" I said.

"The Kind in the United States are scattered, self-governing pockets. They did not centralize like we did in Japan and Europe. There are two big populations—in San Francisco and New York. Neither of them will care much what's going on here."

"You mentioned the Council?"

Ken's eyes narrowed. "No," he said. Only that one word and it was like he'd slammed a door.

"Well then," I said. "It'll have to be the old-fashioned way." I went back to my laptop and searched for Hayk on the PCC website's faculty list.

"Mangasar Hayk. Born in Abovyan, Armenia. Surprise, surprise. Professor of Eastern Languages and Linguistics. He's only been at PCC two years."

"Where was he before?"

I clicked the research agenda link under his bio. "He's been a busy, busy beaver. University of Mexico, Frankfurt, even Waseda in Tokyo, University of Queensland, and most recently, the University of Alaska, Fairbanks. Only a year or two at each location."

"He's searching for something," said Ken.

"For disappearing languages, apparently," I said. "All his papers in the past ten years are on endangered languages. I scrolled through his list of publications. He's here in Portland working on the Siletz Dee-ni."

"What's 'Siletz'?" said Ken.

"One of the Pacific Northwest first nation peoples."

"Like the Ainu in Hokkaido," said Ken, scratching his chin.

"Wait, there's a link here for people interested in translating for him," I said. "He's got a wish list here for native speakers of certain languages."

The list was a mix of active and dead links. Herai and another Tohoku dialect were active, as well as the Siletz and Okanagan links. Mayan and Sahaptin were dead.

Like the woman in the hall from Hayk's fragment. She was a piece of this terrible puzzle. If I could just replay that fragment I might know how she fit in.

Just the idea made my stomach clench. To willingly experience that fragment, dwell in it even on the slight chance some detail could shed light on Hayk's plan? It would be bathing in evil. If it even worked at all.

"We need more information. If only I'd thought to search his office," said Ken.

I closed my eyes, shutting out the false brightness of the computer screen.

"I can text a friend back home to see if they know anything about Hayk and Ullikemi, but I think they've moved under the radar," Ken continued. I wasn't really listening. Ken didn't need to know what I was doing, especially if I failed.

You can do this. Stay calm. Breathe.

The first brushstroke of the kanji character "ichi," formed itself in my mind. No. I didn't want to chase away the fragment, I wanted to experience it. Exhaling in a long stream, I made the kanji fade to gray. The gray deepened in color, and prickles danced across my skin. My entire adult life I'd spent trying to repress fragments during my waking hours. So freeing, and oddly familiar, to let it percolate up through my accumulated layers of filters.

Remember cardamom. Brown-on-black shadows of a darkened hallway. The woman's pale skin and dark hair, her prominent, hooked nose over a slashed neck still seeping blood. Bloodstained papers like dead leaves scattered on the dirty carpet.

The fragment settled in eagerly, and it was hard to understand how I'd missed its powerful, unhuman vividness before, despite Hayk himself being human. It was other.

Cardamom, then copper flooded my mouth. My tongue ached as if I'd bitten down on it. The fragment swelled into my brain, filling up the small spaces between cells, and then overflowed. It spilled down my spine and into my fingertips and toes.

Buzzing restlessness overwhelmed me, a keen *wanting*, like the bloated hunger of a ten day fast.

Swallowing down the urgency, I forced the fragment into focus on one of those scattered pages, like a movie camera swiveling in on a close up.

Even obscured with bright red blood-drops, I recognized the rounded-shapes-within-squares of the characters printed on the papers. Not Chinese or Egyptian, but similar. Mayan hieroglyphics. A fat hand beneath rope tied around a sun.

And then in spiky, irregular writing, that could only be Hayk's; 'a short time before returning to business.'

What had Hayk said to me when I agreed to come down to his office after Kaneko-sensei's class?

I'm sure you have a-short-time-before-an-important-errand to lend me, he'd said. And then things went fuzzy, and I had agreed to meet him despite how little I wanted to get near a man who dreamed of murder.

The dead woman was so achingly bright, so clear, I wanted to shut my eyes, but the memory gripped me with ruthlessly tight fingers. She'd been Mayan, I was sure of it. Triumph washed through me, mixing with the buzzing hunger bloating my limbs, strengthening and twisting it into a bitter seething barely contained by my fragile ribcage.

I gagged, tasting bile that burned like acid. I struggled to swallow it down, and it ripped my throat raw with keen-hot edges. The seething settled into an uneasy lump in the vicinity of my belly.

Anger. The uneasy lump burned with the heat of my anger. Hayk was awful, evil, and this horrible fragment was *inside* me. I wanted it gone!

The lump flared, and a flash of heat went through me, leaving my neck clammy with sweat as it faded.

Gingerly, I flexed toes and fingers which no longer felt like swollen lumps of flesh. Bitterness leached away, my body slowly returning to me like a battered beach abandoned by a receding tidal wave.

I opened my eyes. The cardamom, the dead woman, they were all gone and only traces of the fragment, like a faint pencil outline on blurred paper, remained when I closed my eyes.

Ken's face hovered very close, his hands, warm and heavy pressed on my clenched fists. Sweat trickled down my spine. Oxygen was having a hard time making it into my lungs despite great gulps of air.

"He gets native speakers of endangered languages to translate for him, and then he *murders* them," I said between gasps.

"What did you just do?" He spoke in clipped syllables but his anger was such a pale echo of the seething rage I'd felt gripped in Hayk's fragment that it hardly registered. "You were frozen, but your eyes jerked crazy underneath your eyelids. You gasped and turned ghost pale. What was it? Ullikemi?"

My insides roiled from the acrid mix of anger and elation still churning inside me from the fragment. This close, awareness of Ken made my skin prickle with a thousand skittering ants. His dark eyes tried to pierce through layers of protection and reach inside me, brow knit with anger. *Who does he think he is? Demanding answers like he has any right to tell me what to do?*

"Back off!" I said, pushing him away with a hand splayed across his chest. Ken flew back against the refrigerator with a bang, toppling a half-open box of wild-berry granola over to spill out its contents in a steady stream over his head.

For a moment, I felt a kind of triumph. That would teach him to crowd me.

Then, reality sunk in and anger turned to acute embarrassment. "Sorry, sorry," I said, shaking my head. What was wrong with me?

Ken brushed granola from his hair and rose to his feet in a move more graceful than a granola-covered man had any right to. "You are upset," he said in a carefully neutral tone. "I was worried you might be under some kind of attack."

"I tried to call up Hayk's fragment. I think it was a memory dream, of the woman lying murdered in a hallway."

"A memory dream?"

"Memory dreams are stronger, more detailed because they're based in reality," I said. A faint flush crept to my cheeks. "The fragment I got from you, running in the forest, that was a different kind of dream, foggy, not true memory."

"Hayk's fragment revealed something about Ullikemi's plan?" said Ken. He was now completely clear of granola, but a wild berry still clung to his collar.

I shook my head and reached out to brush the wild berry away. Ken flinched. My mouth went dry. I busied myself sweeping the spilled cereal. He didn't flinch from the brush of my fingers when I took the dustpan from him.

Maybe I'd misread him?

"I'm sorry," I said to the closet when I put the broom away.

"Yes, you said that before." His mouth was still pressed in a firm line.

"This time I'm apologizing for throwing you across my kitchen. I didn't know I could do that. I can't do that. How did I do that?"

"I'm not positive," said Ken. "But you're Baku. My guess is that by consciously recalling the fragment you took some kind of power into yourself."

Oh god. "I ate the dream."

"Possibly."

Who is the monster, now? I looked over at the sleeping form of Dad on my couch. It was like some mad version of bring-your-daughter-to-work day. Only it wasn't his sushi business we shared, but this freaky dream-eating thing.

My head felt hot and buzzed like I'd downed a triple-shot mocha, but nothing else seemed different. Did eating evil just make you seriously cranky or were there other, more invisible, things I should worry about?

"It wasn't you," said Ken. He kept his arms folded, and sat down on the kitchen bar-stool. Keeping himself from towering over me. Purposefully taking up less space in the small area. "That energy that threw me across the room."

I spread my palms in front of his face. "Yes it was."

"No," he said. "That wasn't you, that wasn't your anger or your power. It smells different. Death power, just the faintest echo of blood. No wonder Hayk is bound to Ullikemi."

"So Hayk researches dead languages, kills translators, and keeps his attack-dragon, Ullikemi, bound up in that Vishap stone in his office, trying to get power enough to destroy the thunder god? Whatever that is."

"The thunder god is the key to knowing what Hayk will try next. But you've got the first part backwards. Hayk is only human. He is Ullikemi's servant, not the other way around."

"The thunder gods around here aren't likely to be Middle Eastern," I said. I nudged my laptop back to life. Google gave up nothing for the search terms "thunder god, Portland" other than links to a Swedish death metal band's gig and a gelato shop's list of coffee names.

When I looked up, Ken was rinsing glasses in the sink. The pizza box was empty. I put a hand on my stomach. Was the leaden weight in there pizza or leftover Hayk-fragment?

Ken jammed the faucet handle closed with a thump. He leaned over my sink, his shoulders hunched, and his hands gripping the side of the sink so tightly I could see the skin turning white around his knuckles.

What did I say? Is he actually angry at getting thrown across the room?

"I didn't know what I was getting into when I agreed to come here," he said in that gravelly voice that made the hairs on my arm stand at attention. "No matter what Herai-san made of himself in Portland, it was never my intention to interfere, just to…to convince…"

"I have no clue what you are talking about," I said curtly. Something about this weirdness had to be clear and straightforward. I got up from the computer, battling irritation and unease in equal measure, but I had nowhere to pace. Dad effectively blocked my living area and the kitchen was too small for Ken. I ended up leaning on the opposite side of the counter, a fist pressed into my side.

The waves of frustration coming off Ken were almost visible.

Good. Why should this be any easier for him? What with all his mystic Kitsune secrets and Council talk.

Ken straightened up to face me. "This wasn't supposed to be a fight. That's why they sent me, half—," he gulped down whatever he was going to say. "Someone who appears non-threatening."

We were so close, only a breath away. Any movement would spark the tension and set something into motion between us that scared me down to my toes.

Ken's gaze raked over me, raw and scathing. Fear surged through me. My own? Leftover from Hayk's fragment? I couldn't tell.

Not fear, no. An answer to the strength of the emotion in Ken's voice, to the white-knuckled grip of his hands. His pupils had bled into the whites, darkening his eyes into two slashes of midnight against pale skin.

His face *changed*. The planes of his cheeks lost the amiable roundness, his eyebrows arched high over those eyes I couldn't stop staring into.

"I won't let Hayk hurt you. And not just because of the promise I made to Herai-san."

"Ken—"

"Just let me," he said, vaulting over the counter in a blur of motion. "I need some of your simple strength. Something unstained by ghosts," he finished, standing so close that I felt the warmth of his breath on my face.

I brushed the sides of his arms in a touch meant to be tentative, but as soon as my hands closed on his bare skin, the energy buzzing between us took over. I gripped his elbows and pulled him against me.

"Koi," he said, his lips brushed my ear while his arms stayed rigid at his sides.

"This feels good." He pulled back so his gaze could bore into mine. "But last time you pulled away. There was fear."

Words were barriers. My body ached to move, to feel. My hands gripped his shoulders and kneaded his flesh. Musky *kinako* enveloped me.

"There's no fear in me now," I murmured and reached up to stop his mouth with my own.

When our mouths met Ken held nothing back. His lips opened and a low groan filled his throat. He pulled me deep into his mouth with surging strokes of his tongue, while the firm softness of his lips slid over mine, trying to find the closest possible fit.

Finally, finally. I felt his fingers weave into the hair at my temples, leaving his thumb free to circle the outer edge of my ear in feather-light touches. I gasped for air, rearing back a little and when I tilted my face upward again, Ken kissed the corner of my mouth.

Pulling away? I felt a stab of disappointment that slowly dissolved into tingling awareness as his mouth moved down the column of my throat. He nuzzled the tender skin along the inside of my collarbone, and then carefully tugged the hair band from my ponytail and combed through my hair, his fingers lingering at the top of my chest. He rubbed his face at my neck, inhaling deeply.

The urgency inside me didn't want these light caresses. I tugged at his shoulders, angling for a kiss, but he pulled back.

His eyes were all darkness now. I lunged in, but he held me still with a gentle pressure at my temples.

Doesn't he want to...? Certainty fled. The seething I'd felt since experiencing Hayk's dream slowed to a trickle. I became uncomfortably aware of the garlic on my breath, the slight burn around my lips where his nascent beard had rubbed at me, and the coiled feeling of electricity in the air. Here I was again. Kissing and feeling up a man I'd met the day before. Letting him inside my guard.

A flush burned down my neck. Ken traced a path from my ear to my cheeks with a firm fingertip.

"Here it is again. You're blushing," he said quietly. His nostrils flared slightly.

I nodded slowly, feeling tears burning behind my eyes. *God. What is wrong with me?* His silent regard was too much to bear. I turned my face away. My eyes fell on the muffled hump of my father on the couch. My cheeks burned even more. With Dad right there on the couch!

Ken took a deep breath and let go of my face very slowly, his fingers lingering to brush my cheek and then tucking hair behind my ear.

I shivered at the light touch.

"This isn't you," he said, still in the gravelly voice. His features softened a bit, returning to that amiable version I'd met outside Stumptown Coffee yesterday.

"No," I said, my hand coming up to brush the backs of my fingers against his cheek before my sane voice could interfere. He flinched back, stranding my hand in the tense air between us.

"I mean," I said clearing my throat and taking a step back. I couldn't even trust my own body. Hands, stay down. "I mean, you don't have to use your illusion like that. The other one is your real, um, face, isn't it?"

Ken nodded. "Ah," he said. "Yes." He half-turned away, defenses going up. Transparently brittle. Did I look like that when I talked to Marlin? Readying myself for the next blow?

"They are both me, but I thought this face would help. Be more settling," he said. His features sharpened, resolving back into the face I had been kissing.

I had been *kissing*. Him. The Kitsune.

The Koi I thought I was didn't touch people willingly in an intimate way. He hadn't tasted of pizza or *kinako* this time at all, but of something bitter and compelling.

I barely knew him, despite how he'd helped me. My insides felt all jostled up and bruised like a dropped bag of peaches, but I still wanted to touch him. His presence was an ambient hum all along my skin.

If he tried to kiss me again right this moment I'd let him.

This isn't you, he'd said.

It *had* been me kissing him, but where was that urgency I had felt just an instant ago? Gone, along with the last dregs of Hayk's fragment. Maybe crankiness wasn't the only side-effect of evil-dream eating.

"I think you're right," I said, the absence of that restlessness leaving me hollow. The room was suddenly too bright, the lamination on the counter unbearably gray. Great, just what I needed; a headache coming on.

"That my face illusion calmed you?"

"No, that the, uh, kissing part wasn't me."

Ken's jaw went tight. That had stung.

Oops.

"I should have recognized what I felt rising in you wasn't exactly you," he said. Back to serious Ken.

"It was like when I threw you against the refrigerator, wasn't it?" I said.

Ken winced, and then gave a short nod. "Hayk's fragment."

"So Baku eat dreams and become violent and sexual?"

Ken went all grave and gloomy. "I wish I had answers, Koi. Unfortunately, I just don't know." He waved in the direction of the couch. "Your father is the one with the Baku answers."

Dad. He always had these blackout-like periods after an episode, but never this long.

I pressed thumbs to the place where my neck joined my skull. The headache had arrived and made itself at home.

When the room's awful brightness had dimmed, I went to kneel beside the couch. Dad hadn't changed position at all. Breath tickled the back of my knuckles when I put them to his face, but his chest barely moved.

"Is something wrong?" said Ken from the kitchen.

"Dad?" I said, poking at his cheek. The stubbly beard growth rasped my skin. "This isn't natural sleep."

"Can you wake him?"

I grasped his shoulders. An ache started in my chest at how thin and fragile those shoulders felt under my hands. Shaking him got no reaction. "I don't think so." My throat tightened.

Ken came over to the couch and laid a hand against Dad's forehead. "No fever."

"I should call Dr. Brown. Marlin just made me write that phone number down," I stood up, scraping my shin on the couch. "Where's my phone?"

"Wait a moment," said Ken. He leaned over the back of the couch until his nose touched Dad's. He inhaled deeply. "This might not be entirely organic in origin."

"What?"

"Herai-san smells of the same energy that was inside you. And there's a trace of something else…an energy maybe of this place? Can you enter his sleep like you do the dreams?" said Ken.

I came back to the couch. "I don't know." Frustration made my tone sharp. "I've never gotten fragments from Dad. Never. I don't even know how to begin."

"You've never had a fragment from a Kind before today, have you?"

I shook my head, even as we both realized that was wrong. I had experienced Kind fragments before. "Hayk's fragment. That murder dream was more vivid, more urgent than anything I'd felt before."

"Ullikemi's power inhabits Hayk's fragments by their bond."

"That's why I couldn't repress them during the day? Unlike fragments from normal people." As if I didn't have enough to worry about already. I thought I'd at least conquered keeping fragments out of my waking life. But Kind fragments were a whole new kettle of awesome-sauce fish.

"Okay," said Ken. "Well then, there's no other choice."

"No other choice?" I repeated.

"The reasons I came to Portland are complicated," he said in a firm tone that did not invite questions. "To get permission to come, I had to make certain promises to the Kind here that I wouldn't make waves. But this," he swallowed something slowly and deliberately. His next words came out in a too-carefully even tone. "This Ullikemi thing is not a result of my actions. It is connected to Herai-san. That could put us all in danger."

Was he trying to convince me or himself? The dull ache in my head made it hard to think. Maybe Ken was wrong about this not being organic.

My jacket! That's where my phone was. Ken stopped me with a hand on my arm. "What are you doing?"

"I'm going to call Marlin." I shook off his hand.

"Wait," he said. "It's dangerous to drag your sister into this."

"My Dad is in a coma!" I said.

"If Hayk and Ullikemi are behind this, nothing you or your sister can do will help," said Ken. For a second, I hated him, hated the whole Kitsune, Baku, dragon bag of craziness. It meant I could do nothing for Dad by myself.

"So what do *you* suggest we do?"

Ken ran both hands through his hair, killing the tired mousse completely. Hair fell across his forehead in a droopy-cute wave. My fingers itched to push it to the side.

"Call Kwaskwi."

"Excuse me?"

"You asked before if I had contacts with the Kind here. I do have a local contact. Kwaskwi."

"Who?"

Ken gave me a considering look. "He's a first peoples Kind. Pacific Northwest tribes have legends about him."

I tried to imagine what a Native American Kind would be like. It was hard enough getting my mind around Ken. No, that wasn't true. There wasn't a bit of Ken my mind hadn't been around yet.

A bit of my blush returned. I ducked my head so Ken wouldn't see. The sudden movement made my temples throb.

I was fiending for ibuprofen.

"How is that going to help us?"

"Kwaskwi's got access to resources. He's kind of a spokesperson for the Portland area. We're going to need more than just your Google skills to help us figure out what drew Hayk here. What Ullikemi thinks the thunder god is."

"I see. And meanwhile I just let Dad slumber away?"

"He isn't showing signs of distress; his heartbeat and breathing are steady. His skin is dry and cool. Let me talk to Kwaskwi first."

"Fine."

Ken's hand rose in the air like he meant to touch me. I held my breath, but he pulled it back, taking the motion with him as he turned away. In the space of a few minutes we'd gone from angry to hot to tense. I let my breath go in a slow, steady stream.

Ken spent a few minutes on the phone speaking in a mix of English and a language I'd never heard before. He gave little bows even over the phone, an ingrained Japanese physical response that reminded me of Dad.

"Kwaskwi wants to meet us," said Ken, slipping his DoCoMo cell into a side pocket. Too controlled and precise, like he was wound so tight any sudden movement would make something come unraveled.

"Us?"

"Yes. He made meeting you a condition. An hour from now, at the Mt. Hood viewpoint at the top of Hoyt Arboretum. I assume you know where that is."

"What? He doesn't like Starbucks? We can't take Dad to the Arboretum like this and there's no chance I'm going to leave him alone."

"Call your sister." A new timbre entered Ken's voice, that of command.

I glared at him. "What happened to 'it's too dangerous to drag her into this'?"

"We need Kwaskwi to deal with Hayk. There are only a few places he's willing to meet, and Hoyt arboretum was the closest one. He's somewhat...tricky. Marlin and Herai-san should be fine for just a few hours. It's possible that you did eat that fragment."

"So?"

Ken shot me a sideways look. "So it's possible Hayk and Ullikemi will be slightly less aggressive for a few hours."

He knew more than he was letting on. But I couldn't dwell on that. The headache was a blossom, unfurling spikes of pain through my temples and at the nape of my neck. I squeezed my eyes shut for a second and felt a wave of vertigo. Ken's hands were instantly at my elbows, supporting me.

"What's wrong?"

"Nothing. Just a really bad headache. A few ibuprofen will make me fine," I said, wishing I could lean into him like my body was telling me to do.

Not a good idea. I shuffled away.

Ken let me go. There it was again, that impression he was controlling simmering anger or frustration. A muscle ticked in his jaw.

Angry at me? For getting him mixed up in something he wasn't supposed to handle?

I made a beeline for the medicine cabinet and dry swallowed three of the orange pills. Dialing Marlin's number, I saw that Ken had taken a seat in front of my laptop. He glanced at me for permission.

I nodded, impatiently drumming my fingers on the counter as Marlin's phone rang and rang. I hung up and speed-dialed her number again. No answer. Maybe she was with a client? I texted her.

Need U. Urgent.

I peered over Ken's shoulder. He was Googling nearby businesses.

"What are you looking for?"

"Dentalia."

"Teeth?" I said.

"No, a kind of shell. A mollusk shell that looks like a tusk. Native peoples used it as currency long ago."

"What? Kwaskwi demands a tribute?" I said. Why didn't Marlin text me back? Usually she was freakishly responsive.

"Something like that," he said over his shoulder to me.

"You've got to be kidding."

Ken mumbled something in response that I didn't quite catch. My phone had buzzed and I was reading the incoming text message.

Ur sister speaks Herai 2.

"Oh God," I said. The text was from Marlin's cell.

CHAPTER SEVEN

"Hayk has my sister."

Ken caught me by the arm halfway out the front doorway.

"Where are you going?"

"Hayk's office," I tugged, but his grip became a manacle. "Let me go!" *Less aggressive, huh? Less aggressive my fat ass.*

"You don't even know Hayk is there. And what about your father?"

Enough with his grabbing! I brought my clenched fist down on top of his wrist as hard as I could. Ken let go abruptly, sending me stumbling into the hallway to bang my head against the rain-slicked rail.

He followed me, using his body to block the hall. "Calm down for a minute and *think*."

"I can think and run at the same time," I said between clenched teeth. Pain drove sharp spikes through my scalp. "You wanted to help. You can watch Dad."

He stepped in closer, imprisoning me against the rail. I felt the rain soak through my hoodie, and the scent of cardamom saturated the mossy-dank hallway.

"Koi, listen to me. Hayk and Ullikemi are dangerous. There aren't any rules, no police to save you when dealing with the Kind. You can't just rush down to his office like this."

"He's got *Marlin*," I said. I had tasted Hayk's fragments. I knew better than Ken what he was capable of.

"Let me call Kwaskwi again, we can—"

"No!" I shoved Ken's chest but the energy from Hayk's fragment had completely dissipated and he didn't even flinch. "Please," I said, half sobbing, "please let me go."

Ken cupped my chin, forcing me to let him search my gaze. He slowly lowered his nose to mine, breathing in deeply of my startled exhale. Then he blew air gently over my nose and mouth.

He stepped back, releasing me. Just like that. I didn't waste my chance. I raced down the rain-slick hallway, hopping down the stairs two at a time. Bursting out into the rain, the taste of cardamom and age-old hunger surrounded me, soaking in with the raindrops weighing down my hair and eyelashes. A weighty presence settled over my shoulders, pushing all my thoughts into a swirling ball of confusion.

I stopped at the sidewalk, hesitating, all that desperation urging me to action. I needed a car. I needed to reach Marlin. I made a little jumpy circle as I turned one direction and then another.

My fists curled into themselves, my ragged-bitten nails cutting into my palms. *Damn it!* Hooper was out of town. Ed lived way up in Vancouver. Too far away. There was nobody, not one person I could call on to help me get back to PCC.

"I called a taxi," said Ken from behind me. He stood inside the doorway with Dad draped over his left side. Dad's eyes fluttered half-open and his sparse, gray hair stuck up in disarray.

"Dad," I said, running back to support his other side. He sagged against me like a bag of bones. "What are you doing, Ken? Did he wake up? He can't be out here."

"We'll take Herai-san to Kwaskwi. Then we can find Hayk."

"I'm not entrusting Dad to a stranger!"

"You trusted him to me," said Ken.

"You're not a stranger...you're...you're—"

"Is there somebody else who can watch him?" said Ken.

I wiped stinging cardamom droplets from my eyes, pushing my wet bangs out of my face. The scent made me gag. Crap. Coffee cake would never appeal to me again.

A black Rose-City taxicab pulled over to the curb.

"Stay here with Dad. Please. I trust you."

Ken shook his head. "I made a promise. You can't go without me." The cab driver gave an impatient beep.

Time was ticking. The longer I fought with Ken, the longer Hayk had Marlin to himself. Even stopping at the Salvation Army and arguing the draconian nurse in charge of adult day care into a last minute drop-in would take too much time—she only liked Marlin. I leaned over and pulled open the cab door. Together, we lugged Dad into the backseat between us, ignoring the questioning look of the driver peering out from under a mass of blonde dreadlocks.

"Kwaskwi better be trustworthy," I whispered in Japanese.

"Mostly," Ken replied in English.

The cab driver knocked his walkie talkie on the steering wheel. "Where to?"

"Hoyt Arboretum," said Ken. The driver shrugged and pulled out onto the street, his meter ticking merrily.

Dad's head rested on my shoulder. His long legs curled to the side. His eyes had closed again, and he looked vulnerable in a way that made me want to shake him.

In Japanese, Ken said, "Do you have any jewelry? Necklace? Earrings?"

I showed him my bare earlobes and neck. All I had was a pinkie ring Marlin had given me for my last birthday; just a plain band of gold with a stylized carp.

"It'll have to do," he said.

"What are you talking about?" I said, begrudging him even those words. I was so furious I didn't want to speak.

"Kwaskwi can take it as a marker for now."

"The hell he will." I pictured each word ringed in flame. Did he not realize he was about to push me over the edge of reasonable?

"Trust me, you don't want to come empty handed. He might just take your father as 'payment' instead."

"You stay with Kwaskwi and Dad," I said, switching to English.

"Because you can take on Hayk and Ullikemi all by yourself? That went so well this morning. I am not an oath breaker. I do what I say I will, Koi."

I glared at him. If only Dad had bequeathed me useful powers, like laser eyes.

In a gentler tone, Ken went on, "Kwaskwi is tricky, but if we make a deal, he will be forced to protect Herai-san."

"Fine. We get your pal Kwaskwi to babysit Dad, but then we are storming Hayk's office."

The cabbie gave me a startled look in the rearview mirror. *Oops.* I'd forgotten that last bit was in English. I tried to smile reassuringly at him, but it must have come across more as a grimace. The cabbie floored the accelerator, running a yellow light in the next intersection.

It took only ten minutes to reach Highway 5, but each minute felt like an eternity as I watched for each of Dad's slow, laborious breaths, wanting to kick something or someone to release the tight, coiling spring of panic inside my belly.

As we rounded the forested curve just above the Willamette River, Mount Hood's snow-covered peak emerged from cloud cover to lurk like a genial, eccentric uncle over Portland's rain-shiny downtown. A tingling scatter of goose bumps raised my flesh down my back and across the backs of my arms. The usual heart-lifting effect Hood-sama had on me warped into a painful awareness of the two men beside me.

After another few, torturous minutes wasted negotiating the tourist rental car maze in the zoo parking lot, the cabbie pulled past the zoo with an audible sigh of relief. He veered left at the lower entrance of the Vietnam memorial spiral walk.

"Here you are," he said.

Crap. Of course I'd rushed out of the house without my bag or money or anything useful whatsoever. Ken pulled out a wallet of battered, black leather and slipped two weirdly crisp twenties to the cabbie. We slid a limp Dad out of the seat, heavier than a man mostly skin and bones had any right to be.

This was so wrong.

But Marlin. I pictured her face as she'd looked today leaving the apartment. Nothing could happen to her.

Nothing.

Ken and I pushed and prodded Dad over to the oak shaded bench next to the arboretum map. His head propped in the crook of his elbow atop the bench's armrest, Dad looked like he was dozing. Not that anyone would believe he'd fallen asleep in this afternoon drizzle.

His pulse and breathing were still steady. I fought an urge to curl up next to him on the bench and hide like I'd done so often in childhood. Moisture formed a drip at the tip of my nose, and I caught Ken staring at me with an odd, surprised expression.

"Okay," I said, the urgency returning to unsettle my stomach, "where's your pal?"

Ken pointed up the steep path—half wooden steps, half gravel—leading up the hillside away from the Vietnam Memorial's manicured concrete. "Up there."

"There's no way we can drag Dad up there."

"No," said Ken, meaningfully. His eyes flicked between me and the bench.

"If you make me wait here, I'll go crazy. Marlin could be…" I let the sentence trail off, unwilling to give voice to what I truly feared.

Hayk wanted a sacrifice. Marlin was Dad's daughter, too.

"You must trust me," said Ken. He put a hand lightly on my arm, guiding me under the thickly clustered leaves of the oak tree. I couldn't speak.

His other hand grasped my shoulder, and he gave me a little shake. "Marlin is okay. Ullikemi doesn't really want her, he needs you. Hayk won't do anything drastic until we show up. But I'm not going up to meet Kwaskwi until you swear you'll stay here and not go off all vigilante."

"I promise. Hurry up." I took a seat next to Dad. His hand was hot and fever-dry, despite the rain. "Hurry," I repeated.

Ken reached out and I dropped my pinkie ring into his hand. He turned without another word, taking the wooden steps two at a time, disappearing into the cherry tree varietals lining the path.

I shivered, nestling closer to Dad, feeling the fearless closeness in the press of my hand on his that I never felt with any other living person. Although, that wasn't true, now. Ken, if he counted as human, also had joined that tiny club. I covered my eyes with the backs of my hands. *What am I thinking? Dad isn't human, either. And maybe not me.*

The last headache flares settled into a dull buzz at the base of my skull.

Baku. Eater of dreams. It was crazy, and yet it made sense, and a part of me was glad. Glad I wasn't just insane. Glad that the connection I'd always felt with Dad was a real thing, not just the self-delusion of a socially stilted adolescent.

I bit down on the inside of my cheek. What the hell was wrong with me? I should be planning Marlin's rescue. The thought of myself as a rescuer made me give a despairing laugh.

A minivan drove by, stuffed to the gills with tow-headed children on their way to the zoo. A fierce envy pierced me. What did it matter I wasn't insane? I'd eaten Hayk's dream and felt that energy fill me, the energy that had let me throw Ken across the room. How was that normal? It was evil. And I'd taken that evil into my very core.

I pressed my fists to my ribs, pushing hard as if I could make the ballooning worry inside my chest flatten to nothingness. It didn't help. Tears gathered at the corners of my eyes just as a young couple, probably high schoolers, ambled into view. They were so engrossed with each other, they didn't even spare me a glance. Still, I turned away, feeling so raw and sensitive I would combust into smoke if their eyes touched me.

The high schoolers took the spiral path toward the marble-dotted landscape of the memorial. I touched Dad's cheek again. How long did it take to talk anyway? When would Ken get back?

This sucks so bad.

A large bird landed on the wooden top of the arboretum map and bobbed there, fixing me with a beady, black eye. The bird was big, the size of one of the giant crows that ruled PCC's dumpsters, but with feathers a vivid blue except where bars of black and white striped its wings. A blue jay.

"What?" I demanded, the word exploding from me in a burst.

I made a shooing motion but the jay didn't even flinch. "No crumbs here," I said, feeling like an idiot.

Jays and crows creeped me out. They tore open garbage bags, and aggressively chased all the sparrows away from the bird feeders I hung every winter.

The jay extended his wings, vividly gleaming despite the gray drizzle, and swooped down to land at Dad's feet. I held perfectly still, watching it scratch at the ground as if there were worms hiding in the concrete.

"Shoo," I said again, my voice sounding solitary and soft in the blanket of rain-patter on leaves. Unease joined my other, urgent, feelings. The jay's unwavering attention wasn't natural. I slid Dad down the bench toward me. His head lolled on his neck like a broken doll. My chest ratcheted a niche tighter around my lungs.

"Now would be a great time for you to wake up," I whispered in

Japanese.

The jay cocked its head at my words. Without warning, it spread its banded wings and flew directly at Dad's face. I twisted sideways, curving my torso over Dad with my face buried in his hair, my breathe coming in little pants.

A beat passed and I realized I felt no scratch of bird feet. I straightened and almost jumped right off the bench.

A young man was sitting on the bench on the other side of Dad.

He smiled at me, showing very white, very crooked teeth that were so large they dominated his face.

"Greetings," said the man.

There was no sign of the jay. I wiped my palms on my damp pants, prickles traveling down my neck and the fine hairs on my arms as if I'd had a static shock.

"I'm sorry?"

The man continued smiling. He wore faded but pressed jeans and a plaid shirt buttoned to the neck. His hair was dark, and moussed into generous spikes at the crown of his head. Despite my raised hackles, he didn't instantly creep me out like Hayk.

He held out his hand, but I shook my head, keeping my eyes on his face. I wasn't about to *touch* him. There was the jay, and now there was this man, and I couldn't help equating the two.

"I think we have an appointment," he said. He withdrew his arm with a wink and placed his hands, palms down on his knees.

"Kwaskwi?" I squeaked.

"Guilty as charged."

"But Ken just went up the hill to meet you."

"Ken? Ah, the Kitsune. You have something you wish to ask me?" He leaned a bit forward, expectantly, his eyes gleaming black.

Dad still unconscious between us made me very uncomfortable, but if this was Kwaskwi, I had no time to lose. "I...yes, um well you see there's this dragon Kind trapped in a stone at PCC and the professor that owns the stone has kidnapped my sister, and so I was hoping that you could—"

"Koi!" came a shout from above.

I broke off to see Ken hurling himself down the steps, rain plastering his hair to his forehead in a crazy tangle.

"Please continue," said Kwaskwi. His voice warm and deep, drawing me in. Unease still tickled at the nape of my neck. His eyes did not reflect his voice's warmth, their gleam was…avarice.

"We need you to watch Dad while—" I began again.

Ken yelled in Japanese from the landing at the top of the stairs right above us. "Don't say anything!"

I blinked, my mouth still open. Kwaskwi stood up, his hand gripping Dad's wrist.

"You come without token to make bargains with me. Tradition states I may name my own token. I name Herai Akihito."

"What?" I said, jumping to my feet. My hand hovered over Kwaskwi's forearm for a second until I settled for grabbing Dad's other wrist. I'd rather grab a naked knife blade then touch this guy. I didn't need to see the fragments lurking behind those black, black eyes and too-wide smile.

Ken came tumbling down the last bit of stairs and inserted himself between us.

"Don't presume on her innocence," he snarled.

I prodded at his side. *Damn it.* He was in the way! Ken grimaced at me over his shoulder, but shuffled a little to the side. Kwaskwi didn't look at all put out.

"I do not presume. She came here under the guise of your truce, a *Kind* negotiation," he said.

"We had a token!" I said. I reached over and grabbed Dad's other arm right above where Kwaskwi held him. It was like surreal twister.

"You did not offer it before making your plea," said Kwaskwi. He let go of Dad with a shrug.

"I brought it to the assigned meeting place," said Ken, holding out my pinkie ring.

Kwaskwi gave a burst of laughter. "Please, even you, Bringer, can't be foolish enough to insult me this way." His smile stretched wider, but those teeth and his narrowed eyes made him look fierce. "The Council made it quite clear you have no authority here. You cannot *break the rules* without consequences."

"This is a marker for our token," said Ken carefully. He bowed his head a little. "Of course we shall bring you something more worthy of our regard for your people, Kwaskwi. There was a time constraint."

Kwaskwi rolled back onto his heels. He laughed again, a guffaw like a horse. Tension drained visibly from Ken's shoulders.

"You can't blame me for trying. The Baku is valuable. Even to us." He plucked the pinkie ring from Ken's palm.

Ken nodded. I settled back down on the bench, curling my arm behind Dad's shoulders. Apparently we had reached some kind of understanding, but I didn't trust Kwaskwi.

"We need sanctuary for Herai-san. And anything you know about Mangasar Hayk and Ullikemi."

Kwaskwi's arched his eyebrows. "I agree to provide the Baku sanctuary. But I know nothing of Hayk." He licked his lips, considering. "So the taste borne on the rain is not yours?"

Ken shook his head, bowing at the waist slightly. "I endeavor to fulfill the terms of my presence in your territory."

I almost snorted at the ponderous tone he used. Were interactions among Kind always this full of crap? I mean, really, these two talked as if they sported lace cuffs and cravats in a ballroom somewhere surrounded by champagne-laden waiters.

I sniffed. Ken gave me a quelling look but I sniffed again, pouting. It was not my fault Kwaskwi found me first.

"Ullikemi is dragon-Kind, yes? We haven't had dragons in the Northwest since St Helen's erupted," said Kwaskwi. "The seeking power in this rain is troublesome. Herai Akihito made a pact with us to keep his daughters ignorant of the Kind in return for excluding them from our...curiosity. All Kind in Multnomah lands, from Sauvie Island to the Tualatin plains abided by the pact for this girl's lifetime. But it backfired, eh? She pays the penalty for her father's self-imposed exile. Just the two of you up against a dragon Kind?"

Jerk. He came here knowing who I was, knowing I was vulnerable, to trick me.

"Not just a dragon Kind. Ullikemi is bound into a human myth, Middle Eastern. Don't let Herai-san's long retirement fool you into believing the Herai lineage is weak. Koi may not have her father's knowledge, but she is *Baku.*"

Kwaskwi bowed his head at me in mimicry of Ken's formal posture. He smiled broadly again and two spots of color appeared high on Ken's cheeks. Ken had let slip too much info about me, info Kwaskwi was clearly able to use to manipulate things for his own gain. "I shall endeavor not to underestimate you, daughter-of-Herai."

My hand itched to form a fist and plant it smack dab in the middle of those teeth.

"Dad's sleeping off an episode. He needs shelter and rest. If he shows sign of fever or agitation here's my cell number." Ken pulled me up from the bench.

What was I doing? How could I leave Dad with Kwaskwi? "Do you have a car somewhere? It took both of us to get him here." I glared at Ken, but he made a barely perceptible shake of his head.

"I gave my pledge to care for Herai Akihito as a guest in my home," said Kwaskwi. "Cars really aren't my style."

Thunder rumbled far away and the sky above the hill cleared, a patch of blue in the gray. Portland's trademark liquid sunshine; sun-streamed drizzle fell all around us.

Ken jerked his chin toward the sky, indicating a large object that filled the cloud break. It spiraled down with long, lazy strokes of wings extending the length of a man on either side of its gold and crimson-feathered body.

I stared, trying to get my tired brain to translate what I saw into something that made sense; like a painted plane or a lost kite or something. But my brain refused to cooperate. It kept telling me a giant bird, a gorgeous eagle, was coming to a landing on the first black marble block forming the Vietnam Memorial Walk's wall of names. Giant talons gripped the stone as its magnificent wings tucked in around a body the size of a pony, golden eyes glowing like miniature suns.

"Oh my god," I breathed.

"You are honored, daughter-of-Herai. Thunderbird comes himself to tend your father," said Kwaskwi.

"I didn't know his Kind still existed," said Ken in a soft voice. Awestruck.

Kwaskwi stepped close to Ken, his arms straight at his sides but menace vibrating through his body. "A message for your Council. Thunderbird isn't the only one of us 'tainted' ones who survived the long centuries under human influence in the Americas. Interference from those who value bloodlines and old ways over the sacred diversity of life are unwelcome."

Ken bristled, his face shifting into the sharp planes and darkened eyes of the face I'd seen when we'd gone hunting for Dad. His Kitsune face. "Message received," he said through gritted teeth. Tension arced between them like static electricity.

Thunderbird shifted on its perch, rustling its great wings with a sound like distant summer clouds clashing.

Ken and Kwaskwi each took a carefully synchronized step back, muscles bunching in Ken's shoulders.

Kwaskwi turned to me with a disarmingly earnest expression. "Come back, soon, little carp. It has been a pleasure meeting *you*." He bent to scoop up Dad in his arms, striding over to Thunderbird as if Dad weighed nothing more than a sleeping child.

The bird jumped to the ground a few paces away, massive and golden against the concrete. With a high, piercing cry, it lowered head and shoulders at Kwaskwi's feet.

This was so wrong. Dad should be in an emergency room cubicle, not on the back of a mythological beast. I started forward, my hand outstretched as Kwaskwi placed Dad on the feathered back.

"Koi." Ken pulled my arm so that I came to a halt midstride.

A tickling sensation rippled over my open palm. The bird's expression pulled at me, calling me closer. I tugged at Ken's grip. Among white-gold feathers, twin pools of molten yellow shot through with jagged streaks of fiery orange held me fast. Distantly I heard Ken swear in Japanese.

I wanted, no *ached*, to touch the soft feathers on the bird's downy neck. Thunderbird beckoned. What dreams would a being of such mesmerizing power, such beauty, give me? Powerful ones. I licked my lips, giving a last, sharp jerk to escape the prison of Ken's grip. How dare he keep me from this sweet drowning in brilliant orange and fluid gold topaz?

In a blur of motion, Ken was suddenly between me and the bird. A sharp crack, and my cheek burned. I blinked away tears of pain. Ken had slapped me!

"Ouch!" I said, rubbing my cheek.

Thunderbird opened its beak and screamed. The sound tore through me like razorblades slicing paper. Just over the hill, thunder crashed, the echoes falling away across the soaked city.

Ken staggered to the side and shook his head like he was clearing water from his ears. Kwaskwi stood with legs braced apart, solid as a tree, showing all his crowded teeth with the widest grin yet. His twinkling eyes trained on me.

What was that all about? Had the Thunderbird tried to *make* me touch it? Would a fragment from this godlike Kind have somehow bound me to it? To Kwaskwi?

"Be careful with her, Bringer," he said, holding back laughter and adjusting straps over Dad's back. Thunderbird fidgeted, half opening those massive, elegant wings.

I flinched back.

Echoes of Thunderbird's scream still rang in my head. I rubbed my eyes with my fists, pressing until the painful aftermath faded.

I opened my eyes to find Kwaskwi gone and a blue jay perched on top of the marble monument. It cocked one eye at me, glaring.

"Take care of him," I said firmly. "Or else."

A light patter of rain started, gluing my bangs to my forehead while the open sky above us darkened with storm clouds. When had things gotten so crazy that trusting Dad's care to Kwaskwi and his giant eagle seemed the safest path?

Thunderbird's muscles rippled under golden feathers as it leaped into the air with Dad draped still and limp over its back. Another deep rattle of thunder sounded, farther away, and the eerily soft beating of Thunderbird's wings filled the silence left by its passing.

Thunderbird circled over us, disturbingly heavy and solid to have overhead. A flash of yellow topaz eyes in my brain, and then it wheeled north, Mount Hood's perfect triangle peak obscuring the bird's rapidly disappearing form in white glare.

Tingles ran down my spine, like they had in the cab coming here and I heard a ragged sigh behind me. I turned to find Ken on his knees on the soaked concrete, his head buried in his hands.

"Can't stand being laughed at by the blue jay?" I said.

Ken turned his face up into the streaming rain. Anger darkening his eyes to thin slits, his jaw set in a grim line.

His nostrils flared and suddenly the scent of cardamom was acrid and sharp in my nose, across my tongue, gagging my throat. I coughed, trying to expel the palpable weight of the presence behind that smell.

Ullikemi. Here. All around us, coating my body, the trees, and the hill; a noxious layer with a tinge of…triumph.

Desperation spurred me. I raced up the steps to the first landing as if I could call Kwaskwi and Thunderbird back from the empty, pitiless sky.

We'd led Hayk right to Kwaskwi and Thunderbird. *Stupid, stupid,*

stupid girl.

"Dad," I said. Not safer with the giant eagle after all.

"If I'd known Thunderbird still dwelt with Kwaskwi, I would never have...Thunderbird is an ancient spirit of the Kind. Now it begins," continued Ken, getting to his feet slowly, hunched over like an old man with rain ache in the deepest marrow of his bones. "Bringing shadow to Multonomah lands. Another precious light at risk. We are so few, so few. I was supposed to help Herai-san make things better. And now Ullikemi's found his thunder god."

CHAPTER EIGHT

My phone beeped again as our new taxi pulled into the mega-parking lot at the top of PCC Sylvania's hill. I flipped it open, my heart pounding so hard in my chest I wished I could reach inside my own ribcage and beat it into submission the same way Ken had squeezed the bench's armrest into splinters back at Hoyt Arboretum.

Face etched in livid lines, Ken had taken out a heaping load of hurt on the bench, then stood there, bleeding fists closing and releasing on empty air.

I'd wanted to punch something, too. Or beg forgiveness on my knees. At least curl into a ball under Mom's quilt and forget my part in leading Ullikemi straight to Thunderbird.

And Dad.

Marlin was right. Ken was right, telling me not to bury my head in the sand. I'd dug my own hole, and here I was at the bottom of it, alone with no one to turn to now that creepy Hayk had kidnapped my sister.

No one but Ken. Instead of breaking an innocent bench, I'd called the taxi.

Ken sat next to me now with that awful, careful stillness he'd lapsed into when the taxi pulled up. I stared at the blinking battery icon on my phone's screen. Low battery. Not another text from Hayk as I feared. I sighed and resisted the urge to throw the stupid phone out the window.

Ullikemi's unfocused hunger had coalesced into a purpose that burned through the rain like scented smoke, and the taxi driver coughed when the heavy, hunger-silted air seeped into the car through our opened door. I was sympathetic, the cardamom taste in my mouth made me want to hawk and spit.

The PCC brick and concrete buildings huddled together at the bottom of the hill, barely visible through the blurring rain.

"Koi," Ken said, voice harsh.

I put up a hand. Anything he said now would tip me over the crevice of wallowing guilt. Before she was hospitalized, Mom said on bad days she pretended everything was going to be okay and somehow, the world was fooled just enough for things to work out that day. Hopefully there was enough of that Pierce strength of will in me to fool the world just for this hour. For Marlin's sake. *Please let her be okay. She has to be okay.*

I pushed past Ken in the narrow space between cars. He followed close behind.

"Listen," he said, louder.

The maze of cars was making me crazy. I headed for the slippery sidewalk. All of a sudden Ken's impassable frame blocked the path.

"I *hate* it when you do that!"

"Let me check Hayk's office," he said. Rain slicked his hair into a curled mess, emphasizing the sharp, pale lines of his face. All grim determination.

I shook my head. "My sister. My father. I go. It isn't *you* Hayk wants."

"It's you and Thunderbird he wants now." Ken shifted to block me again when I tried to slip past him. "Are you listening?" He'd switched to Japanese, using very rough, male-speak.

I moved into him, my head tilted up. The fear simmering in me churned to a boil. "You told me Hayk wants a sacrifice, mortal blood, right? You're not mortal."

Ken flinched. A strange expression flickered across his face.

"He's. Got. My. Sister." I pounded a fist on his chest. Hot fear roiled out through my hand and passed into him.

"I'm more like you than you think." Ken lightly gripped my wrist, uncurling my fingers one-by-one to press my palm flat on the damp cotton of his shirt. His heart racing, his whole body thrumming.

Not safe, came a distant warning. *Pull away*. No more close contact. No more of his seductive, mist-filled dreams. Ken's physical hold on me was solid, as if he could force the rising panic to subside with warm hands and a solid chest.

His eyes went feral, the iris bleeding out into the white. Dark eyes. Animal eyes.

"Let me go," I said, wanting a commanding voice and getting plaintive plea instead.

"You barging into Hayk's office will just make it worse." His voice was a growl.

Anger was getting me nowhere. I forced my shoulders down.

"Marlin's all I have left," I said, letting fatigue and sorrow seep into my voice. My forehead tilted forward to rest next to my imprisoned hand. "If something happens to her because of me..." I let the words muffle themselves into Ken's sweatshirt. He relaxed his grip for just an instant, intending to gather me close with both hands.

I twisted under his arm, and took off, slipping and stumbling down the hill on the rain-slick sidewalk.

I made it to the bottom of the hill where a sprinkling of other students in raincoats and sodden hoodies milled the paths between concrete buildings before Ken caught up to me, pacing by my side just as I reached the stairs at Hayk's building.

"That wasn't playing fair," he said.

"You used your strength to hold me," I said. I brushed past him, taking the stairs two at a time. Ken waited at the bottom. It seriously pissed me off how fast that man could move.

"I made promises," he said this time. "To the Council, to your father, to *myself*."

One hand on the door handle, I stopped to glare at him. "Forgive me for not giving a damn about your promises."

Ken followed me into the corridor. I had to stop again, one hand on the grimy plastered wall to keep myself from falling over. Cardamom. Hunger. The pressing and voluminous presence of Ullikemi all around.

"Do you even know what you're going to do if he's there?"

"I have a plan," I said.

Ken coughed and shook himself like a dog emerging from water. "Why didn't you enlighten me about your *plan* back in the taxi?"

"I just made it up now." I paused, needing a moment to catch my breath. "I'm trading myself for Marlin."

"Not acceptable."

"This is not your fight!"

A muscle throbbed in Ken's temple. He pulled back. "Not my fight," he repeated. He slipped his phone out of his pocket.

"Glad that's clear, then," I said, though my stomach sank down to the stale, gray carpet. Excellent plan, alienate the one super-creature on your side.

"Hayk's agenda is more than just helping Ullikemi get to Thunderbird. He must want something for himself, too," Ken said. His fingers danced on the surface of the phone. I looked away, a tight feeling in my chest.

His last words followed me down the hall. "Don't sacrifice

yourself to a murderer."

Hayk's office door swung open a few feet away, a golden square of light on the hall carpet.

"Damn it, I'm tired of coming here to retrieve my family," I muttered.

From inside the office came the rumbling scrape of stone on concrete, and all of a sudden Ullikemi's pressure gripped my head in a vise. I fell to my knees. Behind me, Ken grunted in pain.

I clawed myself to a standing position against the wall. It felt ice cold on my fingertips as I swam through the thick miasma of Ullikemi's presence, inching my way through the door.

"Welcome to our little study session," said Hayk. He lounged in the black vinyl swivel chair behind his desk, the self-satisfied curve of his disturbingly fleshy lips showed off movie-star, white teeth. Marlin sat ramrod straight in one of the folding chairs in front of his desk, her glazed eyes unfocused on the orderly piles of papers on Hayk's desk.

I sagged against the doorframe. My lungs could barely process the air so close to the Vishap stone.

"What do you want?" I coughed.

"Marlin was kindly helping me with research," said Hayk, indicating a sheaf of papers with a lazy hand.

I sensed Ken creep to the edge of the doorway, flattening himself against the hall-side wall. The back of my neck prickled with the urge to look, but I quashed it. He must have some reason for not showing himself to Hayk.

"Marlin," I said, "I think we're late for that thing we have."

A choked, mewling sound escaped my sister's throat, but she didn't move.

"Now, now, Ms. Pierce," said Hayk. "Your sister has been ever-so-helpful. You can't take her away when we're right on the cusp of a really exciting breakthrough."

I dragged myself through the doorway. Marlin's flesh was clammy where I touched her arm. "What have you done to her?"

Hayk's smile widened. "You never got back to me with those translations I asked you for. Luckily, when your sister showed up for my apartment redecorating appointment, it turned out she knew as much Herai dialect as you. She was particularly helpful with a phrase I've been particularly eager to discover."

Hayk stood up suddenly, revealing his hidden right hand. A slender, curved silver dagger flashed in the fluorescent light. He licked his lips, slow and deliberate, and then sliced a shallow cut on his index finger.

I yanked at Marlin, but she was stiff and unmovable. I yanked again, with all my might and dragged her, chair and all, halfway across the floor. Hayk strode over to the Vishap stone and grasped it with his bleeding hand, adding a bright smear to the faint brown stains marring the top of the stone.

"You'll appreciate this one, Ms. Pierce," said Hayk. He mumbled something very low and quick in a language I did not recognize. Stone scraped on concrete. I tilted Marlin's chair at an angle and yanked with both hands.

The Vishap's carved face darkened, the lines writhing and congealing into thickened strands of metallic-green, like an ancient patina of verdigris on copper. The lines twisted off the stone to hover three feet off the ground. Slowly, a shape outlined itself in midair. Long, crocodile snout, teeth double-rowed and jagged like a shark, and huge eyes that glowed phosphorescent in the smothering smoke. A dragon. Ullikemi.

I gasped.

"Don't be tiresome. You're no stranger to otherworldly things, baby *Baku*. We'll skip the lengthy explanations," said Hayk in an impatient, professorial tone.

Where the hell is my cavalry? Why didn't Ken rush in all Kitsune-feral and help me lift Marlin from the damn chair? Was he afraid of Ullikemi? With all my flagging strength I wrenched her upright, and the chair folded in on itself, sending my sister into a tumbling heap on top of me.

"Such haste to leave," said Hayk. "Don't you want to know what phrase your sister helped me with?"

I clawed myself out from under Marlin. Her heartbeat spasmed like a hooked trout. What had he done to her?

Keeping one eye on the pulsing, floating head of Ullikemi, I manhandled Marlin into a standing position. Hayk said something else in the harsh language, and Ullikemi's jaw cracked open.

Cold, wet air flowed from the dragon's mouth, spiraling through the air in a dingy stream. Headed straight toward me.

"Your sister taught me the Herai dialect for *an instance of total surprise that freezes you,*" said Hayk. The last phrase was spoken in a stiff, over-dramatic way that would have been ridiculous if a strange, tiered harmony hadn't surrounded the phrase. The dragon's essence inflated the phrase with an overwhelming blast of cardamom, giving it power—Ullikemi's power. My eyes stung with tears.

Suddenly, the rapid beating of my heart was the only movement I could make.

That phrase. Just like before when he'd called me out of Kaneko-sensei's class with something about having a moment in between errands. Hayk's mouth formed English words, but it was like he droned a chorus of other languages around it like a Tuvan overtone singer. I could pick out the Herai dialect, Spanish, German, along with a host of unidentifiable others. As if every language in the world were combined in the speaking of that single phrase.

Hayk stepped away from the stone to close the distance between us. Ullikemi's visage trailed him with eyes that shimmered like flashes of sunlight on fish scales.

"I could spend all evening picking your sister's brain for more useful phrases for my research. Alas, my *friend* has a different goal in mind," he said and placed a hand on Marlin's shoulder.

"You'll be more polite now, won't you, Ms. Pierce." His other hand made a slight jerk, pulling my attention to the slender dagger, now smeared red along the edge. "Or should I name you properly, Herai-san?"

More of that harsh language from Hayk, and the icy stillness released me. I sagged, barely keeping myself upright.

"Let her go," I said after a couple of deep breaths. My hands clenched and unclenched in frustration.

Hayk laughed, leaning in closer to Marlin so his cheek brushed her hair. "I'm a reasonable man. I'm willing to give up a valuable resource, but not without a little something in return. A small thing. A trifle."

I stared in defiance, my jaw clenched, little aftershock shivers racing up and down my spine. I'd never truly hated anyone in my life. Until now.

I hate Hayk.

"What?" I snapped.

"I propose a trade. Your sister goes free, *unharmed*," said Hayk, lingering on the last word, making it a chilling, travesty of a word, "and you lead us to the native Kind you were with this afternoon."

I had been convinced he would ask for me in exchange. A sick disappointment tightened the back of my throat. What kind of twisted self-centeredness was my plan to sacrifice myself? Useless now.

He wanted Thunderbird. Just as Ken said.

"How about I call the police and you let us both go," I said.

Hayk shook his head. "Tsk-tsk, Ms. Pierce. You disappoint me. Even if they listened to your crazy stories, do you think that I am vulnerable to the likes of the police?"

"Your position at the university would get complicated. I could claim harassment, maybe even get you fired," I said.

His hand crept up Marlin's shoulder, stroking her neck like she was a kitten. "It doesn't matter anymore. My job, this masquerade. Once we take care of Ullikemi's little errand, my years of painstaking research will bear fruit." His movements grew rough. Red welts formed on my sister's neck where he groped her. Wide-eyed and frozen, she could barely blink.

"Don't touch her," I said, pulling Marlin out of his grasp. Hayk let her go with a grimace of distaste.

"You have no idea what I've gone through to dig up all those languages, the people I've had to deal with," Hayk spoke with his hands, weaving a complex pattern with the dagger. "Just a handful of phrases that were suitable, phrases that existed in a small enough proportion of languages that I could collect all the iterations."

He was mad, rambling. I couldn't see what any of this had to do with Thunderbird or Ullikemi. I shuffled backward a step, still-frozen Marlin like a block of wood in my arms. *Now* would be a good time for Ken to bust in with a rescue.

"And then finding Ullikemi's stone. It gets very cold in the desert at night, young lady. But it was worth it," he said, his voice soaked with a sick kind of passion, like a religious fanatic. He edged closer.

"You know all about magic, don't you, Ms. Pierce? The Kind keep their power close. Understand my dilemma. I would like nothing more than to have no further association with you or your sister. But without Ullikemi, all my years of hard work are for nothing. His needs must be met, first, or I'll be stuck lugging this stone around forever. Take me to the place where you met with the native Kind." He was no longer a ranting super villain but his implacable calm was more terrifying than that false politeness had been. "Now."

"No," I said, and turned to book out the door. But Hayk's monologuing had lulled me into a false sense of security. Before I'd taken a step, he lunged, imprisoning Marlin's wrist against his chest and pressing the silver knife's edge tightly into her skin.

"Not as clever as I first supposed," said Hayk, "I was sure you'd understand my priorities."

I weighed the damage his silver knife could do. A slashed wrist and escape versus betraying Thunderbird, Dad, and no guarantee of our safety.

Hayk tsk-tsked into the silence.

"Surrender to fate, Ms. Pierce. You were meant to bring culmination to my studies. For so long the Portland Kind eluded me—Ullikemi's nemesis hiding so close, yet out of reach—then you came to PCC and for the first time since I moved to this soggy city, I had hope."

A slender thread of blood trickled down the vulnerable skin of Marlin's wrist. Would it be so terrible to lead Hayk to the arboretum? Surely Kwaskwi and Thunderbird couldn't be traced from there. Even if Hayk could somehow track them through the air, they were far more capable of taking on this maniac than me. Behind Hayk, the roiling smoke of Ullikemi's form darkened, the green-glass glints of the eyes flaring.

No, that wasn't entirely true. The danger wasn't just Hayk, but Ullikemi, too.

"Take me," said Hayk. A quick slice and a diagonal cut across Marlin's blue veins seeped blood. Hayk smeared the blood across the blade and his fingers. Marlin didn't flinch. Couldn't. Hayk had her perfectly frozen.

"Okay," I said. *He cut her. He hurt Marlin.* Panic frosted my lungs. Marlin's blood was too red, too bright. I pictured Hayk's silver knife buried in her throat. "Just don't hurt her anymore. I'll take you."

Hayk smiled. The silver knife flashed again, this time opening a longer cut along the inside of Marlin's elbow. Marlin cried out, twisting in his grasp.

"What the hell? I said I'd take you!"

Hayk pressed his palm to Marlin's wound, covering his hand in blood. He thrust her at me so quickly I barely had time to snag her around the waist.

"Just making it official." He strode over to the Vishap stone. His hand slapped the surface, leaving a bloody handprint that sank into the stone with a hiss.

"*Im kyanqi xostuma misht uji mech klini,*" Hayk said, the harsh syllables cutting into the room's thick air.

The world dropped itself from under my feet, as if I were in an elevator going down way too fast.

"Your promise binds you," said Hayk, folding his arms.

The rushing sensation came to an abrupt halt as Marlin gave a wracking cough. "He cut me!"

The pressure to leave, to rush away steadily built. My legs took me a step toward the door before I caught myself with a shake. This urgency wasn't coming from me.

"Oh god, get me out of here," said Marlin, fumbling in her pockets for her phone. It refused to appear.

"What did you do to us?"

Hayk considered my words. "Don't play at ignorance."

He'd done something just now with Marlin's blood and Ullikemi's power. I couldn't not go to the arboretum now. My promise to bring him to Thunderbird drew me like flannel-shirted brew-geeks to the smell of Stumptown's Probat drum roaster at work.

"I have to…I have to go to the arboretum."

"Yet you are Kind, or Ullikemi's power would not bind you," said Hayk.

"Koi," said my sister, low-voiced and shaky. "Let's go. Please."

"Okay," I said. The sleeve of her sweater stretched up just enough so I could use it to put pressure on the long slice still oozing blood on her arm.

Hayk's freeze magic no longer held her, but she was weak and confused. I had to get her away from here, to a safe place. A fleeting thought, instantly overwhelmed by a surge of need to go toward the arboretum. I had to go right *now* or my insides would burst.

Out the door it would have to be, the compulsion left me no room to *think*. I stepped through the open door. Ken was nowhere in sight. Something crumpled to a small, slimy ball in my stomach. I had been hoping.

Compulsion propelled me into motion. Dragging Marlin behind me, I started for the exit. Hayk followed close behind, forcing Marlin to tread on my heel.

In Herai dialect I murmured to my sister. "You're going to get out of here. Your apartment isn't safe. Do you have Dad's old condo keys?"

Marlin didn't answer. I paused with my hand on the metal push bar of the exit door. *Where the hell was Ken?* I couldn't, didn't want to believe that he'd run away and left me to deal with this alone. All that talk about promises? How was I supposed to get Marlin to safety by myself? My locked knees unbuckled, sending me lurching through the door like a drunkard.

"Marlin!" I said, squeezing her wrist.

"Yes," she said. Her voice was a hoarse gasp, forced through a clenched jaw. I'd never seen her so wordless, my self-centered, uber-manager sister unraveling.

"Do you have Dad's keys?"

Hayk caught up with me before she could answer. His eyes were no longer pale blue but iridescent spots gleaming in the drab hallway.

"Lead on, we'll follow," he said in a deep, bell tone of a voice, not Hayk's carefully manicured accent. It wasn't just Hayk pausing on the bottom of the concrete steps. Ullikemi rode him; I was taking the dragon with me.

CHAPTER NINE

I held my breath at the bus stop, waiting for the line of students to freak out about Hayk. His eyes were glowing! *Come on, even Portland isn't that weird.*

The black-haired guy at the front of the line never even glanced back once. I scanned down the row of girls lined up in front of us, wishing fiercely for an off-duty cop or even a heftier member of the Rose City Rollers. *Turn around. Notice us.*

But nobody noticed Hayk's eyes, or the strange way he stood, his arms undulating at his sides as if he were caught in an unseen current. Nobody did double takes at Marlin's haggard face or her blood-streaked arm. Dragon glamour? Hayk? No smell of cardamom, just the usual musty rain and tang of Sitka spruce.

Was this how Kwaskwi and his Kind had hidden among humans so long; were we all so startlingly oblivious?

We. Ha! I no longer counted among the 'we.'

"There's a key under the aloe plant on the back verandah," said Marlin in English.

"Speak Japanese," I snapped.

Her face paled.

"Sorry," I said, and pulled her closer. She'd always been the shortest, among our short family, and she looked as small and vulnerable as a child tucked under my arm. Panic rose in me again, as strong as the compulsion. *I have to keep Marlin safe. Have to.* In Herai dialect again I said, "When we get on the bus, stay behind. Hide. Promise me you won't go back to your apartment."

"I will telephone the police," she said. "Text me your location."

I shook my head. "No. You know what he did to you. The police have no defense against that."

"I don't understand. He must have drugged me somehow—"

I squeezed her tighter, channeling some of the frantic urge to move into a hug. "It's not drugs, Marlin. You know what this is. You know Dad and I are different. Let me take Hayk where he wants to go, and then he'll leave us alone."

"And Dad?" she said, lapsing into English.

I turned my face so I could lay my cheek on top of her head. She was trembling. Me, giving *her* comfort. Telling her what to do. All topsy-turvy.

"He's somewhere safe," I lied into her tousled hair. *Please make him safe. Please make her safe.*

The metal squealing of brakes sounded. The bus made its ponderous way down the hill, window wipers going full blast. Ullikemi/Hayk was so focused on the bus, he might not notice if Marlin got left behind.

"You can do this, right? This...magic stuff."

I ignored her question, pulling out my worn, faux leather wallet and fingering the crumpled bill inside. Marlin shook her head. With a hand still streaked with blood, she closed my hands over the pitiful offering. "Money, I have," she said. "Koi, call me as soon as you..." Her voice trailed away.

How to finish that sentence? As soon as I got rid of the dragon? Saved Dad? Figured out how to find Thunderbird? It was all crazy, and despite Marlin's pretense at calm speech, her shaking hands and too-wide pupils told me she was at the end of her rope. I bounced in place on the balls of my feet, the compulsion making my teeth ache.

She needed to leave this crazy stuff behind and get back to her world, the real world.

I could try to give her that, at least, even if the thought of getting on that bus with Hayk by myself left a taste like the bitter dregs of espresso grounds in my mouth.

"The bus," said Hayk, turning his disturbing green gaze back to me. I gave my sister's hand one last squeeze and stepped between her and Hayk.

He muscled past the black-haired slouching guy at the front of the line, eliciting surprised insults from the trio of girls in front of us, but no one moved to stop him as he jumped up the steps into the bus. Polite Portlanders at their finest, I thought to myself. What I wouldn't give for an irate New Yorker or macho Texan cowboy right now.

Or a Kitsune, goddammit.

Ken had made me think he cared about me, about my dad, but he was nowhere in sight.

I paid my fare with a mumbled apology to the driver. I couldn't quite bring myself to take the open space next to Hayk, but I slid into the seat in front of him, wanting his attention on me.

The door squeaked a protest as it closed, and then we were in motion. I resisted the urge to look out the streaked windows. Marlin needed the precious moments to get away, but Hayk didn't seem to care.

"I thank you, little Baku," he said in that weird voice. Not a bell, more like the reverb of sound traveling across watery depths. I shivered. Was it Hayk or Ullikemi speaking?

The bus crested the hill, leaving Marlin behind. I heaved a sigh of relief and my panic simmered down. My family was more or less safe. Now only I had to deal with Hayk.

"Save it," I said, facing front again.

"Oh, but it's only polite," he continued, his voice a chill caress, damper than October drizzle on the back of my neck. This was Hayk speaking. "Without you, I might never have found Ullikemi's nemesis. Ullikemi allows me so much more access to his power now."

I hunched down, bracing my knees on the empty seat in front of me. Running my hands up and down my arms seemed to relieve a little of the pressure from the compulsion. How was I going to survive twenty minutes of this?

Use your time. Think.

My brain whirled round and round and would not settle. I couldn't overpower Hayk physically, and this compulsion meant I had no choice but to go to the arboretum.

So I would lead Hayk to the arboretum, and if Kwaskwi and Thunderbird were somehow there, they would deal with him.

I hoped. And if they weren't there?

I pictured Hayk whipping out a magnifying glass, crouching down to examine the ground for clues like a demented Sherlock Holmes. Would Kwaskwi leave a magical trace? Maybe Ullikemi had some kind of tracking ability for flying creatures.

A small sound halfway between exasperation and a laugh escaped my lips. I braced myself, expecting a comment in Hayk-Ullikemi's disturbing voice but heard only the moaning of the bus as it took a curve.

Except. Except that not all the passengers in the side-facing seats at the front of the bus had the dozing stare of commuters on a drizzly day. The black-haired guy Hayk had cut in front of in line had his purple hoodie pulled up over his head despite being inside the bus.

The guy's face was turned three quarters profile my direction, and I caught the flicker of his eyes, far too attentive and active.

I sat up and the guy immediately craned his neck around to face forward, leaving me staring at the vivid purple cotton of his hood.

No, it couldn't be. I rubbed my eye with a fist, dismayed to see faint smears of Marlin's blood had stained my cuff. I'd walked right past the other passengers, my social blinders on full. His hoodie had the kanji for "Kitsune" on it next to a stylized graphic of Taiko drums.

Ken? Hope tickled my insides. The guy settled back into his chair. His nostrils flared, once, twice, testing the air. *Oh god. It is Ken.* I made fists of both hands, letting my ragged nails bite my palms.

He hadn't cut and run. He was here, following us. I pressed my nails more tightly into my skin. Damn it, I was *not* going to go all squirrelly with relief at that idea. He clearly had his own agenda, and letting me walk into Hayk's office alone to get Marlin was proof of that. He let Hayk slice Marlin like her blood was no more precious than dirt. Where was Mr. Funny Disguise when Hayk forced me to take him here?

Too little, too late.

How I'd felt when he kissed me didn't matter.

I was on my own.

Sitting in front of Hayk played havoc on my raggedy nails, but the enforced stillness was causing my madly flowing adrenaline and rapidly beating heart to slow.

Other needs piped up with urgent messages. Hunger. I needed to pee. I would gladly strangle Greg-ever-chipper for a latte. Too bad there wasn't a Dutch Brothers at the arboretum. Only over-priced tourist coffee at the zoo corner of the giant tourist parking lot.

My mind persisted on this inane loop-de-loop until I realized the bus was pulling up next to the concrete bunker of the Washington Park Max stop, and I had absolutely no idea what I was going to do beyond leading Hayk to the bench at the bottom of the Vietnam Memorial where I'd seen Kwaskwi.

A quick glance at Hayk confirmed no sign of expectation on his face as we neared the stop. Right. He didn't actually *know* where we were going. Maybe I could skip the arboretum, let the bus take us onward to the Rose Garden. But as the bus doors swiveled open, the compulsion gave such a wrenching jerk to my internal organs, I sprang up out of the seat.

Hayk quickly followed me down the steps and onto the concrete sidewalk. A sunbreak appeared in the clouds. A shaft of light cutting through the murky weather made Hayk's curly hair appear like a soft halo which clashed jarringly with the almost devil-like intent apparent in the green eyes. Not impatient, but intent waiting—like Marlin's cat when you were opening a can of tuna.

No, not a cat. A dragon.

Right.

I surveyed the area as if I were looking for the right path. A flash of purple hoodie was visible through the trees. I took a deep breath and stepped into the crosswalk, forcing several vans full of tourists to screech suddenly to a halt.

On the other side of the street, the path leading to the Vietnam Memorial entrance morphed into dirt, bounded on both sides by dripping evergreens and cypress. A few college-types and athletes dressed in damp running shorts were visible, most walking down the hill toward the parking lot.

I tried a step toward the parking lot myself, but it was like trying to push myself through frozen Jell-O, my limbs would not obey me, and a cold *absence* of heat stroked over my skin despite the multiple sunbreaks that had opened up all over the park.

"Your promise binds you," said Hayk. "Lead me to the Kind."

With a deep breath, I started up the slope. "I met them at the bench in front of the Vietnam Memorial," I said.

"Met?" repeated the Ullikemi voice, cardamom seeping into the pine and mulch smell of the arboretum.

"A neutral place," I said, warming to the idea. The compulsion wasn't kicking in, so apparently my promise to "lead him to the Kind" didn't mind that I wasn't actually able to lead Hayk directly to Thunderbird. Maybe all that worry was wasted.

"The thunder god," said the Ullikemi voice. "I felt his presence, but there was another, too, a lesser servant. Tell me their names."

We entered the little plaza with the Vietnam Memorial map and bench. The purple hoodie guy was slouching right in the middle of the bench.

It somehow didn't seem like a good idea to tell Hayk about Kwaskwi or to name Thunderbird. "My promise doesn't cover that," I said.

Hayk grabbed my shoulder, swinging me around to face him. His other hand gripped the material at my neckline and twisted, putting uncomfortable pressure on my airway.

"Tell me," said the Ullikemi voice, and a feeling like decayed, damp leaves stroked me from head to toe. I shivered, arching away from him, but the dragon's strength was in Hayk's hands.

"Let her go," said a voice behind me. Hayk stiffened.

Purple hoodie guy was off the bench, a branch as thick as my wrist gripped in his hands like a baseball bat. Hayk smiled.

"The Kitsune. I felt you, but couldn't quite pinpoint where, or should I say *who*, you were."

The guy took a step closer, the edges of his face blurring and indistinct. I blinked. Eyelashes full and curved, pupils a warm, Valrhona brown. "Even dragons are vulnerable to Kitsune illusion," Ken said.

Hayk tightened his grip at the base of my throat. I gasped.

"Vulnerable," repeated Hayk. "Ironic you should apply that word to *me*." A strange, shivering awareness ran down my shoulders through my arms to my hands, where my palms itched fiercely.

What a fascinating tableau we'd make for tourists coming down the hill. "Where have you been?" I stage whispered.

"Getting permission to make this my business," said Ken, and swung the branch.

Hayk pushed me to the ground, but he couldn't move fast enough to escape Ken's blow. It landed on his back with a *thwump*. I twisted and my hip hit the ground with a jarring thud, pain and surprise taking away what little breath lingered in my lungs.

The two men circled my prone body. The smell of cardamom thickened, and Hayk's eyes glowed Ullikemi's sea green.

"Don't interfere, Kitsune," said Hayk. *No.* Not the cultured tones of the professor, but the sliding vowels and strange harmonics of Ullikemi. "The dream-eater is not my quarry. It is the thunder god I seek. I am bound."

"Your human ally does you shame," said Ken, hefting the branch.

With a hissing crunch, the branch collapsed inward. Water-logged bits of rotten wood showered down, flecking my face with grit. Ken grimaced and threw away the remains.

Ullikemi's power? Did Hayk do that?

"You will not stop me," said Ullikemi, the human vocal cords hoarse and battered underneath those disturbing multi-layered harmonies, like a Balkan men's choir mashed with a didgeridoo. "The search has been arduous, I long for an ending."

I sat up carefully, shivering as my dampened clothes welcomed the chill air. The men did not move, their eyes practically crackled in challenge. Hayk's face was pale beneath bright spots of red tinting his high cheekbones. Feverish. As if his body was rapidly depleting fuel, burned up from the inside.

Where are clueless tourists when you need them? Not a soul was around.

Ken's presence behind me was comforting warmth, but I couldn't stay curled on the ground. I slid my feet beneath my bent knees.

"We are all bound to certain paths," said Ken. "Yet ever have the Kind chosen how we walk them."

Could I sneak off to the side? Hayk's attention was all on Ken and their battle of over-inflated obviousness. The air between them was thick with tension and the sensation of the dragon's energy still crawled my face.

"You speak of choice? What choice? Human myth has enslaved me too long. I don't remember what came before Ullikemi. Tell me,

Kitsune; is it entirely your *choice* to journey so far from your home island?"

A rumbling sound, like a growl, came from Ken.

"Pretend the human myths don't name you, Kitsune. Pretend the Council isn't moribund with its own importance. Believe your own illusions. I surrender to the inevitable. I long now only to find the end of the story."

Enough with the purple prose. This was worse than the SCA melee battle face-off at a Ren Faire—Ullikemi's monologuing wasn't getting us anywhere. Hayk's gray-trousered knees stared me in the face and an inkling of an idea lit up. *Would Ken follow my lead?* I swallowed down a lump of something bitter in my throat and before good sense could stop me, rolled a half somersault right into Hayk's knees. He went over like a falling tower of blocks, his flailing elbows dealing a sharp blow to my head as I scrambled away.

Ken followed him down, crouching over Hayk's chest, breathing in short huffs. His face was the sharp-planed, dark-pupiled one I'd seen when he hunted my father across the city. The purple hoodie morphed back into his OHSU sweatshirt as I sat up, brushing slimy dirt and twigs from my jeans.

The silver knife flashed in Hayk's free hand, cutting a thin line across his own palm. Ken forced his forearm over Hayk's smiling mouth a beat too late. Ullikemi's power thrummed through Hayk's voice.

"*An instance of total surprise that freezes you,*" said Hayk, sub tones, overtones, a harmony of command.

The chill fear took me, a prisoner inside my own flesh.

Ken groaned, muscles in his back bunching and releasing. He couldn't move.

Hayk pushed him off easily. He stood up, brushing damp pine needles from his arms.

"Now, you will tell me the names I require." Hayk gave an impatient cluck of his tongue. He stepped around Ken, who was struggling against frozenness on hands and knees, shaking.

"The names." The voice was Hayk, his face close to mine, all clipped syllables and disdain.

It was such a simple thing: two words. I could say the words and Hayk would unfreeze me, let Ken take me home. I remembered the mesmerizing draw of Thunderbird's eyes and the menace in Kwaskwi's too-wide smile. Kwaskwi and Thunderbird wouldn't hesitate to use me for their own gain. They were powerful enough to take care of themselves.

Tears welled. Lying to myself wasn't helping. It wasn't that simple. Hayk wouldn't let me go. Conviction settled deep in my chest. Ullikemi wanted Thunderbird, and then he wanted my blood just as Ken had said. Giving Hayk the names would only give away what advantage we had, not set me free.

"Ms. Pierce, I thought you ever so much cleverer than this. There is no shortage of people around you who can be made to suffer," he said, brandishing the silver knife at Ken.

Will this man never stop threatening people I care about?

Something twinged within me. I'd included Ken in that thought. Someone I cared about.

He had secrets, but I trusted him. Probably stupid. I'd hidden my whole life. Anything painful, anything real. From friends, from Mom. From Dad's slow decay. Caring meant watching other people hurt, and then dreaming the depth of their pain in full Technicolor at night.

If I sat by and watched Hayk slash Ken to ribbons, something irrevocable would break.

Don't be a sniffling coward.

Hayk ran a finger from the corner of my eye down my cheek, gripping my chin like Humphrey Bogart in one of Mom's black and white movies.

"Kwaskwi," I croaked.

Hayk gave an over exaggerated grimace. "Mortal blood is required for this next part." His tone truly apologetic. He grabbed my pony tail at the back of my head, pulling tightly. "Your Herai blood is so much more potent than mine."

The silver knife flashed again, and a line of pain burned across my left cheek. Behind him, Ken groaned.

Blood dripped down my cheek. Hayk watched, the tip of his tongue caught between his teeth, a desire as deep and overwhelming as Ullikemi's darkening his eyes. He turned from polite professor to something I'd cross to the other side of a street to avoid even in broad daylight.

Gray static gathered at the corners of my eyes. I'd forgotten to breathe. The chill air turned to frost in my lungs, leaving me gasping like a goldfish out of its bowl. Hayk blinked, my noisy breath startling him from the dark place his desires lived.

His grimace stretched to a hungry grin, and he put a cupped palm to my cheek, soaking up the slow trickle of blood. When his skin touched mine, I felt something vital drain from me, leaving me trembling and upright in his grip, my limbs aching to collapse.

Hayk released me abruptly, and I tumbled back to the wet ground. My teeth closed painfully on the side of my tongue, sour melon taste flooding my mouth.

From the ground, Hayk was out of my line of sight, but I heard him begin a chant in that harsh language he'd spoken to Ullikemi. Grunts and curses told me Ken was still struggling.

The web of tree branches breaking up the expanse of cloud-soaked sky over my head was limned in brightness, Mount Hood's peak like ivory shards shredding the green.

Gray static again threatened to blind me. Consciousness drained away like water through a pour-over filter. I clung to the wavering triangle of Mount Hood with all my might.

Hayk's chant rose to a crescendo, one word distinct among the gibberish.

"Kwaskwi!" he intoned. Ullikemi's power burst from the

harmonics, spilling through the clearing in all directions like an arctic wind.

Struggling against Hayk-Ullikemi's power, I managed to shut my eyes.

Behind my eyelids, Hayk's cold subsided a bit. Enough for me to realize there was a hard kernel glowing inside, deep in my belly. I tried to move my hand to cover it but Hayk's frozenness still bound every muscle.

"Soon, he comes," said Hayk. "Be patient a bit more."

I shut out his voice, the bright pain on my cheek, and the chill damp seeping through my clothes. The kernel was warm.

It was a fragment. Hayk's fragment. He'd touched me when he took my blood, and despite the warmth of the kernel, it reeked of an all-consuming desire.

This fragment felt the same as the murdered woman in the hall, and the boy broken at the bottom of the hole.

Powerful, sharp-edged desire. Hayk's.

I probed at the kernel, felt it inside me like a chancre sore.

I remembered the feeling of throwing Ken across the room. Not my own strength, but power borrowed from *eating* a fragment, from eating Hayk's fragment. I could use that power right now.

Dream eater.

Nausea roiled. No, I didn't want to take Hayk's deranged passion into myself. *But it sure would be handy.*

From somewhere outside my personal darkness I heard the staccato, sharp cries of a blue jay. Kwaskwi.

He's coming. With Dad? Or is Dad safe?

This was my fault. I'd given Hayk Kwaskwi's name, and it was my blood fueling this summons.

Chills crept down my spine.

How did I do it before? It wasn't like I'd dreamed this fragment. This was different. The fragment hovered just outside my consciousness, darting to and fro like a minnow worrying at some piece of food. Only in this metaphor it was my brain the fragment was dipping into.

I reached for the taste of painful desire inside me as a blue jay's shrill cries battered me on all sides. The roiling kernel of Hayk's dreaming *caught*, turning to molten metal, burning up my nausea. It traveled up my spine to my head, seething there in an ever-expanding, rhythmic pulse. My skull throbbed. Every muscle in my body flexed, my back arching painfully high off the wet earth.

Awake, I dreamed the dream.

Endless sapphire blue and watery emerald all around me, indistinct shadows glimmering out of sight. My body glided, deadly, through the shifting blue-green, muscles twisting along my back and sides in strange, but powerful, configurations.

Sea salt and murk covered my tongue.

Thunder cracked overhead—a challenge—and I shot up out of the depths, surfacing to a blinding, brilliant, corona of gold around a fiery ball. An overwhelming want surged through me, shredding my insides. A water dragon's defiance to the sky's existence—a devouring hunger for the sun. Water versus air. A challenge that couldn't be ignored.

Oh god. Not Hayk's dream after all.

I gasped, my eyes flying open. The brightness of the drizzly day stung my vision blurry with tears. After a moment of frantic blinking, I could make out an entire scold of jays—wheeling blue swirls in the gray sky above me.

I was a sandpaper bag of mixed up bones. A pathetic excuse for a human, let alone Baku, and Ullikemi's wanting was like knives in my throat, building and building until the feeling I would burst resolved itself into an insistent pressure in my belly.

But I swallowed. Swallowed. My muscles had obeyed me. Was Ullikemi/Hayk's magic thawing? I exhaled, low and long.

The seething, roiling *want* overflowed through the thin fabric of my skin. It burned, every cell catching fire, as if literal flames bloomed across my body.

The binding of Hayk's frozenness sloughed away.

A cry was torn from me as my limbs tingled with a thousand needles. Tendons stretched, flexed, and cracked into place.

Tears still streaming, I sat up, though the muscles in my lower back screamed in protest. I pulled myself up like an arthritic centenarian, the blue jays screaming murder overhead.

Ken hadn't moved from his position on all fours, but Hayk stood in a wide stance, arms outstretched to the sky, Ullikemi's green-glass gaze burning in his face.

"Kwaskwi," Ullikemi said. "I summoned you here."

The scold of jays dropped from the sky like dead weights, straightening out into a jostling line of blue feathers and chattering beaks on top of the same block of marble Thunderbird had perched on a few hours ago.

At some unseen signal, the birds quieted, going motionless.

Hayk-Ullikemi was so focused on the jays, he didn't react at all when I crept closer to Ken. Shaking, jaw clenched tight, he looked so strange, the planes of his face sharpened and odd, more Kitsune than human.

My hands hovered a few inches from his shoulders.

Ken was so strong, so sure. Touching him now, when he was powerless, felt like a violation.

"Playing these tricks is not worthy of the thunder god," said Hayk-Ullikemi.

I forced my hands to Ken's shoulders, and he moaned, a sound low in the back of his throat. I bent over him, pressing my arms and cheek to his back.

Awful and wonderful. Skin crawled on my neck and back, as vulnerable to Hayk as Ken, but inside the cradle of my arms and chest Ken was *warm*. Burning up. And I reveled in that warmth.

There was barely anything left of the kernel—no, the dream-fragment—I'd eaten, but where Ken's skin rubbed mine, his exhilarating heat burned hotter. I breathed in the smell of sweat and salt, and when I exhaled, our connection flared hot. I jerked back. Pain tightened a vise at my temples and the trees surrounding us went fuzzy around the edges. The ground wouldn't settle under my hands.

Ken groaned and stood up, shaking out his long limbs like a dog drying after a dunk in a lake. He slowly backed away from Hayk, grasped me by the wrists, and dragged me after him.

The jays broke their silence, angry squawks punctuating their mass of agitated wing strokes atop the marble. Hayk held his ground. He gathered in a deep breath and let forth a long stream of harsh syllables. The invective ended on the only word I recognized.

"Kwaskwi."

Jays burst out in all directions like Hayk had lobbed a grenade into their midst. Ken hunched over me, providing cover from the screeching cloud of scratching feet and sharp beaks.

One jay remained on the marble. Jabbing its beak toward the sky, it let loose a long, shrill call that set every hair on my body quivering.

The other birds came to rest in the branches of the surrounding trees, an eerily quiet, intent audience.

"Finally," said Ullikemi, "we are met."

CHAPTER TEN

"Someone's been telling you fairy tales," said a voice behind us.

Ken stiffened. "Stay close," he whispered in my ear. I nodded carefully. The vise was back, and my head throbbed like bags of screws flowed in my veins instead of blood.

Kwaskwi, still in plaid shirt and jeans and with hair as spiky as a New York underwear model's, stepped into the clearing from the parking lot path. Ken's eyes flickered between the two men.

Kwaskwi tugged at the stem of a tall strand of wheat grass. It broke off in his hands. He leaned his elbows back on the marble block of vets' names next to the motionless jay, chewing the ragged end of the grass. Quite the picture of a harmless hick.

"I'm no thunder god."

Hayk's eyes blazed impossible green. He shook his head. "You do not lie."

Kwaskwi spit the stem from his mouth, his lips curling into a slow, wide grin. "Nope."

The drizzle had tapered off, but there was enough moisture in the air to hold Ullikemi's presence, the scent of saltwater and spice.

"Give me the thunder god's name," said Hayk.

"Why would I do that?" said Kwaskwi. Laughter shrieked from the jays jostling for position in the surrounding pines.

Ken tugged me back down when I tried to stand. Crazy, alpha-male. Now was the time to run away, *far away* while these two asshats kept each other busy. *Find Dad, make sure Marlin was—*

Ken touched his mouth, and then indicated Hayk.

Infuriating boy, just has to point out the flaw in my brilliant plan. Hayk could still freeze us with a word.

"Destiny. It is in our fate to meet and decide a victor." Ullikemi's voice this time.

"*Your* mythology," said Kwaskwi, standing straight as one of the pines, prickling with irritation. "Whoever you are."

"Unktehila," said Hayk, "the horned serpent," He gave a smile that tried to be sardonic, but his eyes glowed too fierce. "Sisiutl, three-headed serpent. Your mythology, too, Kwaskwi Kwa'yickuc. U'melth. Even in this land of mish-mash beliefs, no Kind escapes human influence."

Hayk breathed deeply, gathering air and power, but before he could speak, Ken lunged with his fist, hitting Hayk on the side of the face so hard I heard a muffled crack. Hayk stumbled to the side.

"Don't let Hayk speak," Ken called out, arms raised for another punch.

Kwaskwi called out in a language I didn't recognize and the air came alive with beating wings and sharp beaks. Jays showered down from all sides, a cavalcade of dark blue. I ducked, claws tearing at my hair.

Cacophony. Hayk-Ullikemi shouted muffled syllables, Ken growled, and the sinister laughter of jays prickled over skin like talons.

Droplets in the air coalesced, and the dark cloud of angry blue unraveled at the edges as their feathers grew water-logged and heavy. Ullikemi *pushing* back with his power. The jays broke apart, circling, struggling to stay airborne with wings rimed in salt.

Kwaskwi called out again. Salt-taste and spice faded to the familiar, Portland mossy-damp smell.

The cloud of attacking birds wheeled apart into two sets of spirals on either side of Hayk. Crumpled, clothes sliced open with hundreds of fine slashes; he backed away down the path toward the zoo parking lot, Ullikemi's presence barely flickering a faint green in his eyes.

His throat worked convulsively. Hayk suddenly hunched over, opened his mouth wide, and spewed feathers, blue soaked to black with gruesome, viscous liquid.

The dragon-Kind had felt so powerful when we stood before the Vishap stone. Did Hayk lose his connection with distance?

Or had fighting Kwaskwi weakened him?

Or does eating a waking dream somehow *drain* a being of their life energy?

I bit my lower lip. *I am not some kind of energy vampire.* A spike of pain arched across my temples.

Ken stalked to the edge of the path. Lithe. Dangerous. Not in the least human. "Leave," he commanded in growly, alpha-male voice.

Hayk tried to speak, but choked on more soaked feathers. With a hacking cough, blue and white tufts floated from his mouth. Hayk inhaled, a drowning man's gasp.

Ullikemi's green had entirely drained away, revealing a naked, human expression of surprise, but only for a fleeting instant. Then Hayk's features curled in on themselves, a bully regrouping. Disdain. Hate. A sick *wanting*. But all Hayk. No water dragon.

Something unpleasant gurgled in my belly, a cramp like I'd eaten too many street tacos.

"You can't hide from us forever," said Hayk, his voice plain and raspy without Ullikemi's harmonics. "You will give Ullikemi the name."

"Not today, *Professor*," said Kwaskwi. "You're nothing but a flesh trash bag without your master."

Ken took a step forward. "Leave now. Or suffer the consequences."

Hayk did not budge. "Your consequences are an empty threat. Kind law hamstrings you quite nicely."

"Kind law bends for the Bringer," growled Ken. "Test me. Please."

Hayk grimaced, his hands making fists at his sides. An almost subsonic growl from Ken raised fine hairs along the back of my neck and arms.

It was clear Hayk regretted not using his silver knife on Ken while he was frozen, but it was also clear in this empty state, without Ullikemi's presence, that he could barely stand upright. With a choked sound of disgust, Hayk spun on his heel and took off at a brisk walk, while the cawing of the whirling jays overhead mocked his retreat.

Kwaskwi strode over, hands outstretched like a pro wrestler ready to grab and throw me down like a bag of rice. Just as he closed in, a strange shimmer outlined me in wavery green. As I held up my own hand, palm out, the green flashed to deep blue, and then faded away entirely. The last gasp of Ullikemi's fragment?

Kwaskwi halted abruptly. *That's right, punk. I eat dragon energy for breakfast. Dream-eater.*

"Funny way of showing your gratitude," said Kwaskwi, anger sharpening his words.

I brushed feathers from my hair. A layer of blue coated the sidewalk and blanketed the brush. Like a thousand birds had suddenly decided to go commando. I glanced at the surrounding pines. Jays settled, jostling on boughs, still fully clothed.

"Are you purposefully craven?" said Kwaskwi, "or is this some Baku superiority thing?"

What was he getting all pouty about? Hayk was gone. My head was about to split open, and possibly we were all about to revisit my non-existent breakfast. I would literally *kill* for a double-shot latte. I gave him my best version of Marlin's hairy eyeball. "Hayk was going to kill Ken."

Kwaskwi turned his head to give a pointed look at Ken, still bristling and ninja-like as he oversaw Hayk's disappearance into the crowded maze of parked cars. "Hmmm," he said. "In danger. The Bringer. Yes, I can see now why the big scary human attacking your pet Kitsune made you *give up my name*."

"I said I was sorry," I said. He needed to give me some space or this simmering feeling would boil over. I *had* given up his name. When the chips were down, I had squealed like a pig and Kwaskwi was now in danger from Ullikemi. I knew that. But even so, the energy from eating the fragment coursed through me and my hands tightened into fists at my sides. That same power I'd used to toss Ken across my kitchen wanted out, and it didn't care who I hurt.

Kwaskwi made a chopping motion with his hand. "You will retrieve your father now," he said. "All bets are off."

Fine with me, jerk.

Ken kicked at the carpet of blue feathers in front of me and put one hand in the center of my back. His hand was warm through my damp clothes.

"Our agreement is unbroken," he said.

Kwaskwi smiled slowly, those big teeth gleaming a challenge. "Petty human myths haven't entangled Thunderbird since Lewis and Clark first set their blistered feet at the mouth of the Columbia River. Caution, my furry friend, above all. Our people embrace human society, unlike *some*," the heavy emphasis unmistakably directed at Ken.

The comforting hand on my back became a tense fist.

Kwaskwi's lazy mirth evaporated, and he advanced into Ken's personal space. "But we don't hand our asses over to humans on a silver platter, either." Sparks almost flew between the two men.

"Don't," said Ken in a quiet voice. "Herai kept her ignorant. She didn't understand what Hayk was, or that Ullikemi rode him."

"No," I said. "That's not right. I may not know the rules, but I'm

147

not an idiot. Snitching is snitching."

Ken's jaw tightened. Insistent pressure from his arm urged me closer to his side, as if he could defend me from myself. It was dangerously tempting to let him try. My temples and the base of my neck throbbed like they were keeping time with a Fall Out Boy song.

This was how I'd felt after throwing Ken across the room into the refrigerator. Was it withdrawal? Did my body crave evil dreams like heroin?

"Forgive me if your little self-pity wallow doesn't pluck my heartstrings," said Kwaskwi. Jays chattered around us, a supporting cast of mirth.

"Fine. Fly Dad back to us. We'll get out of your hair."

"No mythical bird express this time," he said.

"I'll get a cab to drive us up to Government Camp, then," I said. "Dad will be off your hands."

A light rain pattered down around us, the grove oppressively silent. *Where had all the jays gone?* The boughs were suddenly bare, and Kwaskwi, despite his smirk, looked as exhausted and battered as Hayk had just as Ullikemi's glow left him.

"What do you know of our home?" he said in a quiet voice. A chill whispered down my spine. I much preferred his mocking tone to this serious one.

Ken made a low sound in the back of his throat. We were all three balanced on a precarious anger-cliff, one false step would explode any chance we would leave this place without more blood.

"Lucky guess," I murmured, trying to make myself small and nondescript like I did in the PCC hallways. "But you have to admit that for a thunder god home, Mount Hood is fairly obvious."

Kwaskwi raised empty palms to the sky, cupping his hands so that the rain pooled moisture in his palms. Faintly, the smell of cardamom reached me. *Damn. Wasn't a bad guy supposed to need time to regenerate or whatever after he'd been beaten?*

"That Ulli-whatsis is still with us," said Kwaskwi. "What is he, anyway? Polynesian?"

"Middle Eastern," said Ken. "His human's a professor at PCC."

"Feel free to take offense, but I wouldn't let you or the Bringer anywhere near my home. I'll bring the Dream-eater to you."

"Neutral territory," countered Ken.

"Name your spot," said Kwaskwi.

Ken turned to me. Great. A neutral place. Out of the rain, so Ullikemi couldn't track us. Full of people and places to duck into if Hayk should try to follow.

I pressed the pads of my thumbs into the back of my neck, trying to relieve the dull ache enough to think. *Ibuprofen, ibuprofen, my kingdom for an ibuprofen.*

It was Saturday, wasn't it? "Saturday Market, under the Burnside Bridge."

"You don't get out much do you?" said Kwaskwi. The smirk took on a cutting, knowing edge.

"What?"

"Saturday Market moved to Ankeny Square years ago."

I fought a rising blush. Had it really been that long since I was downtown? "The Skidmore Fountain stop is still under the bridge, though, right?" We could ride the Max, out of the rain, get Dad undercover and maybe Ullikemi wouldn't be able to follow us.

"Skidmore Fountain it is," said Kwaskwi.

"I'm sorry," I said, the words escaping before I could bite my lip closed.

Kwaskwi considered me with a calculating expression that jarred with his casual stance. The hesitation I'd seen before when he almost touched me was there, but an instant later it was gone. Pity. That's what I felt from him. Not a scary dream-eater thing after all.

Pity was worse than fear. Worse even than anger. You couldn't recover from pity.

I turned away before the silence could force some kind word from Kwaskwi I wouldn't be able to bear. Pain pounded at my temples, the trees and pavement oddly bright and distinct in their colors.

"Two hours," said Kwaskwi to Ken. He stuck a hand in the back pocket of his jeans and pulled out a white rectangle of paper. Flipping the rectangle at Ken, he shoved into the brush with eerie speed. Speed like Ken had shown. Not human speed. Foolish to keep forgetting I wasn't dealing with humans.

Yeah. Right. It wasn't like Ken or Kwaskwi had come with instructions, and even hours spent with the SyFy channel hadn't prepared me for this. The monsters were real and way too close.

A brilliant flash of blue and the sudden cry of a jay marked Kwaskwi's disappearance. Departure, more likely, although I still couldn't wrap my mind around how a man became a bird. Where did all the mass go? What about his clothes?

Stop picturing Kwaskwi with no clothes. I had to be more in awe of him, more wary. That went for Ken, too.

Magic. This is magic.

But under the pounding of my temples was the same stifling sense of shame that dogged me when Mom died.

I'd screwed up as a daughter when she needed me most and here was another thing I'd royally screwed up. What a mess. Trying to pawn off my responsibility for Dad had gotten us all in trouble. I should just take Dad and run.

Except I couldn't run away with both Dad and Marlin. Where would we go? And I couldn't imagine living anywhere else but Portland. Just the thought of figuring out new streets, learning how to duck through different crowds made my chest feel hollow inside.

I realized Ken was standing, waiting, not crowding my space, but not withdrawing his arm, either.

He held up the white rectangle. A bandage.

Slowly, as if I were a wild animal he might startle, he ripped open the outer cover and firmly placed the adhesive side of the bandage over my cut cheek.

Why did he risk himself helping me?

A suspicion tickling at the back of my mind turned into a full-fledged stream, carving out even more empty space. I wanted to believe the kiss meant he cared about what happened to me, but the practical part of myself that helped me survive all these years knew the truth; Ken had some mission related to Dad.

What had Kwaskwi called him, "Bringer"? It was pretty certain that name had some ominous meaning.

The weight and warmth of his arm turned confining and I squirmed away. Frustration and my throbbing temples kept me going, past the bench and down the path back toward the bus stop.

Two hours. We were meeting Kwaskwi in two hours.

Time enough to get downtown, maybe get a giant burrito at the food stand at Pioneer Square—my nausea had been replaced by a gnawing emptiness. Hungry. Then…my mind balked at anything past the burrito.

Ken trailed me down the path. The bus stop was deserted. The drizzle had chased all the delicate tourists indoors, their cars streaked with damp and silence.

"You were very resourceful," said Ken. Limbs folded neatly together, he took up little space on the drenched bus stop bench. Making himself non-threatening again. *Bastard.*

"Ah, so?" I said doing my best imitation of Dad refusing to discuss.

"This is all new to you, and your father isn't here to teach you about—"

"Dream-eating," I supplied for him. I picked at the jagged cuticle on my thumb. Kwaskwi had been very hot to get his hands on Dad until Ullikemi had reared Hayk's ugly head.

"You came to Portland for Dad." The ache in my temples lessened a bit with some deep breathing. Maybe I didn't have to throw anyone across a room, maybe all that pent-up energy could just…dissipate if I gave it a chance.

"Yes," said Ken.

I glared at him, not sure how to follow that up when I'd expected some reasonable-sounding explanation that would exonerate him from all suspicions of selfish motivations.

I ached for that kind of explanation.

If he sat there looking so safe and open and rumpled, could I stop myself from wanting some physical, tangible sense of him? A touch of skin. A whiff of that cinnamony *kinako* scent?

"To take him back to Japan?" I said.

"Yes," said Ken. "He's been…estranged from the Council for a long time. I had no idea if he would allow me to find him."

"But you found me," I said.

"Yes."

I hated everything unsaid behind that one word. "Are you planning to leave after Kwaskwi gives him back?"

Ken's posture didn't change, but his face went sharp, the safe sense of him disappearing into a coiled readiness tensing along shoulders and leg muscles. He'd been projecting Kitsune illusion again, making me want to trust him. Stupid me to keep forgetting what I saw of him wasn't necessarily real.

The problem was, it wasn't just what I saw that made me want to trust him. It was his *kinako*-scent, and the uncomplicated yearning in his dream fragment, and how, despite everything, I thought he was on my side.

He ran a hand through his hair, combing out pine needles and making the short, black waves stand almost straight out. "That's not my plan anymore."

But it *had* been his plan. To take Dad and run.

I swallowed, trying to shove a big lump of something in my throat back down into my chest. For a moment, I let myself imagine life without Dad. Without the disruption and the guilt whenever I picked him up from the drab Salvation Army Adult daycare. School. A life not within the walls of my apartment. All seemed possible without Dad and his crumbling mind.

If I could ignore all the dream eating.

I coughed, turning away from Ken and hiding my face in the crook of my elbow so he wouldn't see my wet cheeks.

"Ullikemi has the thunder god's scent now. He won't let Hayk give up," said Ken. "Bus is coming."

I nodded, still coughing, feeling the tips of my ears burning.

The bus pulled up to the stop, squealing brakes and spray as the big wheels hit puddles collecting in the gutter. Muddy droplets joined the already rain- and mud-streaked pattern on my jeans. I fished out my last two tickets for the driver and plopped my tired bag of bones into a seat in the back.

Ken joined me, sitting close enough that our legs touched despite the empty seats on either side of us. *Damn Kitsune and his lack of bus seat selection etiquette.*

"Kwaskwi will have to be careful when he hands over Dad," I said, rubbing my temples. Ibuprofen, a burrito, and a ginormous latte. Then life wouldn't seem so terrible.

"Not just Kwaskwi," said Ken.

"Well I'm sure he isn't stupid enough to bring Thunderbird this time."

Ken put a finger to his lips, his eyebrows drawing together in an adorably cranky way. "Better not to speak that name at all."

I gulped air. "You're kidding, right? I mean, Hayk's met Kwaskwi. How hard is it to figure out "Thunderbird" after seeing the Native American? Thunder god. Thunder bird?"

Ken reached an arm around my shoulders, tracing streaks of rain down the window glass with a blunt fingertip. "Naming is important. Trust me." Looking out the window stretched his neck at an angle, revealing the long, lithe muscles under smooth skin.

His arm radiated warmth like a heat-pack. It wasn't even touching me, just resting on the top of the seat, and every square millimeter of skin on my neck tingled at his presence.

Just an arm. Get over it.

"Hayk's a professor," I said, turning to Ken and surprised heat suffused my cheeks.

Ken was *gazing* at me like he had back in my apartment right before things went electric and fluttery. My bottom lip tingled in a way that made me painfully aware of how close we were sitting.

In a soft voice that belonged in a much more intimate setting than a bus, Ken said "Even Professors don't know everything." His arm curled itself down over my shoulder, tugging me a little toward him. "Take your name, for instance," he breathed. His free hand rose, and with two, blunt-nailed, long fingers, tapped me at the corner of an eye, and then stroked all the way down my jaw, just under the stinging cut Hayk had made on my cheek.

"My name?"

"Koi Pierce." My ear tingled with the warm air from the hard consonants, and his touch lingered, distracting and invasive. "Such short, sharp sounds for one such as you."

"I have another name," I said, blushing. *Dork*. I owed him no explanation.

"Yes, even if I were to use the name 'Koi Pierce', it would not truly *name* you. It is not just the words, but the intent, the *concept* of who you are. Kwaskwi's thunder friend is Kind; his naming isn't simple, but it's better not to risk giving any advantage to Ullikemi. You saw how he called Kwaskwi with only the trickster's single name."

Something penetrated the hazy, warm feeling bathing my body. That's why Ullikemi kept insisting on a name. And I thought giving up Kwaskwi's name was no big deal. It was exactly what that evil pair needed. Names. All the names. Another puzzle piece slid into place. Hayk's magic freezing phrase—it was all the versions of that freezing instant all at once, all the *names* of it in all the languages. And somehow by Hayk speaking it, borrowing Ullikemi's power, it equaled magic.

Hayk was no fool, and a master researcher. What was the name he'd said to Kwaskwi?

Unktehila.

I was sure I'd heard that name before in connection with the first peoples around Portland. Ken was naïve to think Hayk didn't have resources. And Hayk knew two of my names. Did that naming magic thing work on humans?

Dream-eater.

I kept forgetting I was no longer entirely Team Human.

Ken's mouth curved into a half-smile. Sharp glints appeared in the dark depths of his eyes. He wasn't thinking about Hayk. "What is your other name?"

I shook my head. "How can it be possible to know every language's version of a word?" I was working hard to dispel this aura of intimacy. But Ken tugged me even closer.

"What is your other name?" His lips brushed my temple.

"If I tell you, does it give you power over me, like Hayk?"

"I would never use you that way, just as you would never use my dreams, Baku."

I recoiled.

Ken lifted my chin so I couldn't avoid his gaze. "Why do you fear the Baku part of yourself?"

Out of the frying pan into the fire. He'd given up on my name to go after bigger game. Every instinct in me screamed to throw him off the scent. I couldn't imagine discussing that surge of strength, that gleeful wallowing in the power inside me I'd felt when...

Say it. Admit it. When you ate *Hayk's evil dream-fragment. And Ullikemi's. And what's more, you* enjoyed *feeling strong until the hangover headache.*

I shoved those thoughts way down deep inside me, trying to close off the doorways Ken had teased opened with his husky voice and irresistible eyebrows.

"You know more about Baku than you're letting on," I said, trying for a defiant tone.

Ken pulled his arm away with a sigh. He gave me a look that promised this thing between us wasn't over. "Baku are powerful, so powerful the Council is desperate that your father returns to Japan."

"Your mission."

"Yes, I was supposed to bring him back by any means necessary. But then, there's you."

"Me." A flush started down the back of my neck that had nothing to do with Ken's dark eyes. "Oh. Your Council never guessed the Baku had a little Baku-ette."

"Herai-san has lived a long, long time. He is one of the last known of his solitary kind. Most Kind don't...procreate with humans. Children were never considered."

"Yeah, well. Here I am."

"Yes, here you are," repeated Ken, leaning toward me, somehow imbuing the words with intense undertones. Fluttery things started fluttering again.

Tightly shut doorways creaked open, tempting me to confide in this man.

Stupid hormones. This wasn't the time or place for flutters, or even the right man. Who knew what kind of life Ken had back in Japan? Did Kitsune live in packs? He obviously wasn't a hermit. He had no idea what crazy thoughts went through my head when he touched me. A kiss, some hormonal groping in the kitchen and on a bus didn't mean to him what it meant to me.

I needed serious chocolate. A couple pieces of Verdun Pistachio Gianduja and I'd be right as rain, dopamine activators sorting out my mixed up brain chemistry.

Ken's eyes were all Kitsune-dark, showing his real face. Mouth open, that *kinako* scent I loved brushing my lips. A pulse, tangible in the air between us, insistent, urging, *wanting*.

Still, I knew next to nothing about him. For all I knew there might even be a Mrs. Kitsune back in Japan. The first time I met him he had a box of condoms in his hands! Even if the condoms were only some kind of lifehack waterproofing for his phone and not for the more obvious purpose, the man did not kiss like a novice.

It was time to stop acting like a high school freshman on her first date.

But it *was* my first date. Or close enough. And I wasn't afraid to dream Ken's fragments.

I leaned forward, closing that infinitesimal gap between us, and brushed his open mouth with mine.

Ken jerked back as if he'd been burned and, with a muffled Japanese curse, pulled his arm tight against his body.

"Sorry," I mumbled, not meeting his eyes. Could I be more pathetic? He probably was just being nice, and me with my lack of experience being all naïve and...

Ken gritted his teeth. "No, you've got it wrong," he whispered.

"Yes," I said, a flush blossoming from neck to hairline. "I figured that out already."

Muscles ticked in his jaw, holding back fierce emotion. "No, you haven't," he growled softly, and grabbed my hand between his palms. The calloused skin was hot to the touch and my focus narrowed down to where little tickles of awareness caressed my hand.

The bus stopped, the sole passenger got up from behind the driver's seat and stepped off. Nobody got on.

"This, this touching you, wanting you, it's not a good idea," he said.

I jerked my hand away.

"Okay, already. I get the picture!"

"I am not saying I don't want you, Koi Pierce," he said, dark eyes leveled into a stare, pinioning me in place like a butterfly on stick pins. "We could come together for mutual comfort. Enjoyable, yes, and don't think I didn't have that in mind before."

Oh.

Ken continued. "But there's more at stake here now than just a physical interlude. Ultimately it would cost more than I am willing to risk."

"Yeah. Okay. Consider it dropped."

He was completely vulpine now with slitted, dark eyes, sharp cheekbones and hair forming a widow's peak over bushy eyebrows. That controlled storm-energy radiated from him in waves, arousing answering trills of tension all along my insides.

Using his real face to try to scare me.

"You know nothing of who I am. What I do for the Council. I have done…great wrong."

A guffaw broke through the sarcastic words hanging on the tip of my tongue. *What is with these people?*

"Great Wrong? Seriously?" Apparently the Kind all needed to take a giant chill pill. Talk about drama-mongers.

"I am the Bringer. You heard Kwaskwi name me."

"Yeah, I've been meaning to ask about that."

Ken took a deep breath. "Kind don't kill. Not other Kind. Rarely humans. It's not just a law, it's who we are."

"You're serious." All levity drained away. Embarrassed heat flushed my face.

"Yes," he said, switching to Japanese, arms at his side, tension thrumming through him so strongly I could almost smell it. "You grew up in the human world, with human blood in your veins. Humans can't know the inexorable inborn yearning of life for itself. The instinctual recognition of life's energy coursing through another. The utter horror of extinguishing it."

Okay, he is serious, but still a drama queen. And now I felt like he was dissing humanity. "So you're saying you and Kwaskwi could beat each other all the live long day, but not kill?"

"Kwaskwi could not," said Ken. He took a deep breath. "Ullikemi cannot, so he thinks to use Hayk as his weapon."

"Because humans are expert killers."

Ken didn't acknowledge my words. He was hell-bent on wringing some painful confession from himself.

"I'm the exception. I am the Bringer. My background gives me the ability to overcome the compulsion."

A world's worth of hurt underlay the careful tone he used. Background? What did it cost to "overcome" that kind of compulsion?

"I bring Death."

The driver craned his neck around the protective panel to glance at us. We needed to tone down the dramatics a bit. Luckily the bus was still empty.

I leaned closer to Ken. "You're what, an assassin?"

His eyes flickered over my face, searching, and then he turned away. "Death-bringer," he said, bitterness lashing out through his quiet voice.

"This is the great wrong you're talking about?"

"I plunge myself into that black abyss, and the taint marks me. You grew up human. Innocent. Not knowing the terrible grace of the Kind. Not knowing the anguish that grips us all when I kill."

I gave a huff of frustration. In English I said, "You don't go around assassinating willy-nilly, right?"

Ken looked up, meeting my gaze with eyes that were bare slits of darkest black. "I have tasted of death's dire emptiness to do the Council's work."

He clearly expected me to show horror.

"I lived Hayk's murders a dozen times. My hand on the blade, blood-warmth on my skin, the acrid smell of fear. I *ate* that dream, whatever the hell that really means, and took that hunger and power into myself. And I liked it! What does that make me?"

"Baku. There is no evil in taking evil from the world."

He doesn't get it. Not at all. Frustration made me grind my teeth. We hovered in our seats, both inches and miles away from touching each other, and I wanted to scream or shake him or better, kick him until that haunted look left his eyes and he went back to being alpha-male again.

The bus pulled to a shuddering stop.

"And here we are," I said, breaking the tension in my best Greg-ever-chipper imitation voice.

Ken gripped the sides of the seat and breathed deeply as the bus driver made his announcement and the doors swiveled open with a whining protest.

Pioneer square. White Doric columns bordering one side of a wide bowl. The brick steps forming the sides of the bowl dull-red in the rain. Only a scattering of hardy tourists wielding umbrellas milled around by the fountain at the north end of the bowl.

Familiar. Real. Navigable.

"The driver didn't say this was Skidmore," said Ken.

"Get off anyway. I need a burrito."

Ken stood and led the way off the bus. As the bus pulled away, he put out an arm to block me.

"Wait a moment," he said.

Cardamom wasn't in the scent of the light rain drenching the square. Gag-sweet spoiled food, the dirt-concrete of the city, and an undercurrent of bitter roast emanating from the Starbucks over the tourist office forming the north end wall of the square, but nothing that smelled of Hayk or Ullikemi.

I zeroed in on Shelly's Garden Burritos and stepped around Ken's arm.

"Kind are here," he said.

I sighed. "Hayk?"

"No. Native peoples."

I gave him a look. "Kwaskwi doesn't trust us, right? It's natural he'd have us watched."

Ken's nostrils flared, breathing in the rain and Portland smell. "Or he's here to snatch you so his people would control both Herai Baku."

"Suspicious much? I thought it was all word-of-the-Kind is gold, and all that."

"He never promised us anything other than to provide safe haven to your father and return him at Skidmore fountain."

"So he's bound to return him to me."

"Yes," said Ken in Japanese. "But if he snatched you here, before you ever reached the fountain, he wouldn't, technically, be breaking faith with us. The contract binds him to return your father at Skidmore fountain. If you're not there to receive him…"

"He wants nothing to do with me anymore, he's afraid of Hayk."

"Speak Japanese," said Ken.

I threw up my hands, gesturing toward a woman with a yellow flag on a pole surrounded by milling, black-haired tourists with umbrellas.

"Half these people are Japanese tourists!"

He leaned over to capture my gaze, forcing me to look at him, his eyes dark with concern but his mouth set in an angry line.

"Why are you fighting me?"

"Because I want a burrito!"

Ken's face lost the amiable roundness, going sleek and sharp. He stabbed a finger toward the food cart verandah.

Fine. Bone-headed Kitsune. I'd get my burrito and show him he was being paranoid and domineering. A new word for the dictionary: domanoid.

Kwaskwi wasn't bird-brained enough to draw Ullikemi's attention out in public by causing a big scene. *Snatching us. Ha.*

I ordered and paid, and then stepped back to find Ken twitchy and tense. He scanned the faces of business people carrying their lunches back to the office buildings, the tourists, and even a catholic high school-uniformed group of girls on the steps giggling over selfies.

Creepy and testosteroney. But irritation had deserted me when I needed it most. Ken wasn't kidding, he really was worried about Kwaskwi. I didn't want to think too deeply about the reason. Kwaskwi had almost been nice to me. Was I fooling myself to think he would hesitate to harm me based on that supposed niceness?

Marlin would probably tell me in a kind, patient, wise-younger-sister voice that I tended to trust people's outer faces too much without questioning inner intentions.

"Number 12 up!" said the Shelly's cashier, flipping a swath of orange-red bangs out of her eyes. She glared in the way that meant it wasn't the first time she'd called my number.

I jolted forward and picked up my burrito, my hands barely able to circle the stuffed silver foil, hot enough to scald my palms.

"Now," said Ken, pointedly looking at the burrito, "we have to speak of important things." He steered me in a half circle back toward the Starbuck's, switching to a formal, old-fashioned Japanese liberally sprinkled with Herai dialect. "That female in the dress with shiny pieces sewn into the hem and her young companion are Kind of the tribes who settled this place before the European invasion."

I blinked at him, answering in English. "What, you Kind have something like 'gay-dar'?"

"Gay-dar?" repeated Ken. He gave me a sharp nudge with his elbow.

"Okay, okay, I'll speak Japanese," I said. "Do you really think Kwaskwi wants to snatch me?"

"I am full-minded that he should have done so already if not for my fortunate presence at your side."

He sounded so formal and so old speaking that way, so at odds with the high cheekbones and model-tousled hair he was sporting. Like if one of the catholic school girls suddenly started spouting Shakespeare.

I held back a smile. Ken was deadly serious, but it was so cute. A twinge of pain at my temple made me remember the burrito. I started unwrapping. Eating dreams apparently made me ravenous for real food. And it was possible his cuteness was entirely illusion. How old was he really?

"We should hie ourselves directly to the meeting place," said Ken.

"Can you consume your foodstuffs on the bus?"

"Sure, yes," I said, lapsing into English again. "But he knows where we are going. It's not like we can lose them."

"Your words speak truth, but though Kwaskwi has not made promise of safe passage, still he is bound by custom not to breach faith in a meeting place in the presence of your father. In this place there is no such advantage."

I chewed a mouthful of garlicky bean and fresh tomato salsa bliss. Suddenly, the garlic taste on my tongue morphed into cardamom. I gagged, dropping the burrito on the ground.

"Ullikemi!" I said.

CHAPTER ELEVEN

Ken lead me back to the bus stop, leaving my burrito forlorn and abandoned at the feet of the curious onlookers.

"I'm still hungry!" I said.

"Does this bus take us to the meeting place?" he said in English.

"No, but we can hop a MAX to Skidmore Fountain. It's under an overpass, so the rain can't touch us there. That's important, right? Staying out of the rain?"

Right on cue a MAX train rumbled around the corner.

"Stay in front of me," said Ken.

The Starbuck's woman with the shiny bits sewed into her gypsy skirt, a blonde-haired coed, and a duo of bald guys in Ducks jerseys were walking rapidly toward us.

Not a random blonde. It was Elise from Kaneko-sensei's class, and she was unmistakably pointing in my direction and speaking rapidly through a sneer. *What? She was Team Kwaskwi?* Implications soaked in with the light rain, dragging my shoulders down. How long had Elise been watching me in Kaneko-sensei's class?

I finally hopped on Ken's panic train; my heart sped up, and curious fizzy gray appeared at the corner of my vision. The painful ache in my temples relapsed back to a pounding headache, gripping my head in a vise.

A strange, green aura outlined the coming MAX train. I blinked, stumbling backwards against Ken's solid chest.

"Koi," he said in his growly voice.

I rubbed my eyes with a fist, and when I peered over Ken's shoulder the green aura limned every object in my vicinity. All but the shiny-skirt woman who now was only a few feet away.

She raised her hands, palms up. "Kitsune, don't be foolish," she said.

"Kwaskwi breaks faith?"

Elise gave an alpha cheerleader giggle. "You broke it first."

The green aura brightened, twisted away from the objects it was outlining to mass together into a glowing blob between me and the folded-open MAX train door.

Ullikemi. Coalescing from the cardamom-scented rain. How had the serpent gotten so powerful? Had Hayk killed again?

I backed up further, bumping into Ken's immovable mass.

"We just want to bring the girl to her father," said Mirror-skirt. *Oh god.* The shiny bits on her skirt weren't mirrors, but teeth, polished till they shone.

"Don't come any nearer," said Ken.

Elise blanched at the command in his voice, taking herself out of the direct line of fire to stand halfway behind one of the brick tables where people played chess on sunnier days.

"But I am so fond of little girls," said the woman, grinning wide to show a row of pearly whites sharpened to points.

I recoiled.

"Little fish, little carp, so bright and shining." She pursed her lips, blood red now against death-pale skin and blew.

"Huuuuuuuu," came her breath. Bone-chill wind through smoky cedars. It curled around me, tempering Ullikemi's musky spice with smoke and ice-sharp prickles.

A passenger gripping his fold-down bicycle stared at me from the open door of the MAX train, fogged green by Ullikemi's shifting presence.

Two spots of incandescent verdigris flared in the green fog, and answering spikes of pain drove through my temples. Ken's arms caught me under the arms just as my knees buckled.

"Ullikemi," I gasped.

"Don't be stupid," growled Ken, "back away now."

"Huuuuuuuu," came the woman's breath again, mixing with the green fog, lightening it. The cardamom faded for a moment, but the woman's breath sucked warmth from every cell in my body. I collapsed at Ken's feet in the slimy gutter of Yamhill Street.

"Stupid tourists," I heard the bike passenger say as the MAX train doors closed, pulling away with a grinding of gears.

White frosted Ken's features. He snarled, baring canines that rivaled the woman's in sharpness and put out both hands, fingers tipped with wicked, ivory claws.

The Ducks guys formed a wall behind the shiny mirror woman, all poised to tear Ken apart.

Ullikemi's mist re-coalesced from the shiny woman's chilling wind. An intense burst of cardamom assailed my nose and throat. A tendril of green fog shot out from the main mass, questing in the air, finding...*searching*.

The tendril aimed straight for my face, like an alien probe in a B horror movie. I clamped my mouth shut with both hands while gray fuzz ate away more of my vision.

Cold damp blew at my back, evidence of Ken's sudden lunge away. Thuds and the sick sound of ripping flesh came from my left.

"Ullikemi," I gasped again, and the fog tendril dove into my throat. Lightning arced overhead, splitting my head wide open.

Into the breach poured the endless emerald blue of the deeps, muscles twisting and flexing along my sinuous length, straining with all my might to reach for the brilliant gold warmth shining down from the glimmering curtain of the ocean's surface…

My lungs gasped for air, and for a moment oxygen filled my chest, pushing Ullikemi out of my head. The gray fuzz cleared. I made out Ken standing over the body of the bald Ducks guy, using the second one, his jersey ripped and covered with blood, as a shield. Shiny-skirt woman loomed, looking taller and gaunter.

Then, like the tide sweeping in, Ullikemi came rushing back, filling, ballooning inside me, pressing against my skin like my mortal body could not contain the want, the desire, the *need* for golden warmth. A warmth tantalizingly just out of reach above me/us as we surged upwards with all our might toward the glittering curtain where water met air. My jaws wide, aching with the strain, I burst from the water with a mighty roar, fangs snapping together on the tail end of a wisp of golden light, a warmth burning pleasure along the side of my mouth and dripping down my throat.

A fragment? No, not exactly a fragment, more like a living vision. I twisted back and forth in the gutter, my hands flexing uselessly. Behind closed eyelids, I tried painting kanji strokes over and over, but black ink bled into deepest green. Ullikemi's hunger convulsed my throat as he force fed me the overpowering vision. Drowning backwards, back into the vivid blue, back in the sinuous body of a water dragon.

A flapping of gold and crimson wings and the piercing shriek of an eagle cut through the golden warmth. Sharp claws ripped my back. My mouth ached with hollow emptiness as I fell back into the water. The eagle shrieked again, laughing.

Caught by Ullikemi's vision, the name of our enemy bubbled up from the depths where I'd buried it. See how it taunts me/us, see how Thunderbird keeps me/us from the warmth of the sun!

And then Ullikemi's voice, jarring harmonics sending my muscles spasming along legs and arms, my teeth chattering like a skeleton's.

Thunderbird!

Oh god. No.

Ullikemi's vision released me, streaks of green and unbearable blue fading to normal Portland clouded skies.

What had the dragon-kind done to me? Used Baku dream-vision against me?

"Ullikemi knows Thunderbird's name," I said, voice torn from a lacerated throat. "I've betrayed him."

"Kwaskwi will have your little fish," shiny-skirt woman said to Ken.

I blinked past tears and mucous at the corners of my eyes, bringing my hands up to my face only to find them covered in street slime. I pushed myself to a kneeling position.

Two bald Ducks fans now lay along Yamhill's soaked pavement, their arms bent in unnatural angles. Ken was still standing, but looked more like Frosty the snowman than a Kitsune, the shiny-skirt woman's chill breath coating him in layer of sparkling frost. He didn't move.

A staring half-circle of tourists stood a few feet away, whispering among themselves and snapping pics as if this were a staged street art presentation.

Where are the cops?

Shiny-skirt inched closer.

"She endangers us, Kitsune. She betrayed Kwaskwi and now Thunderbird. The Kwakwaka'wakw, the Coast Salish, the Haida and the Tsimshian will not give up Thunderbird for her!"

Rattling polished teeth and exhaling cold wind, shiny-skirt woman moved to tower over me, impossibly larger than the old woman she had appeared to be, a giant.

"The little Baku's life will be payment."

"Don't touch her," said Ken, but his voice was human and weak.

Why doesn't he move?

Panic raced through me. I couldn't let Kwaskwi's people take me, I had to reach Skidmore fountain and force Kwaskwi to fulfill his promise to hand over Dad under the original terms of our bargain.

"Little fish, you are mine," crooned the giantess as she bent down to place clawed hands around my throat and squeezed.

Inside my coat pocket, the opening chords to Beethoven's fifth symphony pierced the air. Marlin's ringtone. I wouldn't fail her. Wouldn't fail Dad. Couldn't let this hag choke me to death kneeling in the gutter, covered in slime.

No.

Little fish had a trick up her sleeve. Shiny-skirt dragged me down the pavement by my throat back toward the Starbuck's.

I reached for her wrists with both hands, and she tensed, cutting off my air. My vision went dark, but instead of trying to drag her hands from my throat as she anticipated, I dug my fingernails into her wrists and held on, tight.

Eater of dreams.

Ken called himself tainted.

What would I become if I ate Shiny-skirt's fragment? Blood pounded in my ears, a frantic, failing heartbeat.

No choice. I *reached* for the hag's fragment which already tingled against my palms.

Snow-dusted cedars, craggy, jutting mountains, and the unending wail of the wind. Sweet, delicious-bitter taste of blood on my tongue, and the hulking forms of bear brothers glimpsed through moonlit boughs, huffing through creaking underbrush.

Dzunukwa, naked, pale-skinned monster of the Kwakwaka'wakw, eater of children, bestower of wealth.

The kernel of her, the fragment of herself she dreamed over and over every night. The sense of her was as heavy as ten pound bags of Kokuho Rose weighing down my shoulders and chest.

"I know you," I gasped, and let that kernel sink down, down deep.

Eater of dreams.

The kernel *caught*, turning to molten metal that burned with a knife-edged pleasure. Muscles spasmed up and down my back. I arched like a bowstring, taut with a thousand fire-hot needles.

Dzunukwa flinched; releasing me and bringing her hands, now smeared red with my blood, to her temples. She screamed, backing away.

I staggered to my feet after her, arms outstretched, growling in a voice like a bear's.

The kernel burned, a flaring heat journey up each vertebra to the place where the back of my neck joined my spine, an ever-expanding, rhythmic pulse filling my hindbrain. Like before when I'd taken Ullikemi's fragment to break Hayk's power, the pressure swelled, threatening to crack my skull.

Dzunukwa let loose another frigid blast of air that turned the air around us into a swirling blizzard of snow. It barely registered on me. This frozen hag was no danger. She cowered on the ground, nothing, just a pathetic bag of bones. I was *Dream Eater*. I was—

"Ken?" I reeled from suddenly unbearable pressure. *What had I done?*

"I got you," said Ken's voice, and I felt him catch me around the waist. An instant later he released me with a little yelp of pain. "You're on fire."

"I can't—" Like an overinflated balloon, my internal organs pressed into my ribcage. Dzunukwa's blizzard had melted into floppy, wet flakes and she was hunched over, pale, the tiny polished teeth trembling all over her skirt.

"You drew first blood," gasped the hag. One clawed hand made a chopping motion in the air, and the swirling snow plopped to the ground, melting into oily-dark puddles. "You took my power, and turned it into death-magic."

A sharp-edged knife, no a *fang* as long as my hand, sharpened to a deadly point, appeared in Dzunukwa's hand. Eyes glittering cruel blue, she glanced up at me, suddenly not as weak as she had appeared.

"Law says I may claim your life."

"No," said Ken, pushing me behind him. "She's not true Kind, she is not bound as we are."

All this pressure had to go somewhere. Dzunukwa's fragment wasn't manageable, not like Hayk's. Two. I had two Kind fragments in me. Power like nothing I'd ever felt.

But death-magic. Me?

Dzunukwa lunged with her fang. Ken twisted to the side, shoving me out of her path.

The scattering of businessmen and map-wielding tourists had come closer, exclaiming about the snow-puddle but wary. Someone in Sketchers and purple velour broke my fall.

Elise.

"Get off me," she said, pushing me away. But her fingertips brushed bare skin at my neck.

An endless swath of cedars in a hidden valley, smoke rising from campfires in the shadowed safety of Mt. Rainier.

Another fragment stuffed in on top of Ullikemi and Dzunukwa.

My head burst.

Colors exploded across my vision, and the ground tilted underneath my feet. Every ounce of breath squeezed from my lungs.

In great, painful heaves, I spewed half-digested beans and salsa all over Elise's shoes.

"Fuck!" She kicked at me.

The sound of cloth ripping. "Behold," said Ken. He'd ripped open his plaid button-down. My vision was blurred so much I could only see a strange, black marking on his chest. "Do you lecture a Bringer about Kind law?"

"Murderer," said Dzunukwa. "Kwaskwi won't allow some Council toady to savage our traditions."

"This isn't over, freak," Elise grated out and kicked me hard in the abdomen. I folded backwards, head banging hard against the brick table. Everything went black. I gasped for air, mouth wide open like a fish flung from its bowl.

A hand on my elbow. I flinched.

"It's okay, Koi, it's me," said Ken.

"What's happening?"

"The old woman is walking away. They've given up for now. We have to get to Skidmore fountain," he said.

"I can't, I can't see," I said, grasping at his open collar with both hands. My hand brushed the skin of his chest.

I flinched again. No more fragments. I was raw and loose inside thrumming skin. Even Ken's harmless dreams of forest-running would break the rudimentary bonds holding my fractured cells together.

"It's okay," he said. Warm breath tickled my cheek, and then his lips touched my skin at the base of my ear. Prickles raced down my neck, the length of my arms.

"Ken," I said. "Don't touch—"

Nothing. There was nothing there. No fragment. No dream of four legs racing through oddly scented evergreens.

Did I burn out? Flip a breaker?

His mouth pulled away, only to be followed by the press of his face against my neck, his arms going around my back to press me forcefully to his chest, slimy clothes and all.

Slowly, I let my hands skim up his shoulders, feeling a stickiness that I tried to ignore. Behind his neck, they curled themselves into a knot on bare skin.

Bare skin. No fragment. No need to brace myself. So warm against me in this shadowy darkness. The world could go screw itself. For the first time in my life I relaxed in the presence of another person, and let the burning tears slide free.

"You're fine," he murmured into my throat at the place where my pulse throbbed. "Everything's going to be okay."

"Something broke," I said.

Ken lifted his head, keeping his hands on my back.

"I had to...take something from that hag. Not exactly a dream.

Like a waking vision. I think I overloaded. Now I can't see."

Air passed in front of my face.

"You really can't see this?" said Ken.

I shook my head.

"And just now, when we touched, I got no fragment from you."

The muscles in Ken's neck stiffened. He released me and covered my interlocked hands with his own, gently disengaging me.

"The Max train is coming," he said. "We should board."

My cheeks flushed red. Remind the man you eat his dreams when he's holding you. Of course he'd stiffen. Not to mention we were both covered in god knows what.

"Here," said Ken, and a plastic something brushed my lips. Water. I gulped it down and then took some in my mouth, swishing it around and spitting. Something damp wiped at my face and chin. Ken's wet sleeve?

"You stopped telling me everything's going to be okay," I said.

Ken herded me forward, taking the bottle from my nerveless fingers. "Step up here," he said, guiding me up two metallic steps. The particular gym-socks, metallic-sweet smell of the Max enveloped me.

I heard the swoosh of doors folding closed. The train's sudden movement made me grasp at Ken.

"It's not good that you can't see," he said.

"No duh," I said. "Maybe it's temporary."

"Probably." His thumbs traced the arc of my cheekbones, brushing my eyelashes. "There's no visible damage in the iris or pupil."

Is he staring into my eyes? I blinked furiously, feeling a flush spread across my cheeks. My hand felt a path to his chest and came to rest, palm directly over the still-open shirt fabric where I'd seen that strange character before.

"What's this?" I said.

Ken stilled underneath my hands and sighed. "When you are

experiencing Ullikemi or the hag's dream you do not seem like you are aware of what's going on around you. You are seeing visions, yes? Like a person caught in a nightmare. This time you looked like an epileptic caught in a nightmare. But you noticed that part?"

I nodded. "Hard to miss that whole 'behold' line. Don't be offended, but all that Kind language you and Kwaskwi and Ullikemi use is super hokey."

Silence.

"Are you going to explain the mark?"

"No," said Ken.

"My Alzheimer's-addled father, who is really an ancient Japanese dream eater, is being held hostage by a Native American blue jay trickster, and I'm being hunted by a dragon spirit and a crazy professor who wants to slice me up with a knife. Oh yeah, and I'm *blind*. You already told me about the whole assassin gig. What could be worse?"

The train pulled to a stop. "Mall/4th Street?" said Ken.

"No, we've got three more stops to Skidmore. Just tell me. I want—I need to trust you."

"I'm sorry," he breathed, "I just can't—" Ken's lips slanted across my mouth, firm, demanding, carelessly rough. Caught off guard, I flinched back for an instant. His hands tugged me back, and then I leaned into him.

Ken broke away long enough for a whisper. "I tried to keep away."

Safety, warmth, said his arms pressed around me. *Desire*, said the insistent pressure of his lips, the slight rasp of a morning's growth of whiskers on his chin, sensitizing the corners of my mouth.

Let go, just feel. No need to hold anything back. No tickle of fragment. You can trust him. Trust this.

I did, wallowing in the breathless feeling that had everything to do with his *kinako*-cinnamon musk smell and how my hands trapped by the press of our bodies felt only supple muscle.

Sensation followed upon sensation, rolling over me in waves that mimicked the rhythm of the press and release of our lips, leaving me light-headed and trembling.

"Koi," he said, his tone making my chest ache. One hand traced up my side, trailing prickly awareness, until he cupped my head behind my ear, pressing a slow kiss, savoring, at the corner of my mouth away from the still-stinging slice on my cheek.

It was too much.

A tear squeezed from my tightly shut eye. The tip of Ken's tongue tasted it, followed quickly by his lips slowly caressing my closed eyelids.

"Don't cry," he whispered.

"Don't do this," I said. I pushed at his chest, a lame, half-hearted attempt. "Don't make me feel this way just to distract. It makes me scared to trust you."

Ken sighed, stepping back so that his hand on the small of my back kept me balanced in the swaying of the train, but there was distance between our bodies.

Uh oh. I'd asked for truth. This felt like the moment of calm before a storm. "Spit it out, fox boy."

"You know I came here to bring back your father."

"And?"

"You used the Baku part of yourself to break Hayk's hold, and now you've had a taste of what you can do even to powerful Kind like the hag."

"Yes," I said. "And now I'm blind and burned out."

"I don't know if it's because of your human blood or because your father has left you untrained, but—"

"This isn't about me," I interrupted. "Tell me what that mark on your chest means you were going to do to Dad."

The train rolled to a stop again. Doors opened, I heard the stomping of booted-feet exiting the car, and then the doors closed again. It felt like we were alone. *Did Ken cast some illusion forcing everyone off? Or at least making us look less battered?*

Ken switched to Japanese. "The Council sometimes decides one of us is too dangerous, too powerful if unchecked. My sigil marks me as a Bringer. You know what I bring."

Murderer, Dzunukwa had said.

A tiny spark flared to life inside my chest. Anger. Bright, hot, enough to give me the strength to pull completely away from Ken, pressing my back against the train's metal pole.

"Not Dad. He isn't dangerous," I said in English.

"An untrained, half-Baku was able to break that hag's magic, and Ullikemi's spell. Imagine what havoc Herai-san could wreak if he were not in his right mind," Ken persisted in Japanese.

I didn't care who might be around. I wasn't going to win an argument in Japanese. Even Dad at his most irate with Mom used English to argue. "Dad isn't dangerous, he's not evil. He wouldn't hurt anyone."

"The Hag that choked the life out of you, is she evil? Protecting her clan against foreign invaders? Would Herai-san hesitate if Hayk held a knife to *your* throat?"

"*Hayk* is evil. Use your special skills on Hayk."

"Hayk is human. Different rules," Ken blurted in English. Ha. Changing languages meant Ken was upset. Chalk up one point for me.

"Is he? If he were completely human, would Ullikemi be able to use him?"

"I am not sure," said Ken. His hand came to rest on my cheek. I turned away, not wanting my stupid skin flushed red like Marlin's electric Christmas candles. Not wanting his hand on me.

Murderer.

Hayk was evil. I'd taken that evilness into myself. Not to mention the hag Dzunukwa and Ullikemi as well. Pot calling the kettle black, maybe, but I had yet to hurt somebody so bad they bled. No matter what I was, or was becoming, that distinction was very, very important.

But if Ken tried out his special 'skills' on Dad…

My stomach rebelled, bitter acid biting my throat.

The doors swooshed open.

"Skidmore fountain," said Ken.

Already?

He took my elbow and helped me off the MAX. As soon as I felt pavement under my feet, I jerked out of his grasp.

Shadows had begun to form shapes. Light gray marked the edge of the cover formed by Burnside Bridge above our heads, opening up to a streaked brightness that must be Ankeny Square and the fountain. My sight. This blindness was temporary after all. No need to panic.

"Koi," said Ken, a warning tone. A hissing breath drawn quickly between closed teeth. "Is it usual for the fountain to be deserted at this time of the afternoon?"

"Probably not."

CHAPTER TWELVE

Beethoven's fifth symphony cut the pregnant silence. I fumbled in my pockets and fished out my phone.

"It's me," said Marlin. "Is Dad okay?"

"I don't know," I said. *Give me another few minutes to cure my blindness, dodge Ullikemi and get Dad back from the pissed off Native American were-blue jay.*

"I'm—I'm scared all by myself here."

"Just hold on a bit more," I said. My tone was harsher than I'd intended.

Marlin's voice broke on a sob. "Oh god, Koi, it's just that, I know you've got all that magic stuff, and everything, but, Koi. It's *Dad*. I can't lose him, or you, or anyone else. I just can't."

Marlin had never sounded so close to breaking in her life. Even at Mom's funeral she'd held it together—held us all together.

I cleared my throat. Blinking definitely made the shadows resolve into shapes. The fidgeting, fuzzy blob to my left had to be Ken. "Little Sister," I said in Herai dialect. "You have to stay put and wait. I know it's hard."

"I called the police," Marlin answered in English.

"What?"

"I didn't say anything about the Baku stuff, or that professor. I just said Dad was an Alzheimer's sufferer with dementia and we couldn't find him, and that you thought somebody was keeping him against his will…"

"Marlin," I said, weariness seeping through.

"I know, I know, it's just that you wouldn't answer calls or texts. I didn't know what to do."

A difficult confession. She was at wit's end. I could all but hear the sound of wringing hands over the phone.

I took a deep breath. None of this was Marlin's fault.

"I know it's hard, but you've got to let me take care of this."

"The police can help. I gave them your cell's GPS identifier code. They told me they'd send a patrol car to check out the situation."

The police couldn't do anything against Hayk and Ullikemi, but Kwaskwi might think twice about trying funny stuff if the boys in blue were my backup.

Ken did the disapproving teeth/air hiss. "It will not be easy for you to explain your involvement in this," he said quietly. "Police tend to complicate things. Witnessing Kind business usually makes them want to interfere."

Great. Terrific. Fabulous. I shot him a 'this is my phone conversation, butt out look.'

"I'm getting Dad. I'll bring him home in about an hour."

"You'll bring Dad?"

"Yes," I said. Or explode into bitty bits trying. "But I need you just to sit tight for a while and not call anyone else."

"Okay," she said in a small voice that made me picture her at age six, short hair mussed from tossing and turning on her Holly Hobbie pillow, Mom insisting in that no-argument voice there couldn't be monsters under the bed. She had been brave for Mom's sake.

Bring on that bravery for me now, little sister. We both knew the real monsters weren't hiding anymore. "And get me a triple latte while you're waiting," I said, hoping my grumpy tone would fool her into thinking everything was okay.

"Hang up," said Ken.

I made a shooing motion with my hand. Ken swatted at me. "Kwaskwi is here."

Flapping wings like the sound of a hundred flags caught in a hurricane came from the square. Squinting my eyes forced into focus blue-on-dark-gray shapes converging on the fountain's round basin. They spilled apart to ring the basin's wall around the sculptured women bearing the square pedestal on their shoulders.

"Gotta go," I said, and flipped the phone shut.

"Stay under the awning out of the rain," said Ken, striding toward the basin.

Even without squinting, things were getting clearer. *Temporary blindness is a good thing.* "No way." I followed him. He stopped abruptly. I banged into his back, nose first.

Soft cotton, the warm strength of a body I could too easily let myself lean on.

I snatched my hands back.

"You'll be in the way," said Ken.

His back firmly planted in front of me. Not a crutch, an obstacle.

"Of what?" I said, brave with his face turned away. "Of your 'skills' the Council prizes so highly? What are you planning to do? Murder a murder of jays?"

Ken whirled on me, his eyes bleeding to black. *Okay, lame joke.* Sending Ken after Kwaskwi just didn't feel right. This wasn't a time for fighting or a Kind testosterone-fest. I owed Kwaskwi for giving up his name, and Ken was in attack fox mode, his breathing harsh. If he handled this, things would go down the toilet, fast.

"Let me talk to him," I said brushing past him.

"You can't see," he said.

"It's getting better." The jostling and cawing stopped abruptly.

Their blue shapes formed a frozen, damp tableau ringing the fountain, going full blast despite the constant drizzle.

Ken growled and I didn't need sight to know he was becoming that vulpine, intense version of himself. There was no time for dithering, not with Ken literally on hair-trigger and the police about to show.

I sniffed. Cardamom all around. Ullikemi was definitely lurking.

Just under the edge of the cover, still unwilling to expose myself to the rain, I stopped.

"Kwaskwi," I said to the waiting birds, "I'm here. Thank you so much for caring for my father. I am ready to relieve you of your burden."

The silence was deafening. Damp air thickened, cloyingly sweet with spice, pressing on every inch of skin, but still the jays did not move a feather.

I cleared my itchy throat. "We had a deal."

A warning tickled down the back of my neck and the sensitive outer shell of my ears.

In the next instant, the jays exploded into a whirlwind of caws. Feathers glowed neon blue in my gray-soaked sight, massing in front of the fountain.

Ken pulled again on my arm, urging me further under the cover, but I stood firm.

"Not so easily startled anymore," said a voice from the center of the roiling mass of jays. "Lost that innocence quick, didn't you?"

A crack split the air as jays pinwheeled away from each other in all directions, scattering to the top of the whitewashed, cast iron arches behind the fountain and the colonnades across First Avenue.

Kwaskwi stepped from behind the fountain, black leather jacket swinging with chains and steel-toed boots clinking on the stones of the plaza. His hair was in tightly braided rows and gone was the good old boy swagger. He was dressed for war, and Ken was a heartbeat away from starting one. *This isn't going to help Dad.*

Blinking 'til tears ran down my cheek, I pressed fists to my eyes and rubbed, hard. When my hands came away they were damp, but Ankeny Square was in sharp-edged focus.

Now we were in business.

"I'm here for my father," I said as firmly as I could, but my heart flopped frantically like live, sweet shrimp fished from Dad's restaurant tank. Only resistance to Ken's tugging kept me upright.

"Come out, come out," said Kwaskwi in a sing-song voice. "Oh wait," he said, "you can't risk it. You have no more names to give up to your serpent buddy in exchange for your own hide."

Ken growled again. *Stay behind me,* I willed. The male posturing was as stifling as the cardamom.

I jumped out from under the Mercy Corps Building's awning into the light sprinkle of rain with a swift tug.

Kneeling on the rain-soaked paving stones in front of Kwaskwi, I bent my head like a samurai in one of Dad's TVJapan historical dramas.

"I am sorry," I said. *Come on Kwaskwi, back down.* "I owe you a debt."

"Don't," said Ken. His legs appeared in my peripheral vision. A disapproving hiss rasped my ears. "You're being a fool. And now Ullikemi knows exactly where you are."

Kwaskwi laughed.

"This is not binding. She is innocent and doesn't know what she's saying."

"Nice try, Kitsune," said Kwaskwi, baring those huge front teeth in a wide grin. "That whole Pioneer Square action where she took down Dzunukwa and the Bear Brothers makes that defense a bit flimsy, yes? She is Kind. Her words are binding."

She is Kind.

No more semantics skirting. I was Baku. I ripped dream fragments from people and ate their power.

I channeled more samurai drama-speak. As official and Kind-formal as I could be in English. "I humbly request you return my father to me as we agreed."

"I do enjoy a skillful grovel," said Kwaskwi. "Spend a few more minutes on your knees and we'll see."

Rain soaked my hair, drenching me in Ullikemi's spice. His sickly green energy zinged around the square like the flickering of a lamp about to expire.

"Her father," growled Ken. He put a hand on my shoulder, urging me to stand.

"Keep your pants on," said Kwaskwi. "Your serpent buddy won't get here for at least another minute."

"I know what I did was wrong, but you know that I did it out of ignorance."

Kwaskwi leaned very, very casually against the wet fountain rim, like he was trying very hard not to come over and grip my hoodie around the neck and twist. "Ignorance, bah. Herai kept you in ignorance. If he apologized would it make your suffering any less?" Kwaskwi took three steps forward. Anger came off him in a heat wave. "There is no excuse for betraying Thunderbird."

Ken did something like a shrug, his muscles rippling all over his body. His shirt fell open to reveal a hidden sheath at his belt and the black sigil on his upper chest. A complicated, old-style kanji character in cursive style.

The long, slender dagger gripped in his hand, and the deadly intent in his feral eyes was easier to read.

"Enough," said Ken.

Kwaskwi went utterly still, a statue of anger. "We finish this, now," he said through gritted teeth.

A Subaru Outback in Portland olive pulled to the curb. The doors slammed open and the Duck Jersey twins, limbs whole and hale, wrestled a limp form from the passenger side door.

Dad!

I ran to the car. The Ducks twins pushed Dad at me. I barely caught the dead weight, staggering under long, floppy limbs. Dad's hand grazed my cheek.

Every muscle in my body seized. The world was a slingshot, and I a missile, flung out of Ankeny Square into a brilliant sapphire blue, shot through with gold. Muscles in my back flexed impossibly in ways they never were meant to. Piercing heat to the core of me, and a screech like knives sliced ribbons from my mind, flensing away all that was human.

I soared, on wings that could carry me forever, over the broad, open expanse of an emerald sea. Harsh smell of ancient rocks covered in the endless weight of ocean. Below me a shadow lurking in the depths, hungering, jealous that I flew free on burning, solar winds lifting my wings, while it drowned endlessly in a watery prison.

Thunderbird.

A twin vision to the one Ullikemi had forced on me.

I gasped for air, and felt Ken's hands touching my back as if through layers of down comforters. I was locked in Thunderbird's vision. No, not vision, this was a fragment, and Dad was dreaming it.

Shock pitched me deeper into the dream. I clawed my way through tattered shreds of will. I never got fragments from Dad, never dreamed his dreams, but here he was, dreaming Thunderbird's overwhelming vision, and I was locked in this trap with him.

A shred of myself still hanging on noted the weight of Dad's body disappeared and a sharp sensation across my cut cheek—Ken slapping me? But the feeling only dragged me from the dream for an instant, and then the brilliant, cloudless sky closed in again.

The unsettling might of beating wings made the sound of thunder, and that screaming call shaved me down to pure, tattered slivers of thought.

The sense of Koi the woman balanced on a knife edge. I had to break free of this fragment or drown in a seamless fugue of dream and reality. Like Dad.

Dad?

Dad needs me. Marlin needs me.

Aching limbs tumbled on cold stone pavement or the breath-stealing glory of the flight?

Koi. Koi A. Pierce. Concentrate.

Sink down, down, inside, shut out the endless sky, the seductive caress of air.

I sucked images from the bare bones of myself: sister, woman, daughter. Mother wrapped in her Hawaiian quilts. The solid brick of PCC buildings in the rain. Blinking lines of code on my laptop screen. Dad at the breakfast table in *jinbei* pajamas, worry lines creasing his brow as he asked me about what I'd dreamed the night before.

I am Baku.

Flaring heat seeped into my bones, forming flesh, the outlined awareness of my own body.

Eater-of-dreams. And a powerful dream was threatening to engulf me. I didn't want to fight it—it would be pure bliss to give into that terrible beauty, to encompass it, to fill this nothing of myself with it, to *devour* it.

A voice, a faint echo of a memory. *Why do you fear the Baku part of yourself?*

Not fear. Overwhelming hunger. For power. For warmth. What if giving into the Baku made it impossible for me to be Koi?

It didn't matter. I would fight this. With both parts of myself. Not parts, it was me, I was all of that, there was no Baku here and Koi over there, it was just me.

I had to eat Thunderbird's dream as I had Ullikemi's. Eat the dream of a waking, powerful Kind. But when I'd done that to Dzunukwa, she'd screamed as if I consumed some vital essence along with her fragment.

I prayed I wouldn't do any kind of lasting damage to Thunderbird.

I stopped straining against the dream and the endless expanse of sky rushed in. A surge of wings shot me forward, a luminous arrow aimed at the sun. Sensation avalanched over me, drowning in molten gold and cutting blue. The sun a scorching, pleasurable pain as I rose higher and higher.

A powerful thrill. *Yes!* I could encompass this power, I could take it in. The vision slipped; cold paving stones rough beneath my cheek, clothes soaked with Ullikemi's rain heavy on clammy skin. Ken's slitted, Kitsune-dark eyes boring into me.

The next instant I was back, flying in an endless sky burned free of clouds by a brilliant and unrelenting sun.

Thunderbird's dream; the living kernel of Thunderbird's story of itself.

Burn, little kernel.

I reached again, coaxing the kernel to life. With each gasping, rib-cracking breath torn from my body the flame burned brighter. Every cell in my body wept from strain, but, finally, the dream burned hotter than Thunderbird's sun, pouring heat and energy into every individual cell in my body, filling me with exultant, molten strength.

An eagle's piercing scream came from overhead, shattering the endless blue into jagged edged puzzle pieces that tumbled away, revealing white colonnades against a sky heavy with swollen stratus. Portland drizzle settled on my face. *Lovely, wonderful clouds. Delicious drizzle.*

"What has she done?" Kwaskwi shouted.

"She's Baku," Ken said.

Only an instant of ecstasy, then the blowback kicked in. A flaring heat journeyed up each vertebra in my spine to the back of my neck. An ever-expanding, rhythmic pulse filled my hindbrain. Burning rings radiated out from the base of my neck through my skull, a constant pressure cooking bone. Spikes pierced my temples on either side. My lungs wrung out a gasping sob. A sour taste on my tongue like Dad's fermented *natto* beans. I'd done it. I'd eaten Thunderbird's waking dream and broken its hold over me. Now I was brimming with Thunderbird's harrowing, golden essence.

Death-magic.

Ankeny square, fuzzy from rain, appeared in full color. Blue jays coated the arched colonnade across the street. Cloudy water cascaded from the granite base of Skidmore Fountain into the pool, the only movement in the square.

Ken faced off with Kwaskwi and a Ducks guy. The men leaned slightly forward, as if fighting to stay upright in gale force wind, the tang of pent-up violence stinging the air.

Distant thunder rumbled.

More energy flowed upward from my belly into my splitting head. I blinked away tears, giving myself a little shake and tottered to my feet. Ankeny Square promptly tilted on one axis, colors threatening to spin like a sodden kaleidoscope.

"Back off," I croaked, stumbling forward. I reached under Ken's outspread arm to tap the Ducks guy on his green chest.

The guy went flying, smacking across the Outback's windshield with a meaty thump.

Ken whirled. "Koi!"

Smacking the Ducks guy had released a smidgen of the molten pressure doing its best to crack my skull. I pressed the heel of my palms to my temples. *Think. Think. What should I do?* Urgency kept my thoughts from settling anywhere useful.

"Where's Dad?"

"Are you okay?"

"Just ducky," I said, and took a step toward Kwaskwi.

"Whoa there." He held both hands out in front of him. "Stand down."

Every bone felt impossibly heavy, dragging down my flesh, aching and pulsing to the same beat pounding at my brain. My eyeballs burned in their sockets. "Where. Is. Dad?"

Ken stabbed his chin in the direction of the MAX stop. "He's under the awning, out of the rain."

"I delivered him safe and sound," said Kwaskwi. "I fulfilled our bargain."

For a moment, the air around me flared golden, burning inside my lungs like I'd swallowed a fistful of Dad's freshly grated wasabi.

Far off, the thin wail of a siren cut through the thick, damp air. Kwaskwi stuck his hands in the pockets of his jeans. The corner of his mouth quirked up.

"No worthy token was offered in exchange for my generous care of Herai Akihito," Kwaskwi continued. He drew a small item from his pocket and held it in a weathered palm.

My pinkie ring.

He flipped it, overly casual, into the fountain.

"Don't do anything stupid," Ken said to the still-groaning Ducks guy uncurling himself from the Outback's hood. His compatriot made as if to slip out from behind the driver's wheel, but thought better of it after a glare from Ken.

"Not exactly safe and sound," I ground out through clenched teeth. It took all my strength not to give Kwaskwi one of my little taps.

"Do you name me oath-breaker?" Kwaskwi drew himself up. Those huge front teeth flashed, and from the high arches of the square's whitewashed colonnades came the angry squawks of jays.

"You did something to him," I said. "He is locked in Thunderbird's dream."

"He is Baku," said Kwaskwi, with a lazy smile. "Just like you."

"This isn't natural, I—" A burning sensation ripped through me, cutting off my words. The world turned hazy, pivoting on the axis of Kwaskwi's grin.

Shafts of sunlight spiked through the square's gray stones, punishingly hot.

"What did you do?" I ground out. Sapphire and gold bled up through the stones, down from the sky, spreading in pools. The top of Skidmore Fountain reflected the blinding light of a summer sun

Portland wouldn't see for months.

Thunderbird's dream seized me again with a taloned grip. The kernel burned and burned and burned, and still my shoulders ached with the remembered strain of flight…

It was too much. Too much to contain in the vulnerable flesh and bone cage of my body.

I would explode.

Ken put a firm hand to the small of my back, keeping me upright. Warmth from his hand penetrated the sodden layer of my hoodie. Along with the pressure, came a forest-cool strength, reinforcing fragile boundaries just enough to keep breathing through the pain.

"We are not backwoods savages," said Kwaskwi. "Your Council's purist dogma is outdated. Now, Bringer, you can give them eyewitness testimony we are not weak. We spit on their rules about how to live with humans."

"You can be sure I will tell the Council of this," said Ken.

Sirens pierced the air, only moments away now, and Ullikemi's spice-thick scent became a choking miasma.

I needed to get to Dad. Then get us as far away from Kwaskwi and Thunderbird as possible.

"Take me to Dad," I said to Ken.

"Slam, bam, thank you Ma'am." said Kwaskwi. "I feel so used. Don't you want to stay for the showdown?"

"Showdown?"

Kwaskwi swiveled, launching himself into the Outback just as a police car screeched to a halt under the colonnades.

"Thunderbird gave your father his deepest dreams. Thunderbird's name will do Ullikemi no good when the two of you burn with his essence."

The door slammed shut on his wide grin. Through the open window Kwaskwi waved a lazy hand. "Bye bye, little carp. Good luck with the dragon." The Outback pulled away.

Fool me once, shame on you. Fool me twice, shame on me. And I'd worried eating Thunderbird's dream would cause him harm.

More doors slammed. Ken's hand tensed into a fist again on my shoulder blades.

"Police," he said. "Can you walk?"

"I don't think so," I said. "Things are going all blurry again…"

Rain pounded us, a sudden downpour redolent with spice and salt. Ken made a frustrated sound. The fist at my back slid around my shoulders, and he picked me up like a sleepy child, cradling me to his chest.

"Sir." A male voice from the other side of the square. "Portland Police, we need to have a word with you."

Ken ran for the awning.

"Please halt!"

We reached Dad's slumped form, propped against the Mercy Corps building's brick wall. I slid down Ken's body, landing on wobbly feet.

"The police will—"

"Trust me," he said, darkness bleeding from pupil into white, planes of his face shifting.

Showing me his true face.

I dropped down to squat next to Dad. His mouth was slack, drool gathered at one corner, but his eyes were open wide, staring and sightless.

Not sightless. Consumed by brilliant gold and ocean blue, flying with Thunderbird.

A trance that could so easily claim me, too.

Hold it together.

Dad's face went blurry. I blinked. He, no, *she* had long, blonde hair tied back into a ponytail and a china-pale face with eyes as blue as the awning above our heads.

What the hell?

I glanced at Ken and almost burst out laughing. He'd changed his true face to a younger, male version of the woman. Kitsune illusion.

"Sir?" said the policeman, arriving out of breath. "Didn't you hear me? I asked you to halt."

"Sorry, dude," said Ken in a California surfer boy voice. "Had to get out of the rain."

The policeman had apple-cheeks covered in a lush, red beard. He should have been wearing flannel and making bio-fuel on his organic farm rather than chasing suspicious men downtown.

"It's always better to cooperate with the authorities."

"What can I do for you?"

Officer Bio-fuel stared at the illusion covering Dad. "We're looking for a Japanese male, possibly suffering from dementia, reportedly being held against his will."

Ken shrugged, his arms spread open. "Haven't seen anyone like that."

"Ma'am are you okay?" Officer Bio-Fuel said to Dad. When he received no reply, the policeman turned to me. Did Ken have illusion covering me as well? "Ma'am," he said, moving to block Ken. "Is this man causing you some kind of trouble?"

"No, no trouble," I stammered.

"Can you explain why your friend was carrying you?" He gestured toward Dad. "And what's wrong with this lady?"

"No, it's okay. I mean, we're fine. I just twisted my ankle a bit. We're going home."

"Have you been drinking?" he said.

"No, uh, my friend just suffers from narcolepsy."

Ken arched an eyebrow at me.

I continued my rambling. "We didn't even drive here, so it's not like you have to worry about a DUI..."

Officer Bio-Fuel began unhooking his radio.

"That won't be necessary," I said, trying to stand when an overwhelming tang of spice followed by the sharp sting of salt flooded my nose.

"No, sir," said a new voice. "It really won't be necessary." Hayk walked around the corner of the building, his eyes glowing emerald-green, his voice redolent with eerie harmonics and Ullikemi's restless, lashing energy. *"An instance of total surprise that freezes you."*

CHAPTER THIRTEEN

Officer Bio-Fuel's eyes went wide with shock. The illusion covering Dad and Ken rippled, and then winked out of existence.

"A pleasant surprise meeting you here," said Hayk...or Ullikemi.

Ken twitched, his face feral, his body in the long, lithe, muscled form I'd come to think of as attack mode.

Pins and needles blitzed my skin as Thunderbird's energy fizzed and popped in my veins, fighting Ullikemi's cold magic.

"Let's take care of boy in blue here first." Hayk pushed at Officer Bio-Fuel, sending him on a stumbling journey back across the square to the police car. He wrestled the policeman into the front seat and slammed the door.

I reached for the kernel still burning merrily in my belly, opening up to Thunderbird's golden energy. I wasn't helpless. Hayk's power was borrowed from Ullikemi. I would borrow Thunderbird's to fight it.

The cold sloughed away.

"What are you doing?" Ken gasped through clenched teeth. "Your eyes are all golden."

Veins racing with Thunderbird's power, I strained some more, welcoming the fire.

Hayk jogged back under the awning, eyes glowing green. He bent over Dad and put a hand on his forehead, and then fingers on his wrist.

His back was turned—this was my chance. Achingly slow, I got to my feet, knees creaking. Ken's closest bare skin was a thin stripe of olive between hairline and hoodie. I reached, my fingers pushing through the damp air as slowly as a wooden knife through sticky *mochi* cake.

The connection engaged with a quick flash of damp cypress needles and *kinako* scent.

Ken's fragment.

He groaned, tensing under my fingertips.

I'd broken Hayk's freeze magic before, but back at the arboretum Ken had radiated heat like Dad's imported *kotatsu* heater—this time, fueled by Thunderbird's dreaming, it was me burning up from the inside. Seconds passed. A bead of sweat trickled down the nape of my neck.

Why isn't it working? I let Thunderbird's kernel flare hot again and tried pushing heat into Ken, straining every muscle in a precarious balance like I was on tippy toes over an open campfire.

Ken groaned again.

Where my fingers touched his neck, the skin turned bright red like sunburn.

I was hurting him. My stomach clenched. Dangerous to play around with Thunderbird filling me to bursting, but there was Hayk, touching Dad, and I needed Ken's help. Pain spiked my head.

"Ken," I said, molasses mouth forming the word with slow syllables. "Let me dream you."

The tension in his neck released with a long moan. Like a burst damn, Ken's dreaming poured in; mist-laced hinoki cypress, the clean, musty scent of damp moss, and the seductive urge to run on muscled, strong legs…

Stronger, more real than anything I'd ever felt before, it pulled me out of Ankeny square, away from the pain. I *was* the dream. Me, Fujiwara Kennosuke, in my heart of hearts. At home in this wild, pure place.

Among the trees, a shadow. A slender, small form, dwarfed by the cypress, yet draped in the coruscated lattice of their branches. Closer, and the features resolved into long, dark hair, eyes with a hint of epicanthic fold, and a stubborn jaw. An unsoiled determination, a strength that drew me to the figure as surely as a moth to flame.

A woman.

Koi.

Me?

The vision broke, tumbling me back into myself. My hand still gripped his neck in a stranglehold, but now that storm-brewing electricity sparked between us.

Ken yelled. His body seized up like an epileptic, and then released. Hands braced on the brick wall kept him upright.

A twist of fear spiked through my first flash of triumph.

Hayk's eyes flared emerald green. "What are you doing, Ms. Pierce?"

"Leave now, Hayk," Ken gasped. "And maybe you'll survive this."

At Hayk's feet, Dad opened his eyes. Thunderbird's blue-ringed golden iris glowed in his familiar, weather-tanned face.

Wrong. Like a gut punch.

"Ullikemi and I have plans for you," said Hayk. He palmed the silver knife, still stained with blood, from a sheath at his belt. "This would have been cozier in my office, but her blood spilled here will still give me enough power."

Dad sat up. His face going from slack to sharp in a heartbeat. "We fly the sun's golden pathways," he said in English, the harmonic undertones raising goose pimples along my back and arms. Fear twisted my gut again.

This wasn't Dad. It was Thunderbird, riding Dad just like Ullikemi rode Hayk. This is why Thunderbird had tried to lure me into taking a fragment the first time we met. Was this Kwaskwi's plan? To ride me? Use me to power his magics? Use me to kill?

A shiver ran down my spine, then another. They morphed into certified tremors, my molars grinding. A rumble sounded. Not thunder, not from above, but a deep vibration I felt through the soles of my feet.

The great hunks of limestone that paved Ankeny Square were shaking. Ken jerked his hand away from the brick wall as a fine shower of mortar dusted down around us.

"Akihito, *shikari shite*," said Ken. *Hold it together.*

Dad? Was this what an overburdened Baku could do? Shake stone?

Thunderbird's kernel of dreaming flared in my belly. The burning spreading up through my chest, packed itself into the tips of my fingers.

My bones kindled into a boiling ache. Too much energy and no place for it to go. My heart beat an erratic, mad tattoo within my breast, and every cell in my body throbbed.

Hayk jerked forward. Ken lunged to stop him, but the lingering effects of Hayk's freezing magic made him slow and awkward. Hayk's knife sliced through my hoodie at the neck, drawing a burning line of pain across my collarbone.

"Pardon my forwardness, I find I am impatient," he said, gripping my elbow while a red stain seeped down my chest.

He jerked me close. "Can you feel that? More power than I imagined." He swiveled, the knife at my throat. "Stay right there," he said to Ken. "I have two Baku to play with now, but I really only need one."

Ken fell back a few steps, hands raised in the air.

"*A memory you knew but you have since forgotten—*" Hayk said. Eerie harmonics rent the air, spiking through my brain.

Images flashed through my mind—bursting through the sandstone rotunda of City Hall to find Dad crumpled inside the mayor's office—Kwaskwi facing off against the mayor, refusing to give up Thunderbird—the mayor ordering Officer Bio-Fuel back to his squad car—Mayor Hayk.

Inside my belly, something burned fierce, hot. The mayor's office turned ghostly, superimposed over an open door in the basement of PCC. I shook my head, confused. Hayk's magic was messing with reality.

Hayk let the knife clatter on the stones and ran the back of his hand through my blood, a rough caress.

"Don't touch her," said Ken. "Not even the Mayor of Portland can..." his words trailed away, confusion on his face.

Mayor? Hayk is mayor?

No. That was the magic.

"Yes," said Hayk, triumph in his voice, "the Mayor of Portland can."

"No," I said, Thunderbird's kernel burning the strange images away. Is that what Hayk wanted? Is that why he bound himself to Ullikemi?

"Just a little cut, and even the Kitsune is affected," said Hayk. "Maybe I won't need to take all your blood after all."

The Mercy Corps building groaned, and mortar dust showered down. An awning pole shrieked, coming loose from its concrete base. A swath of heavy, green canvas thumped to the ground.

"You will not use her," said Dad, harmonics echoing in his voice.

Hayk laughed. "You think to stop me? *An instance of total surprise,*" he intoned.

But his words were strangled by a cry of pain. Suddenly released, I backed away.

A green mist flowed from Hayk's eyes as if his soul were being drawn out. The twin whorls darkened, shifting into sinuous ropes that spiraled around the mayor encasing him in bands of incandescent, shimmering blue.

The mayor—no the *professor* recovered his vocal cords. "You promised me I could use the girl if I gave you the Dream Eater!"

His voice was bare, stripped to mere mortal timbre. The blue bands tightened, a wave that swept him from head to toe, leaving his limbs dangling at awkward angles, loose and *wrong*.

Dad stood up with jerky, fumbling movements, as if a marionette pulled by strings. "Voghjuynner odz," said Dad, his jaw awkwardly shaping the strange words. "Kpareik' indz het?"

Snake, do you dance with me?

The meaning welled up from within my aching bones, seeping into me. Thunderbird, issuing a challenge in Ullikemi's native language.

From Dad's body.

Hayk's mouth contorted into a wide rictus, and Ullikemi's eerie voice issued from it in that same, strange language, a clashing, teeth-grinding sound no human vocal cord could make.

"Take the Baku; ride him, as I ride my servant. I will no longer hide in the Vishap stone. Dance with me. Either the sun within you shall feed me or I will devour it this day."

In a boneless glide, Hayk moved toward Dad.

Yelling, Ken jumped in front of Dad. The planes of his face shifted, pared down to the sharp angles and lean, whipcord strength of his true-form.

Ullikemi ripped a strange, hyper-sonic word from Hayk's mouth and a rush of salt-chill air swirled around Ken, a mini tornado. Blue bands detached from motionless Hayk and, questing like a snake's tongue, circled Ken. The bands of mist pulsed, once, and then liquefied. A wave of water crashed over Ken, sending him sprawling against the hard brick of the Mercy Corps building.

A shriek of metal. The North end of the awning collapsed on top of him.

Hayk stood directly in front of Dad, reaching for him with hands contorted into trembling claws.

I lunged for Dad, pulling him against me.

The sudden movement opened up the knife wound on my chest and fresh blood smeared Dad's polo shirt. He burned in my arms, and all I could think of was his ink drawing of the tiger elephant Baku above my bed. I hung on to that image, and it kept us afloat in the shimmering sea of power of Thunderbird's dreaming. Barely.

Thunderbird's primeval self-kernel flared, burning both from the kernel inside my belly and from the touch of Dad's bare skin under my hands. I belonged to this. To dragons and giant eagles. I would burn!

The dreaming split me wide open, aching bones melting to white-hot agony. *Too much, too much.* I couldn't think, could barely see or feel, caught within Thunderbird's molten heart-of-the-sun. Pain shattered me into pieces, reformed me into impossible configurations, and then shattered me again.

I cried out, the razor-keen scream of Thunderbird.

Brilliant, white light. Up, down, all around me, *inside* me.

Thunder boomed, splitting hairline cracks though the light surrounding me, revealing a pulsing, emerald green layer far below. The emerald invaded my light with questing tendrils of mist. Ancient, cold-of-the-deeps eating away at my fire. The poisonous mist tried to reach me, draw me down but, wings beating furiously, I lifted myself out of reach, back to the endless sky.

Someone touched me. My shoulder. I had a shoulder. Body sense returned to me, the outlines of arms, legs, and head familiar but ill-fitting.

Words carried on the slightest of breaths, Herai Dialect, brushed my ear. "Eat the dream, Koi-chan; or you'll die."

The place inside, where I dreamed myself. Still there buried under white sun-spots and golden feathers. Enough myself to recognize Dad's voice.

Dad, awake and aware…

Pain shattered me again, but this time I forced the pieces around that little Koi-self, still hanging on with a death grip.

Carefully, keeping that little bit of myself to the side, I reached for Thunderbird's dreaming. *Burn, little kernel, burn.*

Pressure twisted my brain, squeezing me from all sides.

"Not that way," said Dad in Herai dialect. "The ancient ones' dreaming will split you apart. Pull Thunderbird's dreaming through another fragment."

Another fragment? Thunderbird filled me, crowding out all but Hayk's murderous visions.

Not those. I would not fill dreams of death with Thunderbird's power.

Dad was here, conjoining us in an unwilling bond to Thunderbird, but he had no fragments to give me.

Nothing else is left, all burned away by white light.

Nothing.

Wait.

Something. A wisp of a memory. Mist of a different kind, real, wet, dew-drop sweetness on my face, stillness like a hushed song in a muffled grove of giant hinoki cypress. Needles shifting beneath sturdy legs.

Ken's fragment. His Kitsune-dream.

Thunder boomed, exploding golden light in the cool darkness. Slipping, slipping, I clutched wildly, felt a sharp sensation in my real, flesh hands. A warm, bittersweet trickle running down my hands and arms. Blood.

Dad?

Slipping…

I *pulled* with every fiber of my being, strained to the limit, and wrapped myself with the scent of *kinako* and cypress, and the gentle damp of dew. And then I let go.

Down, I fell, straight toward the poisonous mist which coalesced into Ullikemi's enormous dragon coils.

Pressure swelled again; my insides were too small to contain Thunderbird. My organs shifted aside, skin bubbled out, rearranging. When the agony overshot the sharp-edged boundary of sanity, still I fell.

Down, up, there was no direction, only white light, and falling.

Abruptly I crashed. My body felt punched flat like I'd taken a header off a diving board into an empty pool. A pool. That was a Koi thought. I was me. Human. *Still alive.*

Breath returned to my lungs with a painful whoosh, and I opened my eyes.

Ah. I was not in Kansas anymore, or even Ankeny square. I was in Ken's forest. Mist obscured the edges of a clearing under a twilight-dark sky. Ullikemi's serpent-green, enormous coils wound around a soldier-straight hinoki cypress. My hand touched shaggy bark the color of old blood when I reached out to steady myself. I blinked. My fingers *glowed.*

My hand, my arm, my whole body, shone, lighting the drifting mist all around me. Thunderbird's brilliance flowing just underneath my skin like lava under a thin layer of congealed rock.

Ullikemi unwound from the cypress, gliding over to me. His emerald-glowing eyes and wedge-shaped head supported on a muscular neck weaving in front of me like a Volkswagen-sized cobra dancing for a charmer.

His passage brought a sharp wave of pine-bitter and smoked paprika.

"Thunderbird," he said. "Do you yet deny me the sun?"

"I am not Thunderbird," I said, spreading obviously human arms wide, but a strange harmony vibrated my throat, cut across my tongue, and made my teeth ache.

"Thunderbird rides you as I ride Mangasar Hayk."

"Hayk isn't here."

"He is human. I thought you human, too. But you are Kind. And you burn with Thunderbird's essence." *Baku, dream-eater.* I ate the dreams of monsters. Their dreams flowed into me, and I savored them. Even as Thunderbird's power threatened to burst me like a bubble, there was a fierce joy, of not being vulnerable, of not being in Hayk's power that gave it a sharp-edged pleasure. I would take care of this. Like I couldn't take care of Mom when she lay dying in the hospital.

Needles shifted underneath my feet, releasing their clean tang into the air. This place, this grove of cypress from some primeval Japanese forest, was formed of Ken's fragment. Given a kind of shape by power drawn from eating Thunderbird's dream. But it was mine.

Mine.

"No matter. Whatever you are, Thunderbird overflows within you. If I consume you I will prevail this day."

What is with all this eating? The Kind are just a bunch of over-dramatic, domanoid cannibals. I smiled. Only I would pull up the word 'domanoid' when confronting a giant dragon in my boyfriend's dream-forest. *Koi is back, baby.*

Ullikemi cracked open his wide jaws, and lunged.

I jerked to the side, but not quickly enough. Ullikemi's snout smashed into my shoulder, sending me sprawling on the ground in a foul cloud of moldering spice.

Goddammit. That hurt! Then Thunderbird's power *flexed* and like a DVD skipping, one moment I was a mass of tangled limbs on the ground, and another moment I was on my feet again, wrapping my arms around the barrel-length of Ullikemi's neck underneath the massive jaw. Straining, my hands clasped in a death grip on the other side.

My cheek pressed to freezing scales, blistering with cold, I squeezed.

Ullikemi went wild. Crashing to and fro, smashing me against the cypress trunk.

I hung on, consuming more of Thunderbird's rich, endless-sky dream to keep my hold on the slippery scales.

Ullikemi scraped me on the ground and reared up to bang on a tree again.

How much damage could I take in this dream world? Ullikemi would beat my dream body to a pulp.

"Wait," I gasped.

The snake threw itself toward the tree. Pain wracked me with a hundred little cracking sounds as my back forcefully melded with the cypress trunk. I released my grip, hands trembling with weakness.

This wasn't me, this death-grip on Ullikemi. Eating Thunderbird's dream filled me with the eagle's violent passion, but it wasn't me.

This was Thunderbird's madness. Maybe Thunderbird ached for violence, but I didn't. If I fought Ullikemi, it would only prove Ken's Council right, sending an assassin to take care of Dad, take care of *me*, rather than risk letting loose a Baku drunk on violence.

Ullikemi unhinged his jaw again, blocking out the green canopy overhead.

"I'll feed you the sun," I said. "That's what you want, isn't it?"

Ullikemi paused.

I tried to sit up, groaning at what felt like shards of broken glass inside me, and scrunched over on my side instead.

The jaws snapped around air right above my head.

"Do not think to parlay with me. I have waited, so long, so very long for Mangasar Hayk to find me a thunder god."

My memory zeroed in on Kwaskwi as he had looked at the Vietnam memorial, clad in plaid and weathered jeans, the harmless façade hiding a calculating ferocity.

You gave up my name.

I quashed a wave of guilt. Kwaskwi had used me. Thunderbird came to the arboretum, trying to snare me in a dream. When that failed, they took Dad instead. I owed them nothing. Certainly not some victory-by-proxy over Ullikemi.

"I could set you free."

The snake wove a frenzied, complex dance over my prone body. Cypress loomed over us, blotting out the sky, Ullikemi's spice fighting with pine for dominance.

Ken said Ullikemi was forced by human myth into this dragon shape. I didn't understand how humans could have that kind of effect on Kind, but Ullikemi clearly wasn't invested in Hayk as a friend. Hayk played his human, killing hand while Ullikemi siphoned the power from the dead translators back into Hayk's weird, magical phrases.

If Ullikemi was freed, Hayk would morph from dangerous, magical megalomaniac serial murderer to merely a human killer.

"You would give me the sun?" Ullikemi's sharp-edged harmonics set up an excruciating vibration in my ears.

"You will break with Mangasar Hayk," I said. "No more being the magical Energizer-Bunny for his phrases."

Pulling on Thunderbird's dreaming enough to set Ullikemi free might do serious damage. *Tough cookies.* Pressure was building at the back of my neck, golden brilliance eroded the tree canopy, and Ullikemi would kill me if I didn't do something.

"I so swear," said Ullikemi. Here in this dream-world, the weight of our binding agreement fell like a cobweb mantle over us both.

"Here," I said, and lifted my hands, reaching for the snake.

The great jaw unhinged. Saliva glistened on the fangs.

"Wait, what are you doing!" I yelled. The snake's maw closed over me with a snap.

Frantically I reached for golden sun-fire. Incandescent miasma flowed, igniting every cell in my body. Thunderbird's unfiltered dreaming, a direct line to the heart-of-the-star called Sol.

Frantic, I *pushed* it out in all directions, a thousand lacerations decorating my skin, all weeping gold.

Agony.

A long moment where Koi was lost, sundered into motes of light.

Then, a creeping darkness lessened the light, consumed it.

Ullikemi's wretched, bottomless hunger, gobbling Thunderbird's dreaming from the edges, inexorably pressing into the center, and then more darkness, and cold and…

The dreaming slowed. Thunderbird, trying to resist our connection as I consumed his utter depths. But I was Baku, eater of dreams, and resistance was futile.

Worse than agony, then, to force that connection open, to feel a gleeful, delicious influx of blazing light, reveling in power. Me. Koi-the-Baku, using Thunderbird. Punch-drunk on power, I willed myself to shine like a sunburst.

Still Ullikemi hungered, relentless, an abyss.

A great wrenching, then, as if the entire universe turned itself inside out to pour energy into me. A tsunami built and built and built and then broke with a crash that shook the universe; release.

Something screamed.

Something else broke away with an ululating cry of joy.

Spent dregs of dreaming trickled from me in rivulets of shining gold.

The DVD skipped again. I was back, human Koi, squeezed into a too-small body recently run over by a Mac truck, a mother of a headache pounding my temples.

Ullikemi disintegrated, the snake faded to a green mist which curled away in eddies of chill, rain-scented air.

I lay on paving stone, blind. Someone touched my cheek with excruciating gentleness. I flinched.

"Koi," said a voice I knew from before I had been consumed, and then blessed, cool, nothingness.

CHAPTER FOURTEEN

"It's been a whole night." Marlin's voice came from a pitch-black nowhere. "If she doesn't give us some sign she's still herself, then I am taking her to St. Vincent's whether you like it or not—"

I groaned. Or actually, I groaned inside my own head, but something must have made it to the outside world because suddenly somebody grabbed my hand so hard bones grated together.

"Koi? Can you hear me?" said Marlin.

I groaned again. She was mangling my hand into mush which meant I couldn't squeeze hers in response. Maybe she'd accept eyelid fluttering, instead? Except the muscles in my eyelids weighed a ton.

"She's awake," Dad said in Japanese.

My insides felt packed with cotton, and every muscle as flimsy as an udon noodle, but still Dad's voice sent a tiny frisson sparking up my spine.

He is alive. I am alive. Marlin must be okay, too, or she wouldn't be permanently maiming my hand.

A rush of images swept the inside of my eyelids; Ullikemi, Thunderbird's incandescent dreaming, the final darkness of the snake's jaws around me.

Let's try that groaning one more time. My lips moved, splitting skin and some dried, gummy substance encrusting them.

"Snake," I tried to say, in a voice full of throat-shards.

With Herculean effort, I pried open my eyes to narrow slits.

I'd been wrong. The gripper wasn't Marlin. It was Ken, sitting close by my couch in a folding chair with Marlin's grimacing face hovering over his shoulder.

"Ullikemi's gone," said Ken quietly. Marlin tried to elbow her way in front of him, but he sat still and immovable, the grip on my hand generating warmth that spread up my arm.

"Dad?"

"I'm here, Koi-chan," said Dad from my left. Neck muscles protested, but some of the warmth from Ken's grip must have worked magic, because I managed to turn my head.

Dad. He was as pale as my couch's fabric and still a bit gaunt around the eyes and hollow-cheeked, but he had no visible wounds or scars and the dark mahogany of his pupils held no trace of fog or confusion. This was Dad. Really Dad. Present in a way he hadn't been for years and years.

A thousand words and feelings twisted around in my brain, an insistent pressure in my throat a barrier to all the questions I ached to ask.

This Baku stuff blew into my life like a tornado, ripping away broken boards and glass shards, and sweeping everything into a twisted mess. Dad was at the center of the storm.

He was alive, and I was glad, but just looking at his face made heat well up behind my eyes. I turned back to Ken.

"Hayk?" I said.

Marlin reached over with a lidded cup and pushed a straw between my lips. I sipped water as Ken ran his free hand through his short hair. He was wearing the sharp-boned face I thought of as "human-normal" without amiable glamour.

"We should have called the police," said Marlin.

Right. Because Officer Bio-fuel totally saved the day at Ankeny Square.

"He's beyond the police," said Ken with a patient emphasis that said he and Marlin weren't having this conversation for the first time. "I let Kwaskwi and the teeth hag have him."

I sipped again. This time the water went down my throat without feeling like glass shards.

"Why can't I move?"

Dad cleared his throat. "It will pass."

"How do you know?" said Marlin, still angry.

"She woke up," Dad said. "If she's not completely comatose after taking in Thunderbird's dreaming, then she'll heal."

"Ullikemi's gone?" I repeated Ken's words from before, a whipcord of acid twisted tighter in my belly. I had to know what 'gone' meant.

Ken reached over and smoothed a lock of hair behind my ear. The touch was a mix of warmth and pressure on the edge of pain, as if my skin was hyper-sensitized. "Whatever happened between you and Thunderbird and Ullikemi, it released Hayk. I was a bit busy keeping him contained." He gave a little grimace and rolled his left shoulder gingerly. Even a 'contained' Hayk had managed to injure him.

"At the end there was a great flash of light, and you dropped senseless to the ground. Ullikemi, his scent, his presence, disappeared."

"Dropped senseless?" said Marlin, building up steam, "I told you she needs to be looked at by a—"

A beeping sounded from the kitchen.

"Marlin, come over here and stir the rice," said Dad in his gruff, sushi boss voice.

Grumbling under her breath, my little sister went, shooting me a glare that promised a tongue lashing later.

"Nothing but pizza boxes and frozen shrimp bags in your

garbage," said Dad from the kitchen. "You need eat more fresh fruits and vegetables."

The sharp bite of garlic accompanied by the mellow nuttiness of sesame oil wafted over. Dad was making his famous chopped vegetable and ground beef Bi Bim Bap.

My stomach gurgled.

"You released Ullikemi, didn't you?" said Ken. His thumb was drawing circles on my wrist, in a lazy way meant to distract me from the seriousness of his tone.

"Yes," I said. "I gave him the power from Thunderbird's sun-dreaming and he broke out of the Ullikemi shell. Do you think maybe he got away somehow?"

Ken gave me a sad smile. "Whether the Kind that became Ullikemi is free or has perished, it was his choice."

His choice. Or had Thunderbird's dreaming been too much, and I caused the death of an ancient spirit?

And what of Thunderbird? Had it, another ancient spirit, perished because I swallowed the last ounce of dreaming, pulling from Thunderbird the sun-energy it needed to live?

Ken's gentle wording wasn't what I needed now. If only I could get my useless limbs to respond, I could storm out of the room or hit something, or curl myself into a pathetic ball of helplessness in my futon.

I thought of Dad's Baku drawing over my futon and suddenly was very glad they'd laid me out on the couch where I wouldn't have to look at it.

A monster. Like me. I was Baku and I had chosen to dream-eat.

"You didn't kill them," said Ken.

I stared at the floor.

"That angry, devastated look you get, it makes me want to shake you, or kiss you, or…" Ken's voice turned to an incoherent mumble as he pulled me up from the couch. Arms locked around me, crushing me to his chest.

I breathed in Ken—*kinako*-cinnamon and sweat and musk—and for a moment, escaped aching muscles, splitting headache, and cracked lips.

Cheek pressed to the soft, body-heated cotton of his OHSU sweatshirt, I gasped for breath, air catching on painful, guilty lumps. Ken's hand, all strong, long fingers kneaded up and down my spine.

"I think my arm can move now," I said, flexing slowly. Ken gave a little growl of disapproval. I whispered, "You said we shouldn't be together."

Ken grasped my shoulders and held me prisoner at arm's length. "There is strength in you," he said, loud enough for Dad and Marlin to overhear.

"Not right now."

Ken gave me a little shake. "This is serious. Pay attention."

"Okay, I have Baku strength," I said, "monster-strength."

"No," said Ken, his voice rough. "It's Koi-strength, it's who you are."

I shook my head, silently.

"You're not solely Kind. You're not solely human. You can't hide from your strength anymore."

"So, not one, not the other, I am a hopeless wreck."

"There is no shame in being mixed," said Ken with a curious emphasis. As if his words were meant to convince himself. "There are but a handful of Kind as strong as Baku. And you grew up with no one telling you what you are or could not be…"

Ken's patronizing grip was getting old. I tried to jerk away. Sadly, my muscles were still limp as udon noodles. Aching udon noodles. "God knows what I've done to Thunderbird, Kwaskwi probably would kill me on sight." I gave a little laugh. It sounded a bit hysterical.

Ken put an index finger on my lips. His mouth, lips slightly pink from anger or worry or something opened. Canines, adorably a bit askew, peeked out. My heart began a slow jog, aches forgotten in a rush of endorphins. Were the tips of those canines sharp? If I touched them with my tongue would they prick?

Ken leaned forward and kissed me. I went tumbling back onto the couch. He followed me down, hand cupping my face to help ease me down safely.

Marlin and Dad were standing in my kitchen!

My hands fluttered weakly on his chest. Limp noodle muscles couldn't have had an effect on him, but he broke off, staring down at me with an arrogant, arched eyebrow.

"What are you doing?"

"Giving your family an important message."

I glared. Then I flushed red. *What the hell?*

"Your father will never consent to return to Tokyo unless you accompany us. And he would never risk thrusting you under the Council's headlights without protection." Ken propped a pillow behind me. "He can't doubt my protection now."

Dad cleared his throat. The look he threw Ken over the kitchen counter would have flayed the scales from a salmon.

"I will not return Tokyo," he said in his accented, uncomfortable English.

I made a clumsy fist and knocked on Ken's arm. "Hello? Excuse me? You didn't just admit that kiss was manipulation!"

Marlin gave a choked giggle. "Stupid, much?"

Ken returned Dad's gaze. "Only the Shishin in San Francisco and the Harpies of New York are organized enough to give you sanctuary."

"The professor will not be a problem now that Ullikemi's gone," said Dad. "I don't need Qinglong or Aello to take care of my family." He thrust my dull chopping knife point first through an onion.

"And who will take care of you? Your cover is blown, Herai-san. Even Kwaskwi's people, unorganized and weak, conspired to ensnare you."

"Do you trust the Council to make better choices?" said Dad.

"Whoa there," said Marlin, putting a hand on Dad's shoulder. "Cover blown? Are you saying the doctors were wrong? Your Alzheimer's is cured?"

"It wasn't Alzheimer's," I said.

"Baku that dream evil fragments, but don't eat them, slowly lose their minds," I said. "Right, Dad?"

There were too many people in my little apartment, too many emotions crammed into too little air. Ken squeezed my hand.

God, I needed coffee. Or the dark bite of Dagoba's Xocolatl chili pepper dark chocolate bar. Or for Ken to turn off the manly swagger long enough to realize he was killing any chance I'd go anywhere with him ever again.

"Yes," said Dad. A stark, lonely, unapologetic word. It wasn't enough. Not for the years Marlin and I had cared for him, not for leaving Mom alone with her cancer, not for *leaving* us.

The horrible miasma of Hayk's murderous dreams still felt like a stain in my mind. Thunderbird and Ullikemi's fates were unclear. Even if they were okay, even if I turned out to be a super-Baku and never had to fear touching people again, I could not simply forgive Dad. He'd chosen the long fog over his family. He'd chosen to make his daughter think she was a fatally messed up slacker.

"You're really okay now?" said Marlin.

Dad dumped a package of ground meat into the hot oil in his wok; the sizzling steam rose up to muffle his grunted reply. Marlin's wide-eyed look of hope and grief all tangled together was more than I could bear.

"Koi made a debt-bond to Kwaskwi in Ankeny square," said Ken quietly. "He won't hesitate to use her. If she were conveniently out of town…"

Dad swiveled around, metal spatula raised like he could strike Ken's words from the air. He sighed, a heavy sound that wrapped around me, sinking me further into the couch cushions like the weight of the world.

"I'll go," he said.

"No!" Marlin cried. "You can't leave. Not now that you're okay."

"Marlin," I said in my sternest big sister voice. She was assaulting Dad with words, as if they could break through his silence. In every line of his stiff shoulders and careful stirring of the meat was evidence of Dad's unwavering resolve, and her words only abraded the air, rubbing us all raw.

Marlin dropped the *shamoji*, still sticky with bits of rice, on the floor and ran to kneel at the side of the couch. Her eyes, so like Mom's, were bright with tears.

"Don't leave me here alone," she said. My confident, bossy sister, cracking at the seams. Who was I kidding? Everyone in this room had their insides leaking out. I put a hand on her shoulder and used her as support to haul myself to my feet.

She rose from her crouch to put a supportive arm around my waist and, for a moment, we rested on each other. A sweet, cutting warmth. This is how it could have been between us during Mom's death, and Dad's decline.

My dreams of self-sufficiency were royally screwed now. How many classes had I missed? And Ed probably thought I was dead. Or wished me so since I'd answered none of his contract queries.

I should feel more upset but strangely, a crushing sense of failure was nowhere to be found. Maybe I wasn't meant to be an accountant. But what, then, should I be? I had the chance to decide for myself. Going to see the Council in Japan wouldn't be a trip to Tokyo Disneyland, but if I didn't go, would I ever understand the Baku stuff?

"Dad and I have to go," I said.

Marlin hugged me tight, a little sob escaping her attempt to muffle her face on my shoulder.

"It will be okay," I murmured.

"I'll make sure of that," said Ken.

Marlin broke away to turn the full force of her glare on him. "If *anything, anything* at all happens to my sister or father, I will track you down, wherever you hide, and cut off little bits of you until you're nothing but a pile of ragged flesh."

Whoa. Apparently untapped ruthlessness ran in our family.

Ken gave a formal nod/half-bow, all seriousness.

My left knee twanged, and I slumped to one side. Ken stood up quickly, a hand on my elbow supporting my other side.

"I need the powder room," I said.

Ken and Marlin helped me hobble to the bathroom. When Ken made as if to help me past the bathroom door, I gave a little embarrassed hiccough, and pushed him away.

The scarred, pressboard door shut on twin expressions of concern from Ken and Marlin.

Safe and blessedly *alone* in my bathroom, I turned on the faucet full-strength, a waterfall to drown out sound and thought. Resting my forehead on clammy palms, I sat, just breathing.

I laughed, a broken sound I was thankful the water mostly covered. My insides felt as full to bursting as my little apartment. Ken's fragment, that wild rushing through a green forest, had saved me at Ankeny Square when Thunderbird's dreaming was frying my insides. He had saved me. More than once. And actually, I'd saved him. Broken him from Hayk's freezing spell. The exhilarating heat of his skin on mine.

Kinako ghosted over my tongue. I swallowed back tears.

I bit the inside of my cheek, hard, to stop the tears welling in my eyes. No crying. There would be *no crying* over a boy. I wanted him. Wanted him to want me, but to want me for myself—not because I was conveniently here, or because I was Baku and he needed Dad back in Japan, or because what had happened in the past few days threw us together in a way that made it easy to fall into intimacy.

What did I know, really? Maybe he kissed all the half-Kind girls mixed up with water-dragons and giant eagles?

Besides, he was all angsty emo-boy over his position with the

Council as the Bringer, or whatever. It wasn't easy to love someone who thought they were tainted. A relationship with Ken was a trap. A trap full of double-edged razor blades.

Wait, had I used the word love?

Aw damn, I was a total fool. Ken had gone from stalker to somebody I thought about like...like Valrhona extra dark or a Stumptown Miel latte. Something sweet and dark I craved to make the world more bearable.

Terrifying.

A knock sounded on the door.

I turned off the faucet and rose. Before the toilet had even finished flushing I heard the knob rattle.

I'd forgotten to lock it.

The door swung open, revealing Ken in full, Kitsune-feral mode filling up the doorway with his broad shoulders and bristling, maleness.

"Don't think you can hide," he growled. I flinched back, and he stalked forward, backing me against the cool porcelain of the sink.

One-handed he shut the door behind him, and I heard the snick of the lock.

"You're doing this in the bathroom?" I said.

"Yes."

"What happened to sending my father a message?"

"He doesn't need this message."

I closed my eyes to escape those slitted eyes, slices of darkness.

"You are hiding in here, talking yourself into some kind of escape. You won't get rid of me that easily," he said.

Eyes still closed, I felt my way up his chest with fingers gone nerveless and cold, pushing with the tips just to feel that I was resisting. "You going to lecture me on avoiding-people strategies, Death-bringer?"

Under my fingers, Ken stiffened.

"Play fair," he growled, this time his breath hot on the hollow beneath my right ear.

"Because you've been open and honest and never once used kissing or that damned *kinako* smell to distract me?"

He huffed exasperation, and jerked my hands away to press his full length against me, an overwhelming sensation of heat and strength and that particular vibrating energy cycling back and forth with each uneven breath.

"You need Japan as much as Akihito, and you need *me*."

"Do I?" I snarled, all that energy and his nearness raising my hackles unbearably. My fingers flexed like I had claws.

"Yes."

"I already said I would go with you. What else do you want?"

"More."

I turned my head to the side, so his mouth landed on the pulse at my neck instead of my lips, his tongue flickering out to caress my skin. Shivers and a different kind of pull, a hungry heaviness, swept through me.

"Tell me your other name," he whispered into my skin.

"What?"

Ken gave a ragged sigh, taking his hands away to run them through his hair, making them stand up in adorable, wilty spikes. I sagged against the sink, feeling untethered without his body anchoring me.

"You hold all the cards. You dream my dreams, you make me crazy with that determined, little mouth and all that curly hair and that fierce look on your face like you'd skin me alive, and all I have is your unwilling agreement to come with me? I'm not stupid enough to try bringing you before the Council with things so ambiguous. At the first hint of danger you'll do a runner and poke your head into the nearest sand bank. And I won't be able to stop you."

I bit my lower lip, hard, to keep my hands from going for his neck. To squeeze the arrogant life out of him. Slowly.

Do a runner?

Maybe the Koi he met just days ago, but there was no sand in my hair now. I was here, wasn't I? Who was he to swagger in here with his *kinako* kisses and some kind of expectation I owed him assurance?

Hmmm, that surge of irritation doesn't feel quite right. Maybe I'm still hung over from dream-eating?

I knew what he was. He'd told me. A Bringer. Death-dealer to the Kind. A Kitsune who could have taken Dad that first night and run back to Japan without having to deal with Hayk or Ullikemi or me.

But he didn't. He stayed.

He'd proved he wasn't a runner. I was unfair to be angry that he wanted the same proof from me.

Could I give it? *Quit stalling.* I was wrong about being able to decide anything. He was already inside my defenses.

Mist drifting over ancient, gnarled red-barked hinoki cypress trees, trunks straight and tall guarding a clearing where pine needles released clean-bitter scent under each footstep. Ken's fragment, the deepest kernel-self of his dreaming. Though he called himself Death-bringer, he didn't dream of death like Hayk. His fragment felt as safe as his arm around me on the bus. A shelter, a way to keep the world at bay.

My fears, my history of wacked relationships—flimsy excuses. I couldn't stay closed off forever. But giving him my middle name would give him some kind of power over me, right? Like my dream power over him.

I guess it is only fair.

If it didn't work out, I would survive. That's what people did, wasn't it? Eat evil, battle dragons, and then come home and make sushi. Only giving up, opting out like Dad had, like *I* had, was unforgiveable.

"Aweoweo," I said, wanting to sound confident, but coming off like a five year old girl holding back tears instead.

Ken blinked.

"My other name."

Ken's shoulders visibly relaxed, and the snarky grin I associated with his Kitsune-self appeared. He closed in, the heat from his body sinking more deeply into me than a real touch.

Some insistent, vulnerable thing welled up in my chest and traveled to my throat, making it hard to breathe. I shrugged, trying to make light of what I had just given him. "Mom was from Hawaii."

"Ah, an island girl. That explains the hair," he said. His eyes darkened, the iris swelling to fill the pupil with black, bottomless shadow.

He raised a hand to tug my ponytail, angling my head back so he could whisper into the defenseless hollow of my exposed throat. "What does 'aweoweo' mean?"

I shivered. His mouth on me made my hands curl into fists with the need to feel his body, contoured muscles, skin solid and real—but touching him now would be too much like surrendering.

"Big-eye tuna."

He snorted, and then returned to tracing a trail up my throat, to other, keenly sensitive places around my ear and then my temple.

After a moment, I tugged at his ear, needing to see his face.

Capturing my gaze, he held still, allowing me to see deep inside him, to where something hungry and needful stared back out at me.

"Koi Aweoweo Pierce," he said, slowly, savoring the hard consonants and hissing sibilants. "Promise me that—" he started to say, but I darted forward and kissed him open-mouthed, trying to channel everything into the way my lips pressed to his, and the rhythm of our mingled breath.

No promises. Just this.

Whatever happened when we took Dad back to Japan, I didn't want a Kind binding on it. It had to be a man and a woman and simple, straight-up desire.

A knock sounded on the door.

I pulled back, slowly. Ken looked a little dazed. His tongue darted out to lick the corner of his mouth as if he wanted to savor the lingering taste of me.

"Guys? Dinner's ready," said Marlin through the door. "And I can't keep Dad from barging in there any longer," she added in a stage whisper.

Ken pushed the door open.

My sister stood, hands on her hips, with an expression caught between a glare and smirk.

"Sorted that out, did you? Good. Let's eat."

Korean stone bowls of rice and perfectly seasoned vegetables were laid out on the counter. Dad, Marlin, Ken and I squeezed together at the table; a strange little family.

We ate.

ABOUT THE AUTHOR

K. Bird Lincoln is an ESL professional and writer living on the windswept Minnesota Prairie with family and a huge addiction to frou-frou coffee. Also dark chocolate—without which, the world is a howling void. Originally from Cleveland, she has spent more years living on the edges of the Pacific Ocean than in the Midwest. Her speculative short stories are published in various online and paper publications such as *Strange Horizons*. Her first novel, *Tiger Lily*, a medieval Japanese fantasy, is available from Amazon. She also writes tasty speculative and YA fiction reviews under the name K. Bird at Goodreads.com.

Thank you for reading!
We hope you'll leave an honest review at Amazon,
Goodreads, or wherever you discuss books online.

Leaving a review means a lot for the author and editors who
worked so hard to create this book.

Please sign up for our newsletter for news about upcoming
titles, submission opportunities, special discounts, & more.

WorldWeaverPress.com/newsletter-signup

MORE URBAN FANTASY FROM WORLD WEAVER PRESS

BITE SOMEBODY
Sara Dobie Bauer

"Do you want to be perfect?"

That's what Danny asked Celia the night he turned her into a vampire. Three months have passed since, and immortality didn't transform her into the glamorous, sexy vamp she was expecting, but left her awkward, lonely, and working at a Florida gas station. On top of that, she's a giant screw-up of an immortal, because the only blood she consumes is from illegally obtained hospital blood bags.

What she needs to do—according to her moody vampire friend Imogene—is just … *bite somebody*. But Celia wants her first bite to be special, and she has yet to meet Mr. Right Bite. Then, Ian moves in next door. His scent creeps through her kitchen wall and makes her nose tingle, but insecure Celia can't bring herself to meet the guy face-to-face.

When she finally gets a look at Ian's cyclist physique, curly black hair, and sun-kissed skin, other parts of Celia tingle, as well. Could he be the first bite she's been waiting for to complete her vampire transformation? His kisses certainly have a way of making her fangs throb.

Just when Celia starts to believe Ian may be the fairy tale ending she always wanted, her jerk of a creator returns to town, which spells nothing but trouble for everyone involved.

BITE SOMEBODY ELSE
Sara Dobie Bauer
Available Summer 2017!

"*Bite Somebody* is the *Pretty in Pink* of vampire stories; fun, self-consciously retro, and not afraid to be goofy...Sara Dobie Bauer knows how to keep a reader smiling."
—Christopher Buehlman, author of *Those Across the River*

MORE URBAN FANTASY FROM WORLD WEAVER PRESS

HEIR TO THE LAMP

Genie Chronicles, Book One
Michelle Lowery Combs

A family secret, a mysterious lamp, a dangerous Order with the mad desire to possess both.

Ginn thinks she knows all there is to know about how she became adopted by parents whose number one priority is to embarrass her with public displays of affection, but that changes when a single wish starts a never-ending parade of weirdness marching through her door the day she turns thirteen.

Gifted with a mysterious lamp and the missing pieces from her adoption story, Ginn tries to discover who...or *what*...she really is. That should be strange enough, but to top it off Ginn's being hunted by the Order of the Grimoire, a secret society who'll stop at nothing to harness the power of a real genie. Ginn struggles to stay one step ahead of the Grimms with the help of Rashmere, Guardian of the lamp and the most loyal friend a girl never knew she had. The Grimms are being helped, too—but by whom? As much as she doesn't want to, Ginn's beginning to question the motives of her long-time crush Caleb Scott and his connection to her newest, most dangerous enemy.

SOLOMON'S BELL

Genie Chronicles, Book Two
Michelle Lowery Combs

Ginn thinks she has problems at home until she magically lands herself in 16th century Prague.

"An exciting new spin on a genie tale. Virginia is a feisty main character who I would love to have as a friend. Captivating!"
— Melissa Buell, author of *The Tales of Gymandrol*

MORE URBAN FANTASY FROM WORLD WEAVER PRESS

LEGALLY UNDEAD
Vampirarchy Book 1
Margo Bond Collins

Elle Dupree has her life all figured out: first a wedding, then her Ph.D., then swank faculty parties where she'll serve wine and cheese and introduce people to her husband the lawyer.

But those plans disintegrate when she walks in on a vampire sucking the blood from her fiancé, Greg. Horrified, she screams and runs—not away from the vampire, but toward it, brandishing a wooden letter opener.

As she slams the improvised stake into the vampire's heart, a team of black-clad men bursts into the apartment. Turning to face them, Elle realizes Greg's body is gone—and her perfect life falls apart.

"Ms. Collins delivered tenfold with her debut of theVampirarchy series, I've found my new favorite vampire hunter in Elle Dupree! In a word…FANGTASTIC!!!"
— Romancing the Dark Side

"Manages to take typical features of urban fantasy and make them its own. Left me desperate for the next chapter in Elle's story. I'll be curious to see where Collins takes the Vampirarchy series next!"
— All Things Urban Fantasy

"I LOVED this book!! This book has it all: humor, romance, suspense and vampires…what more can you ask for!"
—Reading Is a Way of Life

MORE URBAN FANTASY FROM
WORLD WEAVER PRESS

OMEGA RISING
A Wolf King Novel
Anna Kyle

Cass Nolan has been forced to avoid the burn of human touch for her whole life, drawing comfort instead from her dreams of a silver wolf—her protector, her friend. When her stalking nightmares return, her imaginary dead sister's ghost tells her to run, Cass knows she should listen, but the sinfully hot stranger she just hired to work on her ranch has her mind buzzing with possibilities. Not only does her skin accept Nathan's touch, it demands it. Cass must make a decision—run again and hope she saves the people who have become her family, or stand and fight. Question is, will it be with Nathan or against him?

Nathan Rivers' life is consumed by his quest to find the Omega wolf responsible for killing his brother, but when the trail leads him to Cass and her merry band of shapeshifters, his wolf wants only to claim her for himself. When evidence begins piling up that Cass is the Omega he's been seeking, things become complicated—especially since someone else wants her dead. Saving her life might mean sacrificing his own, but it may be worth it to save the woman he can't keep from reaching for.

SKYE FALLING
A Wolf King Novella
Anna Kyle

* * *

For more on these and other titles
visit WorldWeaverPress.com
* * *

World Weaver Press
Publishing fantasy, paranormal, and science fiction.
We believe in great storytelling.
WorldWeaverPress.com

CPSIA information can be obtained
at www.ICGtesting.com
Printed in the USA
LVOW08s0337120917
548362LV00009B/136/P